WHAT HE LEFT BEHIND

L.A. WITT

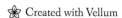

ABOUT WHAT HE LEFT BEHIND

Josh Carver would do anything for Michael Adair, his child-hood best friend. In the five years since Michael finally left his abusive ex-partner, Josh and his husband Ian have helped him leave that horrific past behind him. Michael seems to have adjusted well enough...until he admits he's afraid to date because the abuse has left him terrified of physical intimacy.

Josh is stunned again when Ian proposes a solution—Josh can help Michael learn to enjoy sex again. It isn't like it would be the first time. After all, Josh and Michael lost their virginity to each other years ago.

Michael hesitates, but then takes him up on the idea. It isn't long before Ian's getting involved too... and it's all fine and dandy until emotions come into play that threaten their friendship, as well as Josh and Ian's marriage.

Warning: Contains three guys who will do anything for

each other, a hot tub that's always the right temperature, and a cat with an attitude problem.

This 73,000 word novel was previously published.

To anyone who's ever been a Michael, an Ian, or a Josh.

CHAPTER 1

"Dr. Klein asked me out."

Michael isn't looking at me when he says it. He's across the dimly lit booth, staring down at the piece of bread he's been absently shredding for the last few minutes. Brow taut, shoulders hunched, he hasn't said much since he showed up for lunch, and I knew something had to be wrong. I just wasn't expecting...that.

"Oh." Now I'm mutilating a piece of bread too. "You said no, didn't you?"

The long, resigned release of breath confirms it. Michael sets the bread down, brushes a few crumbs off his fingers and sits back against the fake leather cushion. "I said no."

My heart sinks. He's had the most adorable crush on that doctor for months, and ever since he found out the guy was gay, he's been trying to work up the courage to ask him out. From the sound of it, the doctor—a vet who spends one or two days a week in the clinic where Michael works—has reciprocated pretty hard, and they started flirting cautiously a few weeks ago. I can't blame either of them. The doc is one of those smoking-hot rugged guys with a little gray around the edges, and Michael... Well, Michael is gorgeous. Even my husband ogles him, though he admittedly does have a thing for redheads, and we both get a little breathless at the sight of a man in scrubs.

But Dr. Klein asked, and Michael said no, and I don't know what to say. I didn't know what to say the last couple of times this scenario played out. It happened with another vet tech who worked in the same office last year—they flirted, they danced around the obvious, and when the guy had finally suggested a drink after work, Michael balked. He never has given me a straight answer about that one. Or about the FedEx driver he'd played the same game with for the better part of a year before the vet tech came along.

Except I have my suspicions, and I hope like hell that this time and those other two times were just cold feet, not a throwback to Michael's awful past.

But what the hell do I say?

Come on, Josh. Say something, *for fuck's sake.*

Treading carefully, I ask, "What changed your mind about him?"

Michael leans forward again, pressing his elbow onto the table and kneading the bridge of his nose with two fingers. "God, I'm so stupid."

With anyone else, I'd have thought—and quite possibly said—that yes, dude, you are stupid. Dr. Klein is one of those guys who can turn every head in a room that's already packed full of hot men. Plus he's a vet who's notorious for being extra gentle and kind with animals, and if there's a better way to Michael's heart, I don't know what it is.

I fold my arms on the edge of the table and try to narrow some of the distance between us. It's a struggle not to reach past the abandoned bread basket and put a reassuring hand on his arm. Even after all these years, it's hard to remember that Michael doesn't like being touched. That's one of the biggest tragedies of his past—he'd always been touchy-feely in an endearing kind of way, and it still hurts to see him recoil from even the slightest brush of human contact.

"You're not stupid. What happened?"

"Nothing. Nothing happened." He drops his hand again, and he meets my eyes. "I just couldn't do it."

I swallow. "Have you talked to Dr. Hamilton about it?"

Michael flinches and drops his gaze. The bread is back in his line of sight again, and when he starts ripping crumbs off it once more, his hands are unsteady. Were they earlier? I can't remember now and wish I'd paid attention.

"I left her a message," he whispers. "I doubt she'll be surprised."

"Why?" I chew my lip. "I mean, is this about..." ...*the whole reason you have a therapist in the first place?* "Is it..."

"Steve?"

My hackles go up at the sound of that asshole's name. "Yeah."

"Isn't everything about him these days?" Michael's voice is bitter, and as if for emphasis, he tears off a chunk of crust and tosses it into the basket. Then he shakes his head and sits back again, dusting more crumbs off his fingers. "Every time I think I'm past all that..."

"Dr. Klein is nothing like Steve, though."

"Neither was Steve when we first started dating," he mutters.

The booth is silent for a moment. I still don't know what to say, and Michael's lost in his own thoughts.

Right then, the ponytailed blonde waitress appears with our food and asks with a huge grin, "Okay, who had the veggie stir fry?"

Michael musters something in the neighborhood of a smile. "Me."

She sets the plate down in front of him and turns to me. "So this pesto chicken must be for you."

I nod, but as she lays it on the table, my stomach twists. I could've sworn I was starving when I got here. "Thanks."

"Can I get either of you anything else?"

Michael and I exchange glances, and I shake my head. To the waitress, he says, "No, we're fine. Thank you." Another smile, this time a bit more pronounced, not to mention forced.

"Okay. Enjoy!"

With that, she's gone, and we're alone with two plates of food. Michael eyes his. I poke at mine with a fork. Well. So much for that idea. There are days when I can joke with Michael that we should start a new weight loss program. All someone has to do is say Steve's name at the table, and everyone will lose their appetites.

"I said 'Steve' at every other meal, and lost twenty pounds in two weeks!"

Some days, Michael thinks that's funny in a twisted sort of way. Today, I'm pretty sure his sense of humor has gone in the same direction as his appetite, and I don't blame him one bit. Not if that asshole is still interfering with his life after all this time. It's been five goddamned years since the night I picked him up at the emergency room for the last time, when he said he was really leaving this time and he'd actually stuck to it, and I swear there are days when Steve has a tighter hold on him now than he did back then.

The silence wears on. Michael manages to take a few bites of his pasta, so I make myself eat a bit too. We both have to go back to work after all, and if I know Michael, he's been sucking down coffee and nothing else since his alarm went off. Just like me.

Michael lays his fork down and sits a bit straighter. My mouth goes dry. I quickly take a drink to wash down the pesto chicken before he speaks. At least I know him well enough that I can tell from a mile away if he's about to say something important, and he knows me well enough to wait until I won't aspirate my iced tea.

Once I'm safe from drowning, he finally asks, "You want to know what keeps stopping me from going out with anyone?"

I'm scared to death this will be as hard to hear as the myriad confessions he's made in the years since Steve, especially if it's taken this long for him and his therapist to pry it out of his psyche, and my stomach churns as I nod.

Michael drops his gaze and stares at his food for a moment. He takes a deep breath, and I hold mine.

"Dr. Hamilton's helped me through a lot of the bull-shit," he says. "I can separate everything Steve did from what a real relationship should be. I've sorted most of it out, and I've let enough of it go that I think I can actually be part of a functional, healthy relationship again."

He pauses, and I gnaw my lip. The unspoken "But..." hangs in the air. It's making my hands twitchy, so I slide my wedding ring back and forth over my knuckle to keep them occupied.

"I think I'm okay for almost everything about a normal relationship." He meets my eyes, and the faintest shine in his sends my heart into my feet. His voice barely carries across the booth as he says, "Except I am completely fucking terrified to have sex."

My jaw drops. Immediately, there's a lump in my throat. Dozens of memories flash through my mind—our first time the summer after high school, the night we blew off our own community college graduation, that winter when he fucked me back to life after an overly dramatic breakup—and I can't breathe. That son-of-a-bitch ex-boyfriend of his had dimmed the light in Michael's eyes for a good long time, and he'd put him through more hell than anyone—least of all someone as sweet and gentle as Michael—deserves to go through, but knowing he also took away that passionate, playful, sensual side is... I can't fit it in my head. Even when Michael was young and inexperienced, he'd been so confident and full of life. He didn't care if he performed well, or if he was porn-star perfect. That first time, I'd been all nerves and fear, and he'd seemed so...

Unbreakable.

And now he's gazing at me from across this booth, the faintest hint of tears in his eyes, with his confession still ringing in my ears.

"Michael..." His name comes out as a pathetic whisper. I shake myself and meet his gaze again. "You never told me..." As soon as the words are out, I want to take them back, but he winces before I can, and now it's harder than ever not to reach for his arm. "I'm sorry. I just wasn't expecting that."

"I know." Michael starts picking at his food again, probably just looking for something to do. "I never told anyone except Dr. Hamilton."

There's a million questions on the tip of my tongue, and I bite down on the one that desperately wants to slip out: *What did that son of a bitch do to you?*

Because I know Michael—if he's willing to tell me, he'll do it without prompting. Trying to drag an answer out of him is the quickest way to get him to clam up and shut down. Dr. Hamilton has almost certainly had her work cut out for her.

And I don't ask, because I'm afraid of the answer. The bruises have long since healed, and he doesn't have panic attacks like he used to. The jagged scar beside his eyebrow is the only visual reminder left aside from how hard it still is for him to make eye contact these days. I'm sure he still has a few scars beneath his clothes. I knew about the physical and emotional abuse, and I've wondered plenty of times if that extended to the bedroom, but he's insisted all these years that it didn't.

What have you been carrying alone all this time?

Michael takes a long swallow of Coke and sets the glass down, the tinkling ice giving away the slight tremor in his hand. "I'm sorry. I should have told—"

"Don't you dare apologize," I whisper, struggling *hard* not to reach for him. "I'm always here, and I always have been, but you don't have to tell me anything."

"I know." He sweeps his tongue across his lips. "It actually took me a long time to even tell Dr. Hamilton. And she's helped me through so much, but this..." Michael shakes his head. "The thing is, I really do like Dr. Klein. A lot, but how do I put this far enough behind me to not be a goddamned basket case with him? Or with anyone else?"

"What does Dr. Hamilton suggest?"

He shrugs. "She thinks this might be outside of her expertise. She's tried, but so far, we're just not getting anywhere. She's said a sex therapist might be the way to go." In the dim light, Michael's cheeks color. "But I'm... I mean, it took me this long to even tell you. I don't know if I can talk about this with a complete stranger, you know?" Through gritted teeth, he adds, "Maybe if I were comfortable with that, I could stomach the idea of sleeping with someone I've never touched before. But I can't. So why would I..." He waves a hand and shakes his head.

"Shit," I breathe. "I am so sorry, Michael." It sounds so fucking useless. Especially directed at someone like Michael, who's got every right to be jaded when it comes to apologies.

"I'm just afraid..." He chews his lip. "I've gone out with a few guys over the years, and the second things got physical, I freaked out. It's not as bad as it used to be." He shudders. "The first time, fuck, I probably scarred that guy for life."

"What happened?"

"I panicked." He meets my eyes, and his eyebrows pull together slightly, as if to silently add, *Don't make me go into detail.*

"Was it better the other times?"

"Better, but not..." He rubs the bridge of his nose again. "There's just this wall up. And I don't know how to get over that wall with someone without killing the mood completely, you know?"

I force back that lump in my throat. I remember all too well stumbling over mental obstacles and being scared to death I'd disappoint a guy because I was too nervous and too inexperienced and too freaked out. And I got over those obstacles because of Michael. He was patient, and reassuring, and coaxed me over each and every one of those barriers until we were having the kind of sex I thought existed only in pornos.

"It pisses me off," Michael goes on. "I mean, every time I think I've left that asshole in the past, something else comes up and reminds me of him. I love sex. Well, loved it. And now, I can't even..." He swallows and looks in my eyes again. "I used to get turned on if a guy put his hand on my leg under the table. The last time I went out with someone? He just brushed my leg with his knee, and my skin started crawling. I spent the rest of the evening thinking he was going to touch me for real. When I bailed on him because I was"—he makes air quotes—"feeling kind of sick, it wasn't entirely a lie."

"Jesus."

Michael holds my gaze, but then he shakes his head and picks up his fork again. Stabbing at his food, he sighs. "I'm sorry. I didn't mean to dump all this on you. And you've probably got to get back to work pretty soon."

I glance at the clock on the wall behind him. Yeah, I'm cutting it close, and technically I should bail in the next ten minutes, but I think my boss will understand if I get back late this one time. "I'm not in a hurry."

Michael spears a piece of penne with his fork. "Thanks."

"Any time."

His eyes flick up for a second. We've had this conversation before—Michael knows damn well I mean it when I say I'm always here for him. Day or night, no questions asked. I'd move mountains for him, and right now, I wish like hell I could move this one.

"Have you thought about just going out with the guy?" I ask. "Maybe tell him up front that you prefer to take things slow?"

Michael nods. He nibbles his lunch, and his eyes are unfocused as if he's lost in thought. Then he takes a drink and says, "Honestly? That just makes it worse."

"How so?"

"Because moving slowly is still moving. We'll still get there." He chases another piece of tomato around the edge of his plate. "And I'll be sweating bullets the entire fucking time." He stabs the tomato and nearly puts his fork right through the ceramic. "Sometimes I think it would be better to just dive into bed with a stranger and get it over with."

My neck prickles. "That...doesn't sound like a healthy way to approach it."

He arches an eyebrow. "Got any better ideas?"

I hold his gaze. He holds mine.

And no, I haven't got any better ideas.

CHAPTER 2

By the time I get home from work at ten after seven, I'm starving. If traffic had moved even a little bit slower, I'm pretty sure I would've started eyeballing the steering wheel or the passenger seat's upholstery.

And yet at the same time, the thought of food makes me gag. I've been reeling all day from what Michael told me over lunch, and that's to say nothing of all the things he didn't tell me. I know just enough about that hellish relationship to be able to fill in the blanks. As I'm getting out of my car, a thought smacks me in the back of the head: What if one of those times I met Michael at the ER, when he was shaken and bloody, it had been after Steve—

No. No. No.

Not going there. Not tonight. Not if I ever want to sleep again.

I force my mind to shift gears as I head inside. The instant I open the door from the garage to the foyer, Ariel, our young boxer, comes thundering in from the kitchen, whipping the walls and her own sides with her long tail.

"Ariel," Ian says firmly from the kitchen, and she hurries back the way she came. I follow her. In the kitchen, Ariel skids to a halt, sliding a little on the linoleum before dropping onto her haunches. He taps his thigh, and she moves to his side at the stove, where she sits again. "Good girl." Her tail thumps against the cabinet, and he pets her head. To me, he says, "Hey you. How was your day?" Then he gestures at the stove. "Hungry?"

"Not bad, and very." I greet him with a kiss before I glance at the pot and the skillet, but as soon as I see the food, my gut tightens. It looks and smells wonderful—Ian cooks like a pro—but I'm not sure I can stomach much of anything tonight. Not even when the last real meal I had was the one he cooked last night.

"Hey." Ian tugs my belt loop and brings me closer. "You okay?"

There's that fucking lump in my throat again. No. No, I'm not okay. Because Michael isn't okay. And I don't know what to say to him, and I don't know what to do short of hunting Steve down and strangling him with my bare hands and—

"Josh." Ian cups my face, drawing me out of my thoughts. "What's wrong?"

I lower my gaze. Ariel is staring up at me with those huge brown eyes, her tail still beating against the cabinet, so I hold out my hand. She licks my fingers, and her tail slows.

Daddy, what's wrong?

I sigh and pet her, prompting a little more tail thumping.

Ian kisses my cheek. "Why don't I dish everything up, and we can talk while we eat?"

Wordlessly, I nod. That'll at least buy me a moment to collect my thoughts, assuming our dog's innocent expression doesn't break me down first. Fuck. I haven't been this shaken since the first time I met a bruised, stitched-up Michael at the ER. It's been five years since Steve laid a hand on him, but the wound feels fresh to me because, up until today, I hadn't known. I hadn't fucking known.

What did he do to you, Michael?

Ian dishes everything up, and we sit down at the kitchen table. Ariel lies down beside Ian, ever hopeful of a tossed table scrap, and Rosie, our aloof Siamese, perches on the windowsill, glaring at me like she always does. She's definitely Ian's cat, because she can't stand me. I decided a long time ago she must blame me for her stupid name. I've tried explaining that it was the shelter who named both her and the dog, but to no avail—she hates me.

The thought can't even make me chuckle tonight, and I just sigh and try to eat.

From across the table, Ian watches me, but he doesn't say anything.

I shift uncomfortably. "I had lunch with Michael. And he..."

Ian pulls in a sharp breath and sits straighter. He knows me, and he knows what it means when I'm like this after I've had lunch with Michael. The details are the only variables.

I hesitate. Michael knows I talk to Ian about these things. In fact, he encourages it.

"You shouldn't have to internalize it all," he said to me a few years back. *"And I trust you both."*

So I take a deep breath, and I tell my husband everything Michael told me over lunch.

When I'm finished, Ian sits back against the chair just like Michael did earlier. "Oh my God." He shakes his head and starts absently petting Ariel. "I know I've said it before, but there is a special place in hell for that fucker."

"Yeah, there is."

We exchange glances. That special place in hell has been reserved since long before we found out about this development.

Neither of us says much more. In fact, neither of us says much of anything while we eat. And damn it, I'm still ravenous, but it's a struggle to eat. Ian seems to be having a tough time too, and pasta is one of his favorite things on the planet. Except the Steve diet works pretty well on him too.

I have to wonder how Steve can sleep at night. Or eat. Or just breathe. He'd been such a charmer in the beginning, but my God, the poison in that man is almost visible to the naked eye after a while. During the five long years he had Michael under his thumb, that asshole committed a lot of unforgivable sins, and people still ask Michael why on earth he stayed for so long if it was really that bad. Of course, anyone who's ever been in an abusive relationship knows that walking away is easier said than done. The threats, the manipulation—all of it holds on to the victim like a fucking choke chain.

One chain in particular kept Michael firmly within Steve's grasp—his dog. Any time Michael stepped out of line or so much as hinted about leaving, Steve knew damn well all he had to do was threaten to hurt Cody. Once, after a particularly bad fight, the asshole actually left with the dog and came back without him. He let Michael believe for days that he'd sold him to a dog-fighting ring before finally, after deciding Michael was repentant enough, bringing him home from his brother's house.

In Ian's eyes, that alone cemented Steve's place in the deepest, darkest pits of hell. Ian's an animal lover just like

Michael, and even joking about hurting one makes him see red. Actually threatening to do it? Especially to manipulate someone who once literally jumped into a frozen lake to save a dog? Unforgivable.

I've always agreed with him, and this new revelation about the things that happened in that house makes me wish there were some even deeper and darker pits in hell. Steve deserves nothing less than the worst the devil can offer.

After a while, Ian asks, "Is Michael's therapist helping? With...um..."

"She's trying."

"I guess there's no easy way to come back from something like that. Sitting and talking to someone probably helps, but only to a point."

I nod. "Yeah. I can't imagine what else she can do, though."

"I can't imagine what else anyone can do."

Our eyes meet. Ian sighs and shakes his head. We both continue making a half-assed effort to get through the wonderful meal he cooked. Of course I don't know what the answer is for Michael—I don't even know how to salvage what should have been a pleasant dinner.

Eventually, we've both eaten enough to tide us over until breakfast—or first coffee, as Ian calls it—and we start cleaning up. All the while, I feel like I'm in a haze, part of my mind still stuck in this afternoon's conversation as if my foot's stuck in concrete. Every now and again, as we wash the dishes so we can settle in to watch TV, I manage to forget, but that uncomfortable feeling beneath my rib cage reminds me all isn't right in the world. When I notice it, I remember, and the thoughts start bombarding my brain all over again. I don't foresee a lot of sleep happening tonight.

As we often do, Ian and I spend the evening curled up on the couch with the dog and cat. There isn't much on—mostly reruns and the news—but it's enough to keep us mildly entertained. Or at least distracted. Ian doesn't laugh much, even when it's one of the good sitcoms. I don't either.

I kind of regret telling him what Michael told me—doesn't seem fair to ruin his evening too. But he'd have dragged it out of me sooner or later. Unlike Michael, I crack under interrogation, and Ian's a schoolteacher. He can pry a confession out of the most tight-lipped fourteen-year-old. His own husband? Cake walk.

Still, it bugs me to think of Ian sitting there with the same sick feeling in the pit of his stomach.

I want to text Michael and make sure he's okay. Maybe he's worked up the courage to call Dr. Klein and say he's reconsidered, and yes he would like to go out sometime. I'd like to think that's what he's doing right now, or that they're already on an impromptu date somewhere, but I know Michael. If he's afraid enough of sex to admit he's afraid, then it's not something he's going to shake off with a deep breath and a phone call.

But what *will* it take? I refuse to believe the damage is permanent. Yeah, maybe Michael had turned out to be more breakable than I'd imagined, but not irreparably so. That's just not possible.

Around ten thirty, Ian clicks off the TV. The animals jump off the couch, and we follow, though we're both a little slower. Not that we're old or anything, but a couple of tired thirty-somethings don't quite spring to life the way a year-old boxer and a sassy Siamese do. Especially not this late on a Thursday evening.

From there, it's the same routine as every night. Ian takes the dog out one last time. I top off the cat's food and water while she tries to kill me with her mind. Then the animals commandeer as much of the bed as they can while we brush our teeth and Ian takes out his contacts. For two guys who hadn't caught each other's names until after we'd seen each other's proverbial O-faces, a decade later we've slipped pretty comfortably into the quiet domestic life. And they say you can't find love in a bathhouse.

Those days are behind us now, though, and after all the drama of our wilder years, we're both quite content.

We rearrange the animals and climb into bed.

Ian doesn't kill the light, though. "So, I was thinking."

I shift onto my side and drape an arm over him. "About?"

"Michael."

His name sends a jolt through me, jarring my already tense stomach.

Ian wraps his arm around my shoulders. "About his, um, situation."

"Yeah?"

Ian studies me for a moment. "Maybe you can help him."

I blink. "How?"

"He trusts you. He's..." Ian hesitates. "He's been with you. Maybe you're what he needs right now."

I stare at him because I'm not entirely certain I heard him correctly. "Come again?"

Ian takes my hand, lacing our fingers together on his stomach. "We both know you're still attracted to him."

Heat rushes into my cheeks. "Well, yeah, but that doesn't... I'm not trying to... Ian, I'm—"

"Shh." He squeezes my hand, and a smile plays at his lips. "I'm not making any accusations. You're attracted to him. I have a crush on my boss." He shrugs. "It's life. We're married, not castrated."

"True." I'm still guarded, though. "But we agreed to have a closed relationship."

"We did. Except that was before either of us knew what happened to Michael."

I'm still staring at him, struggling to comprehend that we're even having this conversation.

"Josh, he's your best friend. No one else in the world is as close to him as you are *and* has been physically intimate with him." Ian traces the side of my thumb with his. "Under the circumstances, I'd say what you might be able to do for him trumps any need we have for monogamy."

"But, I mean, even if you're right, I don't want to do some kind of damage to us."

"You wouldn't. I'm not suggesting you cheat on me. I know about it, and I'm endorsing it—it's not cheating." He brings my hand up and kisses the backs of my fingers. "You'd be helping him get his confidence back and undo some of the damage that motherfucker did to him."

A shudder runs through me as my mind's eye tries to show me what might have happened to Michael back then, and I tamp those thoughts down. "I don't... I wouldn't even know where to start."

"Talk to him." Ian squeezes my hand again. "See if he's even on board with the idea, and then play it by ear."

I hold his gaze. "You're really sure about this."

"If it means getting him back to a better place so he can find a better relationship?" Ian nods. "Absolutely."

I chew the inside of my cheek. "What if I make things worse for him?"

"Josh." Ian releases my hand and cups my cheek. "You're

the sweetest and most generous man I've ever been with. You and I both know you'd never push him further than he wanted to go, and you would *never* hurt him. There is literally nothing I can imagine you doing that would do more damage."

"Still. He's already gotten hurt so badly..."

"And I couldn't imagine him being in better hands."

I'm not so confident, but Ian is right about one thing—there's no way in hell I would deliberately do anything to hurt Michael any more than I would do anything to hurt Ian. It's the inadvertent stuff that worries me.

"Talk to him," Ian says again. "Who knows? He might not even be interested. But if he is, just set rules and limits, take it slow, and maybe it'll help."

Fair enough. That I can do. Though I'm not completely sure how to broach that subject. Carefully, I guess. Still, despite my worries, I do feel better knowing there might be something I can actually do to help Michael get back to a better place. *Might.*

I meet Ian's gaze and smile. "You're amazing. You know that?"

He laughs softly and kisses the tip of my nose. "I wouldn't go that far."

"I would." I run my fingers through his hair. "Any rules?"

Ian seems to mull it over for a moment, but then shrugs. "I trust you. And him." He pauses. "Just, you know, be honest with me about anything that's going on. Not necessarily details, just..."

"Just be honest."

"Yeah."

"Okay. I will. I promise."

Ian smiles. He lifts his head and kisses me softly. "We

should get some sleep. Let me know how it goes when you talk to him."

"You'll be the first to hear." I kiss him once more and then settle onto my pillow. "I love you."

"I love you too."

CHAPTER 3

Iᴛ'ѕ ᴀʟᴍᴏѕᴛ ѕɪx ᴏ'ᴄʟᴏᴄᴋ ɪɴ ᴛʜᴇ ᴇᴠᴇɴɪɴɢ, ᴀɴᴅ I ѕᴛɪʟʟ haven't contacted Michael. I tell myself it's because I've been wrapped up in paperwork and PowerPoint, and that I don't want to bother him at work, but that's bullshit.

Sitting in my cubicle beneath the fluorescent lights, playing with my phone, I want to text him, but I don't. I can't. Fact is, I can't figure out what I want to say to him, or how to say it, or if I really should follow through with Ian's suggestion. What would that even mean, anyway? Friends with therapeutic benefits?

And regardless of what we call it, I'm worried sick that this could get complicated. Sex was never complicated for us, but there was never so much riding on it. During those times when we'd fooled around, neither of us had ever been otherwise attached, never mind married to one or trauma-tized by another. Over the years, we'd wandered in and out of each other's beds in between relationships, but it was never a good time for us to pursue something more than sex together. One of us was coming off a breakup, or the other was too tied up with real life to even think of anything more serious.

When life calmed down and we were mature enough to know which way was up, Michael was already happily in a relationship. By the time he'd rebounded from that breakup, I met someone new. We leap-frogged like that all the way through college, until I started working and Michael was in vet school, and then came Ian, and Michael had known before I did that I'd met the man I'd marry. He was the one who told me I was being a dumbass when Ian and I broke up over something stupid, and he was the one who helped us get back together, and damn if he didn't earn his spot as best man at our wedding.

Sometimes I catch myself fantasizing about the sex we used to have, but I never think of him as the one that got away. Just very fond, very hot memories. My relationships with both Ian and Michael turned out exactly the way they should have—I wouldn't trade my husband for anything, and I have the best friend any man could ask for. The best friend who gave me all the confidence I have in the bedroom.

The best friend who's lost all that confidence because of the asshole he started dating six months after I got married.

The best friend who might be able to regain that confidence with my help, if I'm willing to slip off my wedding ring, get into his bed for the first time in over a decade, and...

And no, this can't possibly get complicated.

Cursing under my breath, I rest my elbows on my desk and rub my eyes. This is worse than the helpless feeling I had when there was nothing I could do for Michael. Doing nothing beats the hell out of doing something to fuck him up even more.

Finally, I send a text, but it's not to Michael.

Are you absolutely sure about this?

Ian's definitely home by now, likely grading papers. Hopefully he's in his office or at the kitchen table—if he's kicked back on the couch like he sometimes is, then he's probably got either the cat or all fifty pounds of Ariel in his lap, and his phone might be out of reach.

Within thirty seconds, though, the response comes through: *100% sure.*

And right after that one: *I trust you.*

And he needs me, my brain adds, because it's so fucking helpful.

I'm not nearly as confident about this as my husband, but there is one thing I'm unshakably sure about—how much I want to do something for Michael.

I glance at the clock, and it's five minutes till six. If I want to see him tonight, we need to make a decision soon, because traffic going in his direction will be hellish if I don't get on the road in the next twenty minutes.

So, with the clock inching toward quitting time, I text him: *You busy tonight?*

I hit send and pray for a response of *sorry, got a date with Dr. Klein.*

As I log off the computer, gather my jacket and keys and wait for the minute hand to hit the twelve, I keep an eye on my phone. At six, I leave my desk, and I'm halfway to the parking garage when the phone vibrates.

Already home. Want to come by?

Already home? But it's—

Oh, right. He sometimes has Friday afternoons off after his therapy appointments.

Perfect. This isn't a conversation we need to have out in public.

I text back, *I'll be there as soon as I can.*

And I hope to God the drive gives me enough time to figure out what to say.

I PARK IN THE SPACE BESIDE MICHAEL'S CAR AND TAKE the stairs up to his apartment. My heart's going like crazy, and I've finally worked out exactly how to broach this subject. It'll still be awkward and might make him balk, but at least I can get enough words out for him to consider the idea without making either of us feel like an ass if he declines.

When I reach his door, I pause with my hand on the knob, take a deep breath and go inside—he doesn't like when people knock if he knows they're coming because it pisses off his dog.

"In the kitchen," he calls out.

Cody comes loping down the hallway, so I crouch and open my arms. He jumps up, tail wagging so hard it's shaking his whole body, and I keep my chin up just enough to prevent him from licking my face. That doesn't stop him from trying, of course.

"Cody," Michael says, chuckling. "Get a grip. You just saw him the other day."

"Hey. Hey. He adores me. Don't stand in his way."

Michael just laughs, and when I look up at him, he's standing at the end of the hall with that bright smile on his face, and...

And my mind goes blank.

Absolutely. One hundred percent. Blank.

I came here to talk to him, and I remember why, but the words, they're all gone. Someone straight up unplugged the server, and now I'm staring at Michael like an idiot.

He's staring back at me, his green eyes doing nothing to help me reboot my brain.

Smile fading, he cocks his head. "What?"

Of course he can read me like a book, even when there's nothing on the pages. I gently nudge Cody back, pet him a little and stand up.

Michael's gaze is fixed on me. "You okay?"

"Yeah." I absently brush a few strands of dog hair off my shirt. "I kind of wanted to talk about some things."

His eyebrows lift slightly. "Okay." He glances over his shoulder, then looks at me again. "Coffee?"

"Sure. Yeah. Thanks." Maybe that'll give me time to remember *how* to talk to him.

With Cody hot on my heels, I follow Michael into his kitchen.

While Michael pours coffee, I'm trying hard not to wring my hands, so I play with my wedding ring instead. Somewhere inside my skull are the words I rehearsed in the car, and I rack my brain, searching frantically, but...nothing.

And then there we are, standing on opposite sides of the narrow kitchen, coffee cups in hand. Cody sits between us, tail wagging as he looks at him, then me, then him again. Apparently we're boring, though, because he finally gets up and trots out of the room, tags jingling and nails clicking on the linoleum.

Alone, Michael and I drink in silence. I know the coffee hasn't made it into my system yet, but I'm jittery anyway. Placebo effect, nerves—who the fuck knows. My mental script is irretrievably gone, though, so apparently, if I'm going to give this performance, I get to wing it.

I set my coffee cup on the counter and face him. "So, I've been thinking about what we talked about yesterday. A lot."

His cheeks darken and his gaze drops. "I'm sorry." He plays with the handle on his coffee cup. "I was afraid it might upset you. I shouldn't have unloaded it all on you like that."

"No, no. It's okay." I gulp. "To get right to the point, I think maybe I can help."

Michael's eyes flick up. "Help? How?"

"Um..."

And now we all remember why Josh didn't last very long in drama classes once they got to the improv part...

Michael sets his coffee down and faces me again. "What do you have in mind?"

I rest my hands on the counter's edge, resisting the urge to drum my fingers.

"Josh?" Michael tilts his head.

The pressure's on, and my heart pounds as my stomach threatens to crawl up my throat. The counter is getting damp from my sweaty palms. *Come on, come on...*

Finally, I blurt out, "Do you trust me?" The question startles me, and Michael stares wide-eyed at me.

"What?"

"Do—" I clear my throat. "Do you trust me?"

"With my life," he whispers. "You know that."

"I do. Yeah. I just..." *Well, Josh?* I scrub a clammy hand over my face and exhale. "I was asking because..." *Because I'm an inarticulate idiot at the moment.*

"Josh." He inclines his head. "Whatever's on your mind, just say it." There's a note of uncertainty in his voice, the faintest hint of fear, and I realize he probably has zero idea what I'm trying to say or how it relates to what we talked about yesterday. This must be unnerving him something fierce, and knowing that turns my stomach even harder.

I hesitate, then push myself away from the counter and

step a little bit closer. Not quite enough to make him draw back, but enough I can *almost* reach him if I try. "You know I'd never hurt you, right?"

His gaze still locked on me, Michael nods.

"Then maybe..." The words refuse to come easily. "Maybe I can..." Staring into his eyes like this, certain he'll duck away from me at any moment, I don't know how to say this.

Abruptly, Michael's spine straightens and his lips part. He raises his eyebrows. "Is this conversation going where I think it's going?"

"That depends. Where do you think it's going?"

His Adam's apple bobs. "You first."

Damn it.

I clear my throat again, this time to get the air moving. Not that it helps.

"Just say it," he says. "Be blunt. You know I can handle it."

Not this time, I don't.

But I inhale slowly, hold his gaze and manage to say, "What if I can help you get more comfortable in bed with a man?"

There. It's out. And I don't think his eyes can possibly get any wider.

I hold my breath, wondering where the hell this conversation is going to go now that it's back in his court.

Michael folds his arms. Not tightly, not defensively and not quite enough to mask the shiver that goes through him. I can't tell if he's repulsed, uncomfortable or...something else.

His voice is soft when he says, "Am I right in assuming you're volunteering to be that man?"

There's no point in backpedaling or sugarcoating, so I just nod.

He breaks eye contact and stares at the floor between us. Michael's not easy to read, and right now, I have zero clue what he's thinking. The creases between his eyebrows, the tension in his jaw and his shoulders—they tell me he's deep in thought, but I can't begin to guess what those thoughts are.

He lifts his gaze again. "So you want to sleep together until I can handle it again?"

"If you don't want to, that's—"

"I haven't even gotten that far yet." He waves a hand. "I'm still trying to figure out what you're suggesting."

"Fair enough." I shift under his scrutiny. "The thing is, we've been together before. I'm not an unknown to you."

He studies me but doesn't speak.

I start playing with my ring again. "You know for a fact you can trust me in bed. Maybe that'll get you past those walls that keep tripping you up with guys you *haven't* been with."

"But...what about..." He gestures at my hands. "What about Ian?"

My fingers stop with my ring just above my second knuckle. "This was actually his idea."

Michael's eyes are huge. "Seriously?"

I push the ring all the way on, then hook my thumbs in my pockets and hope that's enough to keep me from being so goddamned fidgety. "His thought was that it might give you a chance to get your bearings before you find yourself considering getting into bed with someone new."

This time, Michael makes no attempt to hide the shudder. "You guys want me to use you? For, what, therapy?"

I shrug. "If you want to look at it like that."

"I don't want pity sex."

"It's not pity any more than it was pity when you slept

with me the first time."

Michael chews his lip again. "That was different."

"How? Because we were young and inexperienced?"

He doesn't answer immediately. Shaking his head, he says, "Look, I don't know about this."

"Do you have any better ideas?"

Michael's eyes flick toward me. Then toward the floor. "No. I don't. And don't get me wrong—I appreciate that you're willing to do this. I really do." He sighs, running a hand through his hair. "I just don't know. I have no idea what to think."

"Do you think it could help?"

He seems to mull it over for a long moment, and then half shrugs. "Maybe?" He meets my eyes, and his are filled with equal parts confusion and pain. "Part of me wants to take you to bed right now because I know that for me, you're the safest man on the planet. If I can't handle sex with you, then I might as well stay celibate."

My heart speeds up. "And the other part?"

He swallows hard, and he's staring at the floor again. "That part is scared to death of breaking that illusion."

It takes me a second to comprehend what he's saying, and when I do, my stomach drops into my feet. "You're afraid I'll do something to make you feel unsafe?"

"It's not rational. I know it's not." When he looks at me this time, his eyes plead with me to understand. "But that's the half that can't let go of the fact that I trusted Steve too." He rubs the back of his neck. "I know you'd never hurt me, Josh. I *know* that. But there was also a time when I *knew* I didn't really have Stockholm Syndrome, and that Steve really did mean well. It's kind of like being on a strong hallucinogen. Once you start seeing shit, you can't trust anything to be real."

Steve, you bastard.

"How can I prove it to you?" I ask softly.

Michael shakes his head and doesn't look at me. "If I knew..."

We're both still and silent for a long time. Then I cautiously come a little bit closer. He flinches, but his feet stay planted.

Slowly, carefully, I bring my hand up, and he's watching it, but he still doesn't back away. He's tense, and I'd bet money that the muscles in his neck are hard as steel right now, especially as I inch closer to his face.

"You can say no," I whisper. "Say the word, and I'll back off."

Still eyeing my hand, he says just as quietly, "Duly noted."

And he still doesn't move. Not toward me, not away from me.

The pad of my forefinger *just* meets his cheekbone, and he flinches again. I do too, because it's heartbreaking to see this man jerking back from a gentle touch, whether it's mine or anyone else's. Especially since there was a time when my touch would have drawn him in—a brush of fingers on his cheek had the same effect as grabbing his shirt and pulling him to me. The instant we made contact, we were in each other's arms.

Now, as my fingertips graze his face again, he closes his eyes and takes slow, ragged breaths, and suddenly he's not a man on the verge of being drawn into a kiss or an embrace. An image of Ripley from *Alien* flashes through my mind—sweating, crying, inches from a monster, awaiting the inevitable, horrible outcome.

"I would never hurt you, Michael," I whisper.

"I know." He shudders hard. "I'm not afraid of you."

You're afraid of who your fucked-up psyche thinks I am.

"You and I are the only ones here."

He meets my eyes. "No, we're not."

Steve, if I ever fucking see you again...

"Do you want this?" I ask. "Do you want—"

"I want everything." His gaze drops again, and he exhales. "I want you to kiss me. I want you to fuck me." He shakes his head. "Goddammit, I want to be able to do this without being scared of someone who isn't here."

Fuck. What do I do?

I let my hand rest against his cheek and wait until the shudder passes. Until he's as relaxed as he's probably going to get. Then, "Do you want to stop?"

"No." He looks me in the eye again. "I don't want to stop."

Sliding my hand from his cheek into his hair, I draw us together, and—

A victory!

He touches my waist. Tentatively, his fingers twitching slightly on top of my shirt, but he's bridged the gap. When I wrap my other arm around him, his hand curves around to my back, and a moment later, his free hand materializes on my chest. I'm still—even with the other on my back, that hand could push me away, and I give him time to decide if it's what he really wants to do.

A fraction of an inch divides our lips, and I'm afraid to cross it. I can feel his uneven breaths, and I swear I can feel his heartbeat over my own, and I don't know if I should move in or back off or—

Michael's hand tightens around the front of my shirt.

He lifts his chin.

And presses his lips to mine.

My heart stops. Neither of us is moving or breathing.

I'm sure he's going to jerk back at any moment, that the traumatized side of him is going to speak up with all its lies about me and every other man in the world, but he doesn't. He doesn't quite melt against me, doesn't quite relax, but in his own way, he does. The rigidity in his muscles starts to subtly ease. The hand on my back slides up a little, though I can't tell if it's a caress or if he's just resituating himself.

Gently, cautiously, I take over—holding him tighter, I tilt my head and nudge his lips with mine. They're taut at first, firm and closed, but gradually, they soften. And then they part. He takes in a long breath through his nose as I deepen the kiss.

He tugs at my shirt, and I'm so light-headed, it throws me off balance. We both stumble a bit, but thank God for Michael's tiny kitchen—his hip brushes the counter, and then I've got him pressed up against it, and he's not pushing me away or trying to stop or doing a damned thing except holding on to me and opening to my kiss. It's all I can do to keep our hips apart—one thing at a time—because I want nothing more than to press against him, feel every inch of him, and pray like hell that he suggests taking this into the other room. But no, no, not yet. Just this. I don't want to overwhelm him.

And that's a risk anyway, because the intensity of this kiss is like nothing I've ever experienced. Sure, there's arousal, and relief, and nerves, but there's something more. A hunger coming from him that I can't quite put my finger on. He's trembling, holding on to me and kissing me like his life depends on it. Not like he wants to drag me to bed, but like he's been waiting for this moment for so fucking long, he doesn't know what to do with it.

After God knows how long, I come up for air.

When our eyes meet, his are wet, and suddenly that

intense hunger not only makes sense, it breaks my heart—
it's the hunger of a man who's been starved for human affection for way, way too long.

He touches his forehead to mine, and my God, he's
shaking. "That's...that's the first time I've kissed anyone
since..."

"That's a damned shame." I pull him into a tighter
embrace and stroke his hair. "Anything you want, Michael,
just say the word."

He sighs. "I don't even know. Where to start. What I
can handle."

"Anything. We can take it as slowly as you need to. Just
like when we were kids—kiss a little. Maybe move up to
going down on each other before—"

"*No.*" The sharpness of his voice startles me almost as
much as the uncomfortable fidget. "Let's... I mean..." His
voice softens. "Slow, yeah. But oral. That's..."

I blink. "No oral?"

"No." He laughs bitterly. "Isn't that a switch? When I
was a kid, I was terrified of being fucked, but totally down
with sucking dick. Now I'd rather be dry-fucked than..."

Jesus. No one, not even Ian, has ever sucked my cock as
enthusiastically as Michael did. I don't even want to know
what Steve did to take that away from him, but I have a
feeling I'll find out sooner or later.

"I'll follow your lead." I smooth his hair. "Anything you
want, it's yours."

He wipes his eyes and then searches mine. "Why are
you doing this?"

"Because you're my best friend."

"This is a little above and beyond for a friend, isn't it?"

"Would you do the same for me?"

Michael tenses, and for a second, I'm afraid of the

answer. But then he says, "If anyone ever did to you what Steve did to me—" He cuts himself off and shakes his head, and then he pulls me in closer. Just before our lips meet, he murmurs, "He'd be a dead man," and then we're kissing again, and alongside that hunger for contact and affection, there's a taste of that passion he'd always had when we'd slept together in the past. That fierceness that came out in the form of desire, resulting in me getting pinned down and ridden hard, but could also come out as protectiveness.

"*He ever hurts you,*" Michael once warned me about one of my questionable boyfriends, "*he'll have me to answer to.*"

"*Do it again,*" he once growled to a guy who wouldn't back off in a club. "*I fucking dare you.*"

Michael breaks the kiss. Against my lips, he whispers, "To answer your question, yes. I'd do the same for you."

"I know you would." I kiss him again.

He draws back and swallows. "This is still a lot to handle. Up until just now, I hadn't even kissed anyone in years."

"There's no reason to rush any of it. We can take it a little at a time. Whatever you're comfortable with."

He's searching my eyes again. Then, tentatively, he pulls me into another kiss. Long, deep, just like the first one, as if the assurance that we can take all the time in the world has given him the confidence to have it all right now.

Anything you want, Michael. Anything.

He slides his hand down my back and draws me even closer, until our hips are *almost* touching, and I'm about to come unglued.

Jesus, I didn't think we'd get beyond a conversation tonight, but now this.

His fingers press into my back. His erection brushes mine. Oh God. I want him so fucking—

"Shit." Michael jerks away and pushes me back, breaking the kiss, breaking the embrace, breaking contact. "I'm sorry, I—"

"What's wrong?" I give him some space instead of pinning him to the counter. "Did I do something—"

"No, no, no." He shakes his head and paces across the linoleum. "No. You didn't do anything wrong."

I watch him, at a loss for what to say. When his back is to me for a second, I quickly adjust the tight front of my jeans, but even alleviating that discomfort doesn't help much.

Michael stops, and he slumps against the counter across from me. "I think I need..." He rubs his hands over his face. "Fuck. I don't know what I need."

"Maybe some time. To get your head around everything."

"Maybe." He sighs. "Probably."

"Do you want me to go?"

He folds his arms tightly across his chest, as if he can't get warm. "I don't want you to go, no."

I study him, trying to read between the lines. "*Should* I go?"

At that, Michael deflates. He cups his elbow and lets his face fall into his hand. "Fuck. Probably. I don't know." Rubbing his eyes, he mutters, "I'm such a goddamned basket case."

"We're going to fix that. Together."

He lowers his hand, meeting my gaze. "Would you be offended if I said I was skeptical that I can be fixed?"

"Offended, no. But I disagree. You've come a long way in the last few years, and you didn't think you'd get that far."

His lips tighten, and he avoids my eyes as he shrugs. "I guess we'll see what happens."

"We don't have to—"

"I want to," he says quickly and quietly. "I can't even tell you how much it means that you're willing to do this, and I want to. I'm just..."

"Not sure how much it'll help?"

He nods.

"Only one way to find out."

He tenses again, flinching slightly.

"It doesn't have to be tonight." I curl my fingers at my sides, desperately wanting to reach for him, but afraid to make contact again. It's so weird, hesitating to touch him after we were just wrapped up in a long kiss. "If you need some time, I can go."

He nods but doesn't speak.

"Call me tomorrow. Even if you're not ready to talk, just, you know, let me know you're doing all right."

"Okay. I will."

My keys jingle as I pull them from my pocket. There's got to be something I can say right now, but I'm drawing almost as much of a blank as I did when I broached this subject with Michael in the first place. So I just murmur, "I'm gonna go."

He nods again.

I spin my keys around my finger, and I still don't have a clue what to say, so I wish him a good night and head out of the kitchen.

I'm halfway down the hall when Michael says, "Josh."

I turn around, eyebrows up.

He hesitates, then meets my eyes from the kitchen doorway, and the subtlest ghost of a smile flickers across his lips. "Thank you."

CHAPTER 4

I SHOULD BE RELIEVED THAT MICHAEL'S OPEN TO IAN'S suggestion, but I don't feel anything like relief as I head home. I'm still too shell-shocked by just how shaken Michael really is. Hearing that his terrible ex did things to him to make him afraid of sex is one thing.

Watching him tremble with fear over the idea of being touched? Seeing the tears in his eyes? Personally witnessing his hellish past turn a kiss into something that difficult?

I wince, my throat aching and my eyes stinging. Knowing how Michael was when he was still young and unscathed makes it even worse. I know firsthand how confident and bold he used to be in bed, and it hurts like hell to realize how much damage has been done.

Halfway back to my house and my husband, I'm struggling to focus on the road, so I pull over. As the engine idles, I rub my hands over my face. Memories are flooding my brain, and one in particular keeps surfacing. It's a memory that still wanders through my mind from time to time, and tonight, it won't be ignored. Not with Michael's kiss still fresh on my lips and the raw fear in his voice still thrumming along my nerve endings. There's no stopping it. The past wants to be heard, and it's either let it say its piece now, or wait until I'm lying in bed beside Ian.

So I close my eyes and let the memories come.

———

WE'D BEEN HIGH SCHOOL GRADUATES FOR ALL OF TWO weeks, so naturally, we owned the world. Driving around our hometown in beater cars, grinning like idiots every time we passed our alma mater, we were flying high and ready for the future to bring it on.

To save money, we were both going the community college route for the next two years. After that, Michael would start at the university for pre-vet, and then veterinary school. He had it all mapped out and planned down to the letter, from graduating at the top of his class to opening up a practice right there in town. My agenda wasn't quite so well plotted. I hoped—and my parents hoped—that the two community college years would be enough for me to figure out what I planned to study at the university, if anything. At the moment, I didn't have a clue.

It was no surprise that Michael had it together and I didn't. He always did. He was valedictorian. I barely squeaked by with a C+ average. He had his driver's license the day he turned sixteen. I failed my driving test twice and finally passed it—barely—just before I turned eighteen. He'd known since kindergarten he wanted to be a vet. Nothing short of a fortune teller or a time machine was going to shed any light on what I wanted to do.

And Michael had figured out this whole gay business long before I had. He'd been out since our freshman year, and he'd confided in me that he'd known since fourth grade.

Me, I'd been a bit slower to creep out of the closet. It took me until well into high school to accept that, no, those hard-ons for guys weren't going away and, no, I really wasn't into girls, no matter how much I wanted to be. Senior year, just before the homecoming game, I finally came out. Naturally, the first person I told was Michael.

He'd blinked a few times, shaken his head and finally said, "Okay. And?"

"What do you mean, 'and'?"

"I mean, I thought you had something big to tell me." He shrugged. "I've known you were gay since forever."

"You—seriously?"

"Yeah."

"Why didn't you tell me?" I laughed. "It took me long enough to figure it out."

Michael turned a bit serious, though. "I thought about it. I've just—" He swallowed hard, and some color showed up in his cheeks as he avoided my eyes. "I didn't want you to think I was trying to persuade you."

"Persuade me? To what? Be gay?"

"Yeah."

"Why the hell would—"

He met my gaze. And held it. And held it. And—

Oh.

Oh.

I gulped. "Are you..."

The color in his cheeks deepened. "Would it weird you out if I told you I've wanted to kiss you since last year?"

Slowly, wordlessly, I shook my head. The guy I'd been fantasizing about for the last few months wanted to kiss me? After a long, silent moment, I said, "Do you still want to?"

Michael nodded. "A lot."

"Me too."

His eyebrows flicked up. "Have, um, have you ever kissed anyone before?"

"Not..." My face burned, and it was probably as red as his was a minute ago. "No guys."

"Girls?"

I nodded.

I thought he might be put off by that or think it was weird or something, but the corners of his mouth curled up and his eyes narrowed a little. As he curved his hand around the back of my neck, he said, "Good. Then you already know what to do."

Before I could protest—*I know how to kiss a girl, not a guy, and I never said I was good at it!*—Michael kissed me.

And if I had any doubts left that I was gay, they evaporated the second our lips met. Kissing girls had been all right, but even the deepest, hottest kiss I'd ever shared with a girl didn't curl my toes like this one did. Then Michael teased my lips apart with the tip of his tongue, and oh, yeah, I was definitely gay. This was easy. Effortless. My chin brushed his, and the lightly abrasive stubble—Michael had had to shave since junior high—was an unexpected turn-on. His lips were so soft, and that roughness was as masculine and hot as the short hair I couldn't stop running my fingers through.

When we separated, I was dizzy and out of breath, and that had never happened before.

Yep. Definitely gay.

Michael licked his lips. "I've been waiting to do that for so long."

"Good news," I said. "You don't have to wait to do it again."

He didn't wait.

We made out a few times after that. A few times? Hell,

any time we could get away from the prying eyes of adult supervision. All through our senior year, any chance we had, we were kissing in cars, beneath the bleachers, in our bedrooms when we could be absolutely certain our parents wouldn't walk in. Sometimes shirts came off, sometimes hands just slid under letterman jackets, and every once in a while, a brave palm would drift over the front of someone's jeans, but it never went further than that. I was nervous and inexperienced, and Michael always seemed perfectly content to make out. He loved kissing, and so did I, so neither of us complained about doing *a lot* of kissing.

But now high school was over, and suddenly I was restless. I wasn't bored, just curious. Adventurous. As if my newly minted diploma and my odometer hitting eighteen suddenly made me far too mature to still be a virgin.

Now that my mind was made up, I couldn't stop thinking about it. Every time I saw Michael, I was so turned on, I could barely speak. And when we finally got some time alone while his parents were at work, I was damn near shaking as we kissed and touched in his twin bed.

I couldn't wait. Not one more minute.

I broke the kiss and managed to catch my breath enough to speak. "I kind of want to go further this time."

Michael looked me in the eye. "How much further?"

I licked my lips, my whole body tingling with excitement and nerves. "Let's see where it goes."

His grin drove my pulse skyward. "I'm in."

"Took a whole lot of arm twisting, didn't it?"

He threw his head back and laughed. "Getting naked with you is not going to take any arm twisting."

I should've laughed, but my breath caught. Getting naked together. Holy fuck. Yes. Now.

He met my eyes, and his laughter was gone, and I knew

right then there was no turning back. This was happening, here and now, and I couldn't wait to be completely overwhelmed by him.

Bring it on, Michael...

Oh, he brought it on. For the longest time, we made out like we always did, but it was different this time. We were breathing faster, holding each other tighter, like our bodies knew this was only the beginning.

Michael made the first move. He slid his hand between us, cupping my erection through my pants, and kneaded with his fingers. I groaned, and I rubbed against his hand, almost like I was fucking his palm, and it felt amazing. Especially when Michael lifted his head and kissed my neck. My neck and my dick weren't connected, but the combination—his light little kisses and the pressure and friction below my belt—was insane.

"Why the hell didn't we do this sooner?" he murmured. "This is *hot.*"

"I dunno. But don't want to stop."

He moaned something I didn't understand, and when I ground against him harder, he gasped. That was when I realized I was pushing the back of his hand against his own cock. Maybe...

I lifted my hips and nudged his hand away. Before he could protest, I came back down, and now the only things separating my dick from his were two thick layers of denim, but holy fuck, we might as well have been rubbing naked skin against naked skin.

Michael pushed me onto my back, and he straddled me. As if having his rock-hard dick pressed against mine wasn't enough to fuck with my head, he sat up and pulled off his shirt, revealing his gorgeous torso. The thick ridge below his belt made my mouth water—I'd felt him against me plenty of times, and I'd even stroked him through his pants before, but tonight, I wanted him out of those tight jeans.

"Clothes," I said, wondering when I'd been reduced to single words. "Clothes...off."

"Good idea. All of them off."

"Yeah. Now."

I shivered—naked in bed with Michael? Why *didn't* we do this sooner?

Never mind that. We were doing it now, and so far, it was well worth the wait.

Belts came unbuckled. Shirts came untucked. Every motion and gesture and touch seemed so...profound. Meaningful. Like every article of clothing we took off was a rite of passage, and in spite of my eighteen-year-old freshly graduated confidence, now I wasn't sure I was ready for any of this.

Michael, though. Michael was ready. He peeled off my clothes like he was unwrapping a gift and wanted to savor the experience—eager to see what was underneath but still in no hurry as he slid his hands under my shirt and pushed it over my head.

I liked the way his palms felt on my skin—warm, lightly calloused and still soft at the same time—and I wanted to know what it felt like to do the same to him, so I pushed his jeans and boxers over his hips. I was suddenly a lot less coordinated than I'd been before, probably because his hands were still on me, and getting his pants off was a lot more complicated than it was supposed to be.

But with some fumbling and struggling, we managed, and just like that, we were tangled up in each other like we'd been a million times before, but with nothing at all between us. Sometimes he was on top. Sometimes I was. Sometimes we were on our sides. Always touching, though, and my head spun as we explored each other from head to toe.

I'd never even thought about how amazing it would be just to feel his warm body against mine—everything from his body heat to the thin hair on his legs drove my senses crazy. I couldn't stop touching him. Everywhere. Not just his ass or his cock or those beautiful abs. *Everywhere.* The lines and grooves defining his muscles. Smooth planes and soft contours. I was so fucking turned on, I was sure with every brush of his hand that I was going to come, but apparently, months on end of long make-out sessions had done a thing or two for my stamina. Thank God—I didn't want this to be over any time soon.

Michael rolled me onto my back and straddled me again, and my spine arched as his cock rubbed against mine.

"Holy shit," I breathed.

"Feels good, doesn't it?" He sounded as blown away as I felt.

"Yeah. Feels..." I moaned and closed my eyes. "Surprised I haven't come yet."

"Me too."

"For the record," I said, gazing up at him, "I have no idea what I'm doing."

"Good." He leaned down and kissed beneath my jaw. "Then you won't know when I do the wrong thing."

I laughed, holding him closer. "Everything you've done so far has been amazing."

"Likewise," he murmured and found my lips with his.

As we kissed, the heat of his naked body pressed against mine was unbelievable. I still couldn't keep my hands off him—following the gentle curve of his spine, tracing his narrow waist, kneading the powerful muscles of his thighs.

He lifted up a little, and when his fingers closed around

my cock, all my breath was gone. I'd jerked off a million times—how the fuck was it so much more intense when it was his hand? I couldn't figure out what made it so different, but I didn't care because it felt great.

But then he stopped.

"What're you doing?" I asked. "I liked what—"

He kissed me. "I want to try something," he said, panting against my lips. "Stay still."

"Okay." I was nervous as fuck, but more excited than anything else.

He kissed the center of my chest, and then started working his way down, and...

Oh God.

Oh fucking God.

He wasn't...

Yeah.

He was.

His lips were inches from my cock when he looked up at me. "Just tell me if you're gonna come, okay?"

I nodded. "Sure. Yeah." Because I definitely wanted the same courtesy if I ever worked up the nerve to go down on him.

Michael ran the tip of his tongue down the shaft of my cock, and I almost had to give him that warning right then and there.

"Holy shit!" My hips thrust up off the bed as if they had a mind of their own.

He did it again, and this time fluttered the tip of his tongue around the head, and before I could make sense of that, his lips were around my cock. Hot, wet, with his tongue teasing sensitive skin that had never been touched like that—so much for that stamina I'd built up from all that making out. As Michael added his hand to the mix, stroking the shaft while his mouth explored the crown, my orgasm was closing in fast. I held my breath and gritted my teeth—this couldn't be over yet. I wanted him to do this forever. I wasn't sure I could handle something this intense for more than a few seconds, but damn, I wanted to try, because it felt so, so good, especially when he moaned and his voice vibrated against my skin

Somehow, I managed, "I'm gonna...I'm gonna come."

I thought he'd stop, but he didn't. He kept going. Maybe he didn't hear me.

"Michael...fuck..." I wasn't even in control of my body anymore. My hips lifted up, pushing my cock deeper into his mouth, and he groaned and stroked me even faster.

And I was *there*.

"Fuck!" I clapped my hand over my mouth, barely stifling a helpless moan, and holy shit, Michael didn't stop. He didn't even miss a beat, and he kept stroking my cock and bobbing his head until I shuddered hard and sank back to the bed.

Michael sat up, wiping his mouth with the back of his hand, and flashed me the most delicious grin. "I've been wanting to do that forever."

I'd forgotten how to speak, so I just gestured for him to come back up to me. He did, and he leaned in to kiss me but hesitated. "I, um, don't know if you want to...after, uh..."

I grabbed him, pulled him in and kissed him. Before that day, the thought of kissing another guy after a blowjob was a little weird, but right then, it was hot, so I went for it. And holy fuck, it *was* hot. Like a vaguely salty reminder of what he'd just done to me, as if I stood a chance of forgetting any time soon.

He lifted himself up, probably to catch his breath. "You okay?"

"Y-yeah. You?"

He grinned. "I'm great."

"Yeah, you are." I lifted my head and kissed him lightly. "Where the hell did you learn to do that?"

Michael laughed softly and shrugged. "I guessed."

"Lucky guesses. It's really good."

"Yeah? What's it like?"

"It's awesome. In fact..." I nudged him onto his back. "You should try it."

His eyes widened, and he squirmed a bit as I leaned down to kiss his neck. "D-don't mind if I do," he said. "Oh my God."

"Same deal." I kissed beneath his collarbone. "Tell me if you're gonna come."

Michael nodded vigorously, and he squirmed as I worked my way down his torso. I'd thought he'd done the same thing to me as a way to tease me, and maybe he had, but it was a damned good way to work up the courage to suck his dick. Inching closer to him, I told myself with every soft kiss that there was nothing to be nervous about.

When my lips reached his hipbone, there was no turning back, and looking up at him, I couldn't imagine turning back. Yeah, I was nervous as hell and had no idea what the fuck I was doing, but that look on his face—eyes round and gleaming, breath coming in short, sharp gasps—killed any hesitation I had left. I'd damn well figure out what I was doing if it meant driving him as crazy as he'd driven me.

I stroked his cock, tentatively at first, and then with more confidence. I wasn't so sure I could take him in my mouth—he hadn't had much trouble with me, but his cock was a little thicker than mine. But I'd also seen pornos with guys who were hung like tree trunks, and they'd managed to fit into all kinds of places where they probably shouldn't have, and Michael was much more...well-proportioned.

There was only one way to find out if I could take him.

Steadying him with one hand, I let the head of his cock slip between my lips. Instantly, I felt like an idiot for ever being afraid to do this. His skin was hot and salty, and I loved the way his hard dick slid between my lips, especially as I took him a little deeper. So that was why he was so into going down on me—this was almost as good as being on the receiving end.

"Oh...*fuck.*" Michael's fingers curled around the sheets at his sides.

I glanced up at him, and my God, his face. His lips were parted, his cheeks and neck flushed, and his forehead was creased as he stared right back down at me with wide, gleaming eyes.

"D-don't stop," he slurred. "That's so...oh fuck..."

I broke eye contact and kept doing what I was doing, not giving a damn that my jaw and my hand were starting to ache a little. As long as I was turning Michael on like this, I didn't care.

A salty-sweet taste met my tongue. He must've been getting close. Was I ready for that? To have him come in my mouth? He'd let me come in his, but could I—

"Oh yeah," he moaned, barely enunciating at all. "God, yeah. I'm...I'm gonna..."

I kept going. I kept stroking him as he got even harder in my hand, and the head of his cock seemed to swell between my lips. He moaned again, and then he whimpered, and his whole body tensed and arched. His breath caught. He ground out a curse, and suddenly, all the tension in his body released, and all the air rushed out of his lungs, and semen rushed across my tongue. There was more than I expected, and before I could even think twice, I swallowed it, and he kept coming, and the way he shuddered and groaned was too hot to be real.

I stopped, and Michael collapsed back onto the bed as if he'd actually levitated off it.

"Holy shit," he breathed.

I joined him up by the pillows, and like I had earlier, he grabbed me and pulled me into a kiss. Fuck. The taste of his orgasm, the tingling in my lips from going down on him, and now his always spectacular kiss? I never wanted to leave this bed. *Ever.*

When we finally separated, I touched my forehead to his. "So that's why people like sex so much."

He laughed breathlessly. "Yeah. That's why. Jesus." He ran his fingers through my hair. "I have no idea if we're doing any of this right, but everything we've done has been amazing."

"I agree." I brushed a kiss across his lips. "Imagine how much better we'll be when we've had some practice."

That grin damn near got me hard all over again. Wrapping his arms around me, Michael pulled me down to him. "You can practice on me all you want as long as you let me suck your dick again."

I shivered. "Deal."

IN MY CAR ON THE SIDE OF THE ROAD ALL THESE YEARS later, I sniff sharply and wipe my eyes. I've thought about that night many times over the years, but it's never made me cry before. Though my dick is hard and my body is trembling, the sting in my eyes is too intense to ignore.

They say losing your virginity means losing your innocence, but everything about that afternoon in Michael's bed was innocent. It was sweet, and gentle, and one of those memories that I hope never, ever fades. It was a night when neither of us knew Steve existed or that he'd eventually find a way to leave his mark on every facet of Michael's being. Before the panic attacks, the ER visits, the restraining orders that weren't worth the paper they were printed on, not to mention all the fighting it took just to *get* one of those worthless pieces of paper. Before Michael watched his life-long dream of becoming a veterinarian go up in smoke after he flunked out of school. He never has told me what happened, why he went from a straight-A student to failing his finals, but the way he averts his eyes whenever the subject comes up, and just knowing who he was going home to every night at the time, well, I can put two and two together.

But that afternoon we went to bed together for the first time, none of that had happened yet. Neither of us had any reason to be scared or cynical about the future, and it remains to this day one of the most beautiful sexual encounters I've ever had.

There was light in Michael's eyes that day.

And so help me God, I will do whatever it takes to bring that light back to life.

CHAPTER 5

I FINALLY GET MY SHIT TOGETHER AND FINISH THE drive home. The whole way, I can't stop asking myself—and the universe, and God and whoever happens to be listening —if I'm in over my head. I'm even more determined to help Michael, and even less certain of my ability to do it. I'm already emotionally exhausted, and we didn't even get past a kiss.

Fuck. It's not a question of whether I'm in over my head —it's a question of how far.

I pull into the garage and park beside Ian's car. As the garage door closes behind me, I shuffle to the door and into the foyer.

Ariel thunders in and bounces, running in circles at my feet.

"Hey, baby," I say with a halfhearted smile and scratch behind her huge floppy ears. "Did you miss me?"

"She always misses you."

Ian's voice makes my heart clench. I look across the foyer into the living room. He's on the couch, grading papers as always, with Rosie on his lap. She glances up at me, and she's about as indifferent to my presence as she is to the papers Ian's using her to prop up.

Ian isn't quite so indifferent, though. His eyebrows arch enough that I know he sees right through me. He clicks off the TV, which he must've been using for background noise. "How did it go?"

"It..." I look down at the dog again because she's easier to face at the moment than he is. And even she seems to be looking at me like "Well? How *did* it go?"

I clear my throat. "I think I need a drink."

"I think I'll join you." He picks Rosie up and plants her on the other cushion. She hisses, and he grumbles "Bitch" as he gets up.

Usually, her attitude makes me chuckle—she really is kind of a bitch—but tonight, I just don't have it in me. I reserve what energy I have left to get me from the foyer to the kitchen.

A glass of wine isn't going to cut it tonight, so it's straight to the freezer for the bottle of vodka that's been in there for the past three years.

"That bad, huh?" Ian asks as I set the bottle on the counter.

Was it that bad? I don't even know if it went badly, per se. Michael's on board with the solution Ian suggested. He feels safe enough with me to do this. I can help. I can do something to *fix* this.

Ian wraps his arms around me, and I exhale.

"You okay?" he asks against my neck.

"I don't know." I rest my hands on his.

He holds me tighter. "You talked to Michael about it?"

"Yeah. He needs a little time to think, but it sounds like he wants to try it."

"Oh. That's good, right?"

"Yeah. I guess we'll see what happens."

"I guess we will." He kisses my neck again but doesn't say anything. Knowing him, he's waiting for me to elaborate.

Finally, I lean against him. "It's just so hard to see him like that, you know? Since I know what he was like when he was younger and hadn't been put through the wringer, yet. It's just—" My voice cracks. "It's really hard to see."

Ian holds me tighter and kisses just above my collar. "I can't even imagine."

"I kissed him. Didn't go any further than that, though."

Ian tenses a little, lips touching my skin but not moving. After a moment, he quietly says, "Oh."

I turn my head slightly. "That's okay, right? I mean, you're—"

"It's fine. It's fine." Ian turns me around and puts his hands on my hips. "I, uh... It might take some adjustment. Knowing you're with someone else. Physically."

"But you said—"

"I know, I know." He shakes his head. "I'll be fine with it. It's, you know, going from 'in theory' to 'in practice'." Before I can ask for the millionth time if he's *sure* about this, he says, "How was he with that? With kissing you?"

I swallow, my spine prickling at the memory. "It was harder for him than I thought it would be. He's definitely got some ghosts hanging around in that department."

Ian flinches. "God, what a travesty."

"It really is." I shudder. "I think this process is going to be slower than I thought. I think..." My brain is threatening to send me back to that place it went while I was in the car. Back to the better times that only make the present more painful to accept. "I need..." My eyes dart toward the bottle of vodka, which is starting to sweat on the counter. Then I release my breath and gently free myself from my husband's embrace. "I think I need a shower. I feel like I've got"—I shudder—"Steve all over me."

Ian nods. "Go. We'll sit down and have a drink afterward, and maybe talk about this some more."

"Good idea."

I kiss him gently and then make my way upstairs, Ariel hot on my heels. She follows me to the bathroom, as she always does. I stop there and pet her, giving her some attention, and then send her into the bedroom to wait until I'm done with my shower. Closing the door is kind of a necessity with her in the house—otherwise it's a good bet she'll end up in the shower, as we've both found out the hard way a few times.

Alone in the bathroom, I turn on the water as hot as it'll go and scrub until my skin is raw. I hope to God this doesn't happen every time I'm with Michael. Hopefully it's just my body reacting to the undeniable reality of how traumatized my best friend is and how much damage that cretin left behind. I've known all along that he hurt Michael, but I never realized Steve's got a ghost like poison ivy.

The water is starting to get cool, and I'm as clean as I'm going to get, so I shut it off and get out.

After I've dried off, I wrap the towel around my waist. When I step out of the bathroom, Ariel isn't there. The bedroom door is closed, and Ian's lying in bed, in jeans and nothing else, but he's not waiting for me so we can go to sleep or go downstairs for a drink. Not with that gleam in his eyes, and definitely not with the bottle of lube conveniently placed on the nightstand.

My shoulders droop. "Ian..."

"I know you don't feel like it." He swings his long legs over the edge of the bed and rolls to his feet. He takes off his glasses, sets them beside the bottle of lube and then crosses the room to where I'm standing. As he slides his hands over my bare waist, he adds, "I think it might be good for you to remember why you're doing this."

"Oh, believe me. I haven't forgot—"

Ian's lips stop mine. Whatever resistance I have is slipping away fast, and in spite of myself, I wrap my arms around him. How he's in the mood is beyond me, but it's contagious. I wasn't thinking positively about sex when I came out of the shower, but even after all these years, Ian can still turn me on when he wants to, and he definitely wants to now. His mouth is taking over mine, and his palms are sliding all over my damp skin, and damn all these goose bumps for giving me away. And if they don't give me away, the hard-on that's swelling against his certainly does.

He guides me toward the bed, and with every step, his kiss gets more demanding. He wants me to remember why I'm doing this, what Michael's been missing all this time and I've vowed to get back for him, but sex with Ian is on a whole different plane. Michael is—was—playful and leisurely, never in any rush. Ian doesn't hurry either, but he's rough and aggressive, the kind of man who leaves marks. Whenever he's done with me, I'm satisfied beyond belief, and yet still begging for more.

Maybe he doesn't want to remind me what I'm doing for Michael as much as he wants me to remember that he's here too.

Oh, Ian. I hold him tighter, kiss him harder. *You don't ever have to worry that I'll forget you.*

Ian nudges me back another step, and though my eyes are closed and I'm moving backward, I take the step without hesitation. His arm is around me, and he can see past me— he won't let me fall or hit something. My mind is reeling with anticipation but not fear. Because there's never been a trace of fear between us in the bedroom. Maybe some first-time clumsiness when we met, but actual fear? None. Never. I can't imagine ever being scared of Ian, or of him recoiling from my touch the way Michael did tonight. I can't imagine us ever touching each other any way besides... this. Like two people who are, for the time being, living and breathing for nothing beyond the other's pleasure.

My calves touch the bed. Ian cups my cock through the towel and squeezes just hard enough to make my breath catch. With a gasp, I break the kiss and tilt my head back, and he goes right for my neck.

"You've done enough thinking for tonight," he whispers, and his lips skate along my throat. "And you've got a lot of emotional shit ahead of you." He kisses beneath my jaw as he tugs the towel free. "So for tonight, I want you to lie back, close your eyes and just enjoy being fucked."

A shiver runs through me. My towel lands at my feet. "I think I like the sound of that."

His lips curve into a grin. He plants one more soft little kiss on my neck and then lifts his head. "Anything you want tonight, it's yours."

A million fantasies rush through my mind—all the things we've done or talked about doing in a decade—but I just whisper, "You."

Ian's grin gets bigger, more wicked, and he kisses me once more.

Then he drops to his knees in front of me.

And everything just...disappears. His lips and tongue, his hands, the way he moans with pleasure as he's sucking my cock—my brain can't even comprehend anything beyond all this. I watch him, barely breathing. This is one of my favorite views ever. His brow is furrowed as if everything he's doing requires intense concentration, and whenever his blue eyes flick up to meet mine, my heart nearly stops. Yeah, so much for not being in the mood.

"You're fucking amazing." I slide my hands into Ian's hair and rock my hips, fucking his mouth slowly, and he groans and bobs his head faster.

Then he stops. Disappointment has about two seconds to set in before he meets my gaze again, and...*Jesus*. As he stands, eyes gleaming like they were when I came out of the bathroom, my whole body is electrified. I know exactly what's next.

"Want me on my back?" I lick my lips. "Or—"

"I want you to stay right there. Don't move."

I don't move. Ian takes off his jeans and boxers, and then he puts his arms around me again. Holding me, kissing me, turning me inside out.

Now we're moving together. Going back. Going down. Even the instinctive fear of falling backward is barely there —Ian won't let me drop.

And he doesn't. He eases me down onto the bed, and sinks down on top of me, kissing me passionately and pressing his feverishly hot body against mine.

He doesn't stay like that for long, though.

"I want you just like that," he whispers, and kisses me once more. Then he sits up and reaches for the lube. As he strokes it onto his dick, I can barely lie still.

Yes. Yes. Fuck me. The sheets gather in my curling fingers. *Right now.*

He starts to guide himself in but hesitates. "On second thought..." He nudges my hip. "Turn around."

Those two words go straight to my balls, and I bite down on a moan. He doesn't just want to fuck me tonight— he wants to fuck me *hard*.

As I shift position, Ian hands me the damp towel I'd worn out of the bathroom.

"Put this down first." He gives me a moment to smooth the towel on the bed beneath me.

Then he's behind me. And he's pressing against me. And my head is already spinning and the anticipation is going to drive me insane.

And just like it always does, the first stroke takes my breath away.

My head falls forward. The towel and sheets are flimsy anchors, but they're something to hold on to, and I hold them tight as Ian's cock slides deeper inside me. As he always does, he takes his time, letting me get used to him before he starts going to town on me. It doesn't take long— we've fucked enough times, my body always yields easily to him—and he steadies my hips as he finds a perfect, smooth cadence.

For a few strokes, anyway. Just as my vision is starting to clear, and I can finally breathe, he speeds up. He has a death grip on me now and holds me perfectly still as he slams into me. Skin slaps against skin. Every thrust knocks breath from my lungs, and I'm pretty sure I'm moaning and cursing, but my brain can't zero in on anything except the way Ian's dick feels and his deliciously painful grip on my hips.

His weight shifts. Ian pushes me all the way down to the mattress, the cool and slightly damp towel beneath me emphasizing the warmth of his skin against mine, and he fucks me deep and hard, and between his cock inside me and his hot breath on my neck, I'm losing my mind. Nothing else exists, nothing else matters—just my husband's amazing body against mine, his cock driving into me, my own cock rubbing against the coarse towel, and the orgasm that's building by the second.

I claw at the bed. Curl my toes. Try to complement his thrusts, but I can't move, so I just lie there. Lie there, close my eyes, enjoy the ride. Holy hell, I love the way this man fucks me. My orgasm is both irrelevant and inevitable—I don't care if I ever come, because I feel so, so good, but I will because it's impossible not to when Ian's body is against me and his cock is moving inside me.

He groans in my ear. "Goddamn, you get tight when you're close. You are...so..."

I bite my lip, squeezing my eyes shut and trying not to come quite yet. He's close too, and I love how he sounds— the way his breath catches, the way his voice is strained and shaky.

Somehow, he manages to thrust even harder, as if he thinks he can possibly get any deeper inside me. I press my forehead into the mattress, gripping the edges of the towel and holding my breath and—

And he sinks his teeth into my shoulder.

And I come.

One second, I'm on the verge, and the next, I'm gone, and Ian knows just how to keep me going, fucking me relentlessly as I gasp and cry out and fall to pieces beneath him.

Then I collapse. All I can do now is lie there and be fucked, taking him again and again while aftershocks ripple through me and my fingers knead the comforter.

"*Fuck.*" Ian grunts. Forces himself into me. Trembles.

And exhales, his whole body relaxing on top of mine as cool breath rushes past my neck.

"Jesus," I breathe.

He drops a light kiss on my shoulder. "You're welcome."

I snort and roll my eyes. "Arrogant bastard."

Chuckling, he kisses the spot where he bit me. "Arrogant bastard who just made you come." He withdraws slowly. "So as I said, you're welcome."

I push myself up on shaky arms and glare playfully at him but can't help laughing. "Well, if anyone's earned the right to be so cocky in the bedroom..." I cup the back of his neck and kiss him.

"Damn right," he murmurs between kisses. Running his fingers through my sweaty hair, he says, "So much for your shower, though."

I shrug. "I'll cope somehow."

We clean ourselves up and collapse into bed together. As the dust settles and the rest of the world returns, that uncomfortable knot in my stomach comes back with a vengeance. That's the downside of forgetting about things for a little while—they always come back, louder and more insistent than before.

I sigh and rest my head on Ian's shoulder. This road with Michael is going to be a long one, isn't it?

"Still worrying about Michael?" Ian's soft voice breaks the silence, startling me.

"Yeah. I don't think that's going to stop any time soon."

"He'll be okay." Ian kisses my temple. "It might not happen overnight, but he's in good hands."

On both counts, I wish I was as optimistic as he is. "I still can't believe you're on board with this."

Ian holds me closer. "If it were anyone else, I might not be okay with it. But if it weren't for Michael, I probably wouldn't have you." He nuzzles my neck. "I'd say we both kind of owe him one."

"Still."

"I promise, Josh, I'm on board with this. I want him to

be okay, and there's no one else in a better position than you to get him there."

"So no pressure, right?"

"No, there's no pressure." He shifts around and props himself up on his elbow while I lie on my back. "A lot of this is on Michael, not you. You're not fixing him. You're giving him a safe place to work through the stuff that needs fixing." Ian touches my face. "Literally all you have to do is be the safe, kind, giving lover that you already are, and let him do the rest."

I swallow, watching my fingers run up and down his forearm. "Then why am I so scared to screw this up?"

"Because you care about him."

The lump is rising in my throat, but I push it back. "I do."

Silence falls, and I don't have the first clue how to fill it. Ian's confident I can help Michael, and I'm terrified I'll make it worse, and there's no point in beating that dead horse. The only thing that'll appease my worried mind is seeing the results, and that'll just take time. There's nothing we can do tonight.

Ian kisses my forehead. "Still need that drink?"

"No. Maybe. I don't know." I pull him closer. "I kind of want to stay like this for a while."

"Then we will. Come here."

I turn on my side again, facing him, and Ian wraps his arm around my shoulders and rests his other hand on my arm. His fingertips run back and forth along my skin, the touch both ticklish and reassuring.

Even in my most volatile relationships, and during the rough patches I've had with Ian, I've never been afraid of someone. In all the years we've been together, and the years I spent with other guys before him, it has never once felt like a novelty to be safe in a man's arms.

Lying there with Ian, safe and comfortable, I let my mind wander back to earlier this evening. It feels like a lifetime ago, standing there in Michael's kitchen and fighting through all his demons for that first hard-won kiss before Michael finally had to back off. I almost feel guilty for making love so easily with Ian; we've been effortless lovers from the very beginning, and it's hard to stomach that we're still that way while Michael's been twisting in the wind all this time.

I take Ian's hand and kiss the backs of his fingers.

You deserve to feel this way with someone, Michael.

And I'll make damn sure you do.

CHAPTER 6

Parked beneath Michael's apartment building, I don't get out of the car quite yet.

So, this is it. Here we go. Time to get in way, way over my head and hope like hell Michael doesn't catch on that I don't have a clue what I'm doing, and pray to God I don't fuck up. How do we even get started with something like this, anyway? It's not like showing up at my old piano teacher's house.

Knock, knock—I'm here for the eight o'clock lesson.

I close my eyes and pull in a long breath through my nose. I've got this.

Right?

"*A lot of this is on Michael, not you,*" Ian's voice echoes in my brain. "*You're not fixing him. You're giving him a safe place to work through the stuff that needs fixing.*"

I gulp. That's all there is to it, isn't it? Michael needs a safe place. I am that safe place. So, with my heart in my throat and my knees a little shaky, I get out of the car and head up to his apartment.

Hand on the doorknob, though, I hesitate again.

"Literally all you have to do is be the safe, kind, giving lover that you already are, and let him do the rest."

What if it's not that simple?

I know people with PTSD. Even the most well-meaning friend can accidentally set off a flashback. One of my coworkers spent a year in Afghanistan, and he seemed okay with everything we would've expected to trigger him. Crowds and loud noises don't bother him. He took his kids to a fireworks show last year without any issues. Even the fire alarm going off barely made him jump. He told someone the only thing he struggles with is driving through mountains or open wilderness, particularly if it's a desert. His wife has to drive through places like that. Otherwise, he's completely back to normal.

And then someone decided to surprise him for his fortieth birthday last year. Apparently, walking into a conference room that he thought was empty and suddenly having the lights come on and two dozen people shout "Surprise!" was...not good for him.

I shudder, my fingers still resting on the doorknob. Michael's been on a relatively even keel, especially after all the therapy he's had. But is there some trigger I don't know about?

Only one way to find out, I suppose.

I whisper a prayer and then open the door.

Cody comes flying down the hall, barking and wagging his tail.

"Hey, you." I chuckle and crouch down to pet him. He immediately flips over on his back, tail still going ninety miles an hour as I scratch his belly.

"Cody!" Michael's voice sends a flutter through me. "Come eat!"

The dog is on his feet again and scrambling up the hall

to the kitchen. I stand, push my shoulders back and follow him.

I've got this. It'll be fine.

I step into the kitchen.

Michael comes into view.

My stomach flips. This is it. Here we are.

I try and fail to will my heart to slow down. "Hey."

"Hey." His cheeks color, and he laughs softly. "So, um. I guess we're..."

"Yeah." I laugh too, which at least means I'm breathing.

"Do you..." He gestures over his shoulder at the kitchen. "Do you want something to drink? Coffee?"

"No. No, I'm good."

Our eyes meet.

"Listen, uh..." I clear my throat. "I'm following your lead on this. I don't really know what we're doing. I mean, where to start." I chew my lip. "Maybe we should talk limits. What's off limits at this point?"

Michael hugs himself and avoids my eyes for a moment. "Definitely not oral yet."

"Okay. No oral." Cocking my head, I ask, "Does that apply to both giving and receiving?"

He nods, but then his lips quirk. "Well, receiving might be okay. Maybe." He gulps. "Just *not* giving."

"Noted. What about anal?"

"We'll work up to that."

The fact that he's more optimistic about anal than oral makes my skin crawl—he used to love oral sex. Giving and receiving. I don't even want to know what Steve did to turn something Michael loved into something he's afraid of.

"So for tonight," he goes on, "maybe we could... Okay, this might be kind of weird."

I'm pretty sure we're long past weird and well into what the fuck, but I don't say anything.

He wrings his hands, watching them instead of me. "So I'm still not too sure about touching. Or being touched." He exhales sharply. "It's stupid, but there it is."

"It's not stupid." I manage to keep the venom out of my voice—that's all for Steve, not Michael. "After what you've been through..."

Michael shudders. "Anyway, if you're really okay with baby steps..." He raises his eyebrows.

"Absolutely. Your pace."

"Okay. Good. Because I'm thinking a small step to start with would be a massage."

"Oh. I hadn't even thought of that. That's a really good idea."

Some of the apprehension vanishes from his expression. "Why don't I start by giving you one, and we'll see where it goes from there?"

I grin. "I'm not going to say no to a massage from you."

Michael hesitates, but then he lets himself smile just enough to crinkle the corners of his eyes. "Bedroom?"

"Lead the way."

Walking into Michael's bedroom is weird as hell. I've been in here plenty of times—Ian and I helped him move in, and I've taken care of his dog while he was out of town—but never under this pretense. My nerve endings tingle. God knows how this is going to play out tonight, and how far this is going to go. Just being here stirs something in me—excitement about being with Michael, uncertainty about whether this will be a good step or an unmitigated disaster, guilt over going to bed with one man while I'm wearing a wedding ring for another.

Tonight, I'm almost hoping he doesn't work up the

courage to take this very far because I'm probably too nervous to get it up. Back when we had sex the first time, I was nervous as hell, but I had teenage hormones as an ace up my sleeve. Now? Not so much. And I'm sure that's exactly what Michael's psyche needs—trying to conquer his fear of sex with someone who can't get or stay hard.

Oblivious to my worries, Michael picks up a bottle of oil off the dresser. "I've had this stuff for ages, but never used it." He tears the plastic seal around the lid with his thumb and peels it off. "You're not allergic to anything, are you?"

"Not that I'm aware of. What's in it?"

He looks at the label. "Sunflower seed oil, some sort of flower extract, and—wait." He looks closer. "Crap. I don't know if this stuff is condom safe." His eyes flick up and meet mine. "Is that okay?"

I study him for a moment. "Do you think we'll get far enough tonight to need condoms?"

Michael tenses. "Um..."

"One step at a time." I smile. "I just don't want you to think we have to get that far tonight." Especially since I don't know if I'm going to make it that far tonight.

He swallows but then relaxes slightly. "Okay. Yeah, I don't know. One thing at a time, right?"

"One thing at a time." I gently take the bottle and set it on the dresser. Then I close my hands around his. He straightens, pulling in a sharp breath, but he doesn't jerk away. Holding both his hand and his gaze, I quietly say, "There's no pressure tonight, Michael. We only have to go as far as you're comfortable."

He swallows. "I guess I..." His eyes lose focus, and then he shakes himself. "I don't know."

"Relax." I smile. "It's me."

"I know it is." His expression is deadly serious. "I don't think I could handle being here with anyone else."

Jesus. What did that asshole do to you?

His thumb rubs back and forth along mine. "For, uh, future reference, though, do you think we need to use condoms?"

I consider it for a moment. "Well, I haven't been with anyone but Ian in years. It's up to you."

"I've been tested." He shrugs. "I'm okay without them if you are. And if Ian won't object."

"Since we won't have to worry about it tonight, why don't I talk to him later?"

Michael nods. "Good idea."

"For the moment, though..." I glance at the massage oil, and when I grin at Michael, he returns it.

With his free hand, Michael reaches up and touches my face. The contact makes my skin prickle all over and speeds up my heart rate.

Then, without a word, he draws me down, and when our lips meet, I release his hand and slowly, gently, put my arms around him. He cradles the back of my head as he deepens the kiss, sliding his tongue alongside mine. My head is spinning and my pulse is racing, both from the kiss itself and from Michael's sudden surge of confidence.

And so much for whatever concerns I had about not being able to get hard.

I try to draw my hips back a little, but Michael presses his fingers into my lower back, keeping us close together. For a moment, I'm back in our early days, when a kiss like this was almost a guarantee that we'd be horizontal and sweating before long, and I hope like hell that this boldness holds out. That whatshisname doesn't sink his claws in and remind Michael of his past and his fears.

Remember our *past, Michael. Not the one you had with him.*

He breaks the kiss and gazes up at me. "Wow," he whispers breathlessly.

"Yeah. Wow is right."

His eyes flick toward my lips, then meet mine again, and he grins. "I'm...I'm definitely in if you still are."

I lick my lips. "Absolutely."

"So, massage?"

"Yes, please."

He kisses me once more, and then he lets me go. He turns down the bed and moves the pillows off to the side, and while he does that, I strip off my shirt and jeans. To my surprise, Michael starts getting undressed too, and I don't question him. This is all about his comfort zone, and if he's comfortable getting undressed, I'll call that a step in the right direction.

It's a struggle not to stop and stare at him, though I do steal a few glances. It's tough not to—he's always had a gorgeous body, and time has been nothing but kind to him. He's smooth in all the right places, sharp in all the others, with a few constellations of freckles here and there, placed as if to deliberately draw attention to his shoulders and pecs.

"Um." I gesture at the bed. "Facedown?"

"Yeah. Use whatever pillows you need. So you're comfortable."

I settle on the bed, which is a challenge now that my cock has definitely decided to join the party. Thank God for a pillow-top mattress. I take one of Michael's pillows, fold my arms under it, and rest my head on top of it. And then fidget a little more until I'm as comfortable as a man can get while lying on an erection.

Michael joins me. I can't tell if he's sitting or kneeling. Hell, he could be standing on his head for all I know—he's just beyond the edge of my peripheral vision, only his body heat and the slight dip in the mattress giving away his presence.

Now I'm starting to see why Michael wanted to go this route. Not only is a massage fairly benign, lying somewhere in the gray area between platonic and sexual, but it puts me in the most passive, nonthreatening position I can think of. I can't grab him or overpower him. I can't even look at him without twisting around.

"Ready?" he asks.

"Whenever you are."

I close my eyes. The bottle top clicks open, then shut. Skin hisses against skin—he's probably rubbing his hands together to warm up the oil.

Then the sound stops.

The whole room is still.

Every inch of my skin is suddenly hyperaware of everything, even the ambient air, as if my senses are searching for that first contact, wondering when he'll make the connection. When, and where.

And *if*.

What if he's having second thoughts? If he's—

There.

Between my shoulder blades.

Fingertips at first, and then more. His touch is tentative, almost ticklish, fingers and palm barely meeting my skin, and my whole body's hyperawareness instantly concentrates itself in that warm outline of his hand.

Slowly, he traces the length of my spine, taking an absolute age to make the journey from the base of my neck to just above my boxers. The contact breaks, and then his hand materializes between my shoulder blades again, and he repeats the same stroke. Again. Then again.

The motion reminds me of someone petting a dog, and maybe that's what he's doing—taking something he does all the time without flinching, and transferring that to human contact. Allowing himself this type of touch so he can move on to massaging and...more.

Take all the time you want. I'm not going anywhere.

He adds his other hand. Starting at my shoulders, he traces the muscles and the outside of my rib cage. "This okay?"

You tell me.

"Feels great." I turn my head as much as I can without snapping my neck, and hope he can see my smile. "You've always been good at this."

He laughs softly, and the next stroke of his hand is more confident. More pressure, less hesitation, and it feels divine. His hands have always been a bit calloused, and the combination of softness and roughness sliding over my skin feels amazing. Little by little, the explorative touch becomes an actual massage. He presses in, kneads muscles that were tighter than I thought and damn near lulls me to sleep.

I'm not hard anymore, which makes it a hell of a lot more comfortable to lie like this, but it's not nerves or even lack of arousal. I'm just...that...relaxed.

I need to return the favor. Maybe not tonight—I'm following his lead, after all—but I want him to feel this way. Comfortable, relaxed, completely at ease.

I'm nearly drifting off when the bed dips beside me. Michael's knee materializes beside my thigh, and then his weight eases down over me.

Though he's barely leaning on me—touching, to be sure, but holding himself up on his knees—it's suddenly difficult to breathe. The heels of his hands glide up my back, but it's that thick hard-on against my ass that has my full attention. Two thin layers of shorts do nothing to temper that solid presence or the heat of his flesh, and lying on my stomach is starting to get *really* uncomfortable again.

Michael's hands stop. "Turn over."

Oh, thank God.

He lifts himself off me, and I roll onto my back. To my surprise, he gets back on top. His hands start just above my boxers, and slide upward, applying almost no pressure at all, just skimming across my skin and forcing all the breath out of my lungs. If having his dick against my ass was maddening, this is unreal. He's rock hard, straining against the front of his boxers, and every time he so much as breathes, he rubs just right to make my breath catch.

The best part, though, is that I can see him now. So many memories flood my brain, and my mouth waters as I see him sitting like this in the past—on top of me, wearing next to nothing, gazing down with those heavy-lidded green eyes and that smile on his face.

I hear his voice from a lifetime ago: *"Stop me if it hurts."*

Years later, *"I'll make you forget that he hurt you."*

It hadn't hurt that first time—he'd been much too careful—and yes, he'd made me forget about the ex who'd stomped all over my heart. All before someone had come along and broken Michael.

Now it's my turn to protect you and help you heal.

Gazing up at him, I want to reach for him, but I don't. Not yet. He's still getting used to all of this. One thing at a time. No matter how much I want to touch all over his smooth skin and his gorgeous body.

Michael lets his hands slid from my chest to my shoulders, and then past them, onto the bed, and he sinks down on top of me. The temptation is almost irresistible now. My fingers curl at my sides, gathering handfuls of sheets and digging into the mattress.

"God, I want to touch you so bad, Michael."

He presses his hips against me, taking my breath away all over again, and murmurs, "Please do."

Our eyes meet.

"Stop me if it hurts."

"I'll make you forget that he hurt you."

Moving slowly, I reach for him, and we both gasp as my palms come to rest on his sides. As I wrap my arms around him, I hold my breath and Michael shivers. He squirms a little in my embrace, but he doesn't pull back.

"You okay?"

"Y-yeah." He swallows, then brushes his lips across mine. "Just nerves."

"We don't have to go any further than this."

"This is a lot further than you might think."

I run my hands up his back. "Tell me what you want me to do."

Michael licks his lips. "Give me your hand." He grabs the bottle and pours some oil onto my palm. Then he guides my hand down between us and under his waistband, and he wraps my fingers around his dick. Instinctively, I start stroking, my slippery hand sliding easily up and down the thick shaft and the head.

Michael groans softly.

I squeeze a little. Twist a little. Squeeze again. "Like that?"

"Mmhmm." He closes his eyes and exhales. "Oh fuck."

With every stroke, my thumb rubs along the underside of my cock through our clothes.

"Sit up a little," I murmur. "Clothes are...in the way."

Michael hesitates for a heartbeat, but then he lifts himself up. I push my boxers down just far enough to get them out of the way, and to my surprise, Michael does the same. When he comes down again, his cock rubs against mine, and we both groan as I close my hand around our cocks. I can't get my hand all the way around, but it's enough, and judging by the way Michael whimpers and starts rocking back and forth, he agrees. He fucks into my hand and against my cock, and I stroke us both, falling into perfect sync with the motion of his hips.

"Is this good?" I ask anyway.

"Oh yeah." He sweeps his tongue across his lips. "D-don't know if I can come, but—"

"You don't have to come," I breathe. "Nobody does. Does it feel good?"

"Very."

"That's all that matters." I kiss him softly and add, "I just want you to feel good."

"I do feel good." His lips graze mine. "This is... Holy fuck..."

"Perfect. Then don't...stop."

Michael kisses me hard, and he doesn't stop. There isn't as much oil now, and the friction is getting more intense. I'm about to ask if he's okay or if he wants to add more, but then he moans and thrusts even harder.

With a shudder, he breaks the kiss and lets his head fall beside mine. I swear to God, his shudder echoes right through my body, curling my toes and lifting my spine off the bed. My eyes won't focus. My mind is a mess. All I can think of is *please, please, don't stop,* and Michael isn't stopping. We've fallen into a perfect rhythm, his hips and my hand moving together like they were made for this, and *holy shit.*

"Fuck," I whisper. "Keep doing that and *I'm* gonna come."

"Good." He keeps doing that, and my orgasm's not stopping for anything, and when my breath catches, Michael thrusts even harder, and just like that, I'm coming. And coming. And coming.

"OhmyGod," I murmur. "Jesus, Michael."

And suddenly he throws his head back and groans. His rhythm falls to pieces, and God only knows whose semen is whose anymore, and who the fuck cares. He trembles and jerks, and then he releases a long, ragged breath and sinks down on top of me.

For a moment, we're just still, holding each other and catching our breath. Michael's arms shake as he pushes himself up, but when our eyes meet, we both smile.

"That was a hell of a massage," I whisper.

He laughs, and I love that sound even more than his moans and gasps. He leans down to kiss me. "Guess we got a happy ending, didn't we?"

Chuckling, I nod. "Yeah. Guess we did."

One more kiss, and then he rolls off me and grabs some tissues from the nightstand. After we've kicked off our boxers and cleaned ourselves up, we pull the covers over us.

Michael turns on his side, facing me, and I mirror him. He cups my cheek. "That really was amazing."

I kiss his palm and smile. "Glad you enjoyed it."

He smiles but then turns serious. As his thumb traces my cheekbone, he says, "I can't thank you enough. I know we didn't go very far tonight, but"—the smile slowly returns—"I'm suddenly a lot more optimistic that we'll get there."

Me too. I haven't breathed this easily since we had lunch the other day.

I smooth his hair. "Same here. And I don't have any complaints about how far we made it tonight. Do you?"

"Not at all."

"Good."

He rests his head on my shoulder, and I kiss his forehead.

Tonight went better than I'd expected. On the other hand, we kept it pretty safe and benign. Sex is a minefield for him, and though I don't know where all the mines are, I'm fairly certain this will get more challenging as we go. Something is making him shy away from oral sex. I'd bet good money that anal isn't going to be easy either. Somewhere between here and being fully confident, there's a conference room full of well-meaning coworkers ready to send him into a tailspin.

But this is a step, and it's a promising one.

I'll take it.

CHAPTER 7

EVER SINCE IAN AND I BOUGHT THIS HOUSE FOUR YEARS ago, we've had a weekly tradition of hanging out in the hot tub with Michael on Sunday nights. We started out getting together to watch movies, but after giving in to the siren's call of the tub several times in a row, we decided to skip the movies altogether.

Sometimes during the summer, we'll pass around a joint, but only when Ian's off school for a few months. Michael's boss doesn't care—she smokes too—and mine hasn't given a drug test to anyone but a new hire in years. The school district isn't so tolerant, though, so between September and June, we just crack open a bottle of wine and relax before the work week starts.

Tonight, however, is the first Sunday since this whole thing started with Michael, and it's the first time I've been nervous about getting into the hot tub with the two of them. Sitting between them as Ian fills all our glasses, I follow their lead. As long as they're comfortable and acting like everything's normal—as normal as they can be, I guess—

then I'll assume everything *is* normal and act accordingly too.

While Ian's turned away to put the wine bottle on the little table beyond the tub's edge, Michael glances at me, eyebrows up.

Is this weird? his eyes seem to ask.

Maybe. But—I raise my glass—*we have wine.*

His brow pinches for a second, but then he chuckles and raises his glass too, so hopefully the message made it across.

Oblivious to our silent exchange, Ian turns around again. "To the start of another week of being gainfully employed."

"Cheers," Michael says, chuckling.

We carefully clink our glasses together—the last thing we need is for a sliver to break off and fall in the water—and settle back against the sides.

Next to me, Ian sinks down into the water until his chin is touching the surface, and closes his eyes. "Ugh. Is the school year over yet?"

"That bad?" Michael asks.

"Worse." Ian stares up at the top of the gazebo. "I swear to God, if I get one more parent asking why their kid is failing, as if *I'm* the problem..."

"Jesus," Michael mutters into his glass.

Ian lifts himself up and takes a sip, then sinks down again. "And they wonder why half the faculty smokes."

"Wait, they know about that?"

Ian swirls his wine slowly. "Of course they do. It's the parents we're hiding it from."

Michael laughs. "Okay, that makes sense."

"Yeah, most of the powers that be just ignore it as long

as we don't show up at school smelling like it. Or obviously stoned."

"Or share it with the kids," I add.

Ian snorts. "Or buy it from them."

Michael nearly spits out his wine. "Please tell me no one's done that."

"Which part?" Ian asks. "Coming to school stoned, sharing it with the kids or buying it from them?"

Michael raises his eyebrows. "Uh, any of the above?"

Ian purses his lips. "Well, rumor has it some kids stole the gym teacher's stash, and when they got caught, they ratted him out."

"Did he get canned?"

"Not after he threatened to pay his dealer to produce a list of everyone who bought from her." Ian laughs into his glass. "The whole thing disappeared pretty quickly after that."

Michael whistles. "Wow, I didn't realize pot was such a hot commodity."

"At a school where we're trying to educate the children of entitled rich fucks who believe grades are given, not earned?" Ian raises his glass in a mock toast. "You're damn right it's a hot commodity."

"Huh. Yeah. I guess I can see that." Michael takes a sip. "I'm sure there are worse ways to cope."

"There are. And believe me—people do those too." Ian scowls. "Last year, two teachers at another school were busted buying Adderall off the kids. You know it's getting bad when the kids and teachers need the same drugs to function."

"Ugh," Michael says. "That's just sad."

Ian and I both nod. We've had many, many conversations

about the teachers and students alike being driven to desperate measures, or out of school entirely. If Ian didn't enjoy working with the kids so much, he'd have walked out and gotten a job at Radio Shack or something just to keep his sanity. But he loves what he does, so he grinds his teeth through meetings with parents, indulges in some wine on the weekends and then loses himself in a little bit of weed over the summer.

The mood in the hot tub threatens to get depressing, but Rosie picks that exact moment to climb up the side of the gazebo. Though she does it every single time we're out here, she still startles the hell out of all three of us.

Indifferently, Rosie wanders along the side, safely on the wood, and stops beside Michael. She bumps her head against his, and he reaches up to scratch her chin. As he does, she puts her front paws on the slippery edge and leans toward him, balancing precariously.

Ian gives an exasperated sigh. "You know, cat, one of these days, your dumb ass is going to fall into this tub."

Michael shoots him a good-natured glare. "And you'll laugh your head off, won't you?"

"Well, you have to admit," Ian says, bringing his glass up to his lips, "it *would* be funny."

"Aww, no it wouldn't." Michael strokes her back with a wet hand, leaving her coat soaked. "He's so mean to you."

"Uh-huh." I laugh. "Says the man who thinks it's hilarious to pet her like that so she'll go dry off on *our* furniture."

"I just can't believe she puts up with it." Ian pauses. "Wait, no, never mind. Michael can do no wrong in her eyes."

"Eh, you don't have any room to complain." I playfully nudge his leg with my foot. "At least she actually likes you."

"Most of the time." He nods toward Michael. "I mean, 'kay, she hates you, but she likes him better than me."

"There's a hierarchy." Michael shrugs. "Not my fault I came out on top."

Ian opens his mouth to retort, but pauses.

And then Michael turns beet red.

And then I get it.

Michael clears his throat. "I, uh...I meant in the—"

"Cat hierarchy." Ian reaches for the wine bottle. "Got it." He tops us all off, but even the wine can't fill this unusual—and totally predictable—awkward silence. So much for things being completely normal.

Michael stares into his glass. "I, uh, don't want to make things weird, but I think we should, you know, talk. About what's going on." He gestures at me.

Ian takes a deep swallow of wine. As he sets his glass on the edge, he nods. "Okay. We can talk about it." His eyes dart back and forth between us. "What exactly..." He glances at his glass again, as if he might drain what's left in one go. But he doesn't. He slides a hand over my knee as he often does. "What do we *need* to talk about?"

Good question. We should address the issue, and we should be open about it, but what needs to be said?

They don't offer up anything. Michael doesn't look up from his glass. Ian can't seem to get comfortable beside me.

My stomach twists and my heart races. "Well, for starters, maybe now would be a good time to address the condom issue."

They both tense a bit.

"Condom issue?" Ian asks.

"Yeah." I glance at Michael, then turn to my husband, lacing our fingers together beneath the water. "Do you have any preference? As far as whether or not we use them?"

"Oh." Ian absently rubs my thumb with his. "Um. Not really, no. I know Josh is clean."

"And I haven't touched anyone in years," Michael says.

"Then if you guys don't want to use them, I..." Ian pauses, reaching for his glass with his other hand. "I guess I don't have any issue with that."

"We don't have to. It's completely up to you."

Ian's eyes lose focus, and he slowly sips his wine. For a few seconds, he rolls it around in his mouth. Michael and I exchange uncertain glances.

But then Ian shrugs and puts the glass aside again. "I trust you both. If you're comfortable going bareback, then I'm comfortable with it too."

"If that changes," I say quietly, "all you have to do is tell us."

Ian nods, a faint smile forming on his lips, and he squeezes my knee beneath the water. "I will. But I don't think it'll be a problem."

Even still, silence falls again, and it stretches well into awkward. I'm not sure we have enough wine for this conversation. Maybe it should have waited until after the school year.

Except it can't wait. We need to clear the air and make sure we're all on the same page before this continues, because I refuse to let this damage my friendship *or* my marriage.

It's Michael who finally breaks the silence. "I guess the biggest question I have is, condoms aside, are you sure you're okay with this, Ian? I mean, let me just put it out there." He gestures toward me. "I'm sleeping with your husband."

"I know." Ian swirls his wine again, watching that 'stead of looking at either of us. "Look, I'm not going to 'nd I don't have reservations about this. I do. I admit it." 'nces at me before he finally meets Michael's eyes.

"But if that son of a bitch did something to you that's still hurting you after all this time, and there's something Josh can do to alleviate that? Then hell yeah, I'm okay with it."

Michael holds his gaze. "Even if it means...?"

Ian hesitates for a split second but nods. "Yeah. And I mean, I'll get over my reservations. The bottom line is that Josh and I both care about you. If there's anything I can do to make this whole thing easier, I'm happy to do it. Josh is just...more suited to this particular approach than I am."

My heart flutters, and I'm not sure why. His blessing? The incredibly subtle—and quite possibly imaginary—implication that if I weren't here, he'd be willing to do what I'm doing for Michael? Just the fact that he is so damned unselfish, even when it comes to me, our marriage and our sex life?

I squeeze his hand. He smiles at me and squeezes back, giving my heart another jolt.

Michael clears his throat. "You guys..." He releases a heavy breath. "You really have no idea how much this means to me."

"You're our friend," Ian says. "It was hard as hell watching you go through all that. If there's something we can do, or one of us can do, then..."

"I know." Michael swallows. "And you guys have both already done more for me than you can imagine. If it hadn't been for the two of you, I might still be with Steve now."

"We never would've let that happen," Ian growls. "Another few months with him, and no one would've ever found that fucker's body."

The fierce protectiveness in his voice makes me shiver. Michael too.

"I know," Michael says quietly. "That's why I'm grateful as hell to have you guys. And what we're doing now, it's—" His voice cracks, and he quickly swallows some wine. "It seriously means a lot." Smiling a bit, he raises his glass. "I can even drink again because of you two."

"You couldn't..." I pause. "Because of Steve?"

Michael shrugs. "Oh, what isn't because of Steve? Obviously I got over this one."

"Was it..." Ian hesitates. "When he hurt you, uh, sexually, was it when he drank?"

The wine on my tongue gets slightly sour. Steve and alcohol had a volatile relationship too—I was pretty sure that was the only kind of relationship he was capable of having.

Michael shakes his head. "When it came to that, the booze was a blessing in disguise, actually. Sometimes I'd encourage him to drink too much because then he couldn't perform." His cheeks color. "The alcohol could make him violent, but..." For a moment, his eyes are distant. Then he brings his glass up again and mutters into it, "That was better than the alternative."

Ian and I exchange wide-eyed glances. We'd seen Michael with concussions, cracked ribs, stitches, the occasional black eye, even a broken wrist. That was better than the alternative? How bad did it *get*?

He must see the question in my eyes, because he adds, "Trust me on this one."

"I do," I say. "It's just hard to imagine."

"Yeah, it is," Ian breathes.

"Well, a lot of it's behind me." Michael pushes his shoulders back and rests his head against the edge of the tub. "Five years of therapy will do that to you." He smiles, and it's more genuine than I'd have expected during a conversation about his ex. "We're still working some bugs but I'm a lot better now."

"You definitely are." Ian smiles too. "It shows."

"Now if I can just forget him in the bedroom, I'll be in good shape."

"Well." Ian turns to me. Then back to Michael. "I'd say you're in good hands."

Michael meets my gaze. "Yeah. I'd say so too."

And I hope like hell that they're right.

WE ALL DRINK A BIT MORE THAN USUAL TONIGHT. Not enough to get sloppy drunk—none of us care for that—but we're probably all pushing the legal limit to drive. There will be some mild hangovers all around tomorrow, but a few gallons of coffee and some more of water will get us through our respective workdays.

Ian's got the highest tolerance out of the three of us, and he stops drinking first, so at the end of the evening, he drives Michael home. By the time they leave, he's sobered up, so I'm not concerned.

While he's gone, I cover up the tub, take care of the animals and try to ignore the creepy-crawly feeling that seems to follow every conversation involving Steve. It's especially pronounced after tonight's discussion. The more Michael tips his hand about what happened, the more I worry about what we're doing. And having Ian admit to his reservations about all this isn't helping. I'm glad he's honest about it, of course. But going forward, knowing he's not sure, is challenging.

Maybe I should've had more wine. Or less. One of the two. Fuck, I don't know. I'm not even sure if a few puffs off a joint would be enough to unwind me tonight.

It's nearly bedtime, so I start going through the motions.

Ariel announces that Ian's home, and I'm just finishing up brushing my teeth when he joins me in the bathroom. As soon as I see his face, my heart skips. His jaw is tight, his brow furrowed.

"You okay?" I ask as I slot my toothbrush beside the mirror.

"I'm fine." Ian wraps his arms around my waist and kisses the side of my neck. "Listen, um, on the drive home, I did a lot of thinking. About Michael. And you."

My stomach tightens. "Yeah?"

"Yeah. I told you guys tonight I had some reservations."

I turn around in his embrace and meet his gaze, but don't speak.

Ian swallows. "After everything Steve put him through..." He takes a deep breath, and the intensity in his eyes startles me as he whispers, "You have my unconditional blessing to give Michael *anything* he needs to put that son of a bitch behind him."

"Are—"

"I'm absolutely sure." He cups my cheek with an unsteady hand. "After tonight, whatever doubts I had, they're gone." He draws me in, and our lips brush as he murmurs, "And he's damn lucky to have someone like you."

"I think I'm the lucky one right now." I kiss him softly. "I can't imagine anyone else who'd let me do this."

"I trust you. I know both of you." He draws back a little, and that intensity is still there, but different now. Clearer. As if he's...*haunted*. "I just can't live with the idea of him struggling through this by himself."

Before I can respond, Ian kisses me, and he holds me so ¡ght, it's almost painful.

He breaks the kiss just enough to murmur, "Anything ds."

"Noted." I nudge him toward the doorway. "Tonight? Anything *you* need."

"Good. Because right now, I need the same thing he does."

His kiss ends the conversation but fills in what he left unspoken:

I need you.

CHAPTER 8

ON THE WAY UP TO MICHAEL'S APARTMENT, MY PULSE is already pounding and my palms have been damp since I left work.

Please, please, let this go well. Michael deserves it.

I reach for the knob, but the door opens.

And I meet Michael's gaze.

He grins. His eyes are gleaming and narrow, as if he's been plotting and scheming.

Oh fuck. It's going to be a good night, isn't it?

He closes the door behind us.

I shrug off my jacket. "You're in a good mood."

"Yep. I am." And just like that, he's against me, kissing me.

My jacket falls forgotten to the floor. We stumble back into the wall, and Michael's kissing me like he did way back when. Breathlessly, passionately, telegraphing loud and clear that he wants it and he wants it right now. But how much can he *handle*?

"Bedroom," he murmurs. "I can't wait."

He takes my hand, and we hurry down the hall to his

bedroom. As soon as we cross that threshold, he's in my arms again. Fuck, this must be a good sign.

"T-tell me what you want to—"

"I want you to fuck me."

I freeze. "Michael, are you—"

"Please. I want... God, I want you so bad."

"But are—"

His kiss answers me. Still...

"Are you sure you don't want to top me first?" I moisten my lips. "Small steps?"

"I'm sure. I've been thinking about this all day." He rubs against my hand—fuck, he's already hard as a rock.

Goose bumps prickle beneath my shirt. "Have you?"

"All day."

"Well then." I pull him in and kiss the side of his neck. "Who am I to deny you something you've been fantasizing about?"

Michael shivers. "Please."

"Then why do you still have clothes on?"

Without missing a beat, he pulls back. His shirt is off before I can even start on mine. We strip down to nothing, and all the while, my heart's going crazy—I had expected this to be a long process, but after just one night together and a reassuring conversation with Ian, he's ready to move this far forward? God, yes.

We climb onto his bed, hands and mouths all over each other, and my head is spinning faster and faster. Now that I have his body against mine, I'm as impatient as he is. I could make out with him all night, stroke him and tease him and turn him inside out, but I want him *now*.

I kiss my way up his neck, and then sit up. "Get on your knees."

Michael starts to turn around but stops. He closes his eyes. Breathes slowly. Deeply.

I touch his shoulder, and he flinches. Subtly but unmistakably. "Michael? You okay?"

"Yeah. Sorry." He shakes his head. "It happens sometimes. Just spaced out for a second. I'm good."

I raise my eyebrows. "We can slow down."

"No! I want to keep going. I'm good."

The hair on the back of my neck stands on end. I don't want to second guess him and undermine his confidence, but I also don't want to push him too far.

Michael faces me fully and curves a hand around the side of my neck. "I want this." He kisses me, and there's that boldness again—he pushes my lips apart, explores my mouth, teases my tongue. Then he touches his forehead to mine. "I'm okay. I promise."

I hesitate but finally nod. "Turn around."

Another shiver runs through him, and he grins. After one long, knee-shaking kiss, he turns around.

Heart thumping, I run my hand over his beautiful ass and up his narrow waist. The thought of being inside him is more than enough to send my body temperature soaring.

I put some lube on my fingers first. As I press my fingertip against him, he exhales slowly, and he curses under his breath.

"You okay?"

"Yeah. Just really, *really* want you to fuck me. Like, *now*."

I grin. "I will. After I tease you a little."

"Fucker," he mutters.

I laugh, and some of the tension in my neck and shoulders eases—his sense of humor is intact, so maybe he really is ready for this.

I tease his anus with a lubed fingertip. He groans and lets his head fall forward. Teasing him drives me as crazy as it does him, and this view is just...beautiful. His muscles, his freckles—I could stare at him all day. The only way this view could get any better is with my dick sliding in and out of him.

"Josh," he moans. "Fuck me."

With pleasure.

I gently press my finger into him, but it takes work. Even when we were both doing this for the first time, back when we were nervous kids, he wasn't this tense. Or maybe I just don't remember. Either way, he hasn't been touched in years, so I take my time. He slowly yields to my finger, though it's still a tight fit.

"Can you handle more?"

He nods. Is he breathing?

"Michael? Are you—"

"More. Please." His voice is tense too, but he leans back against me as I'm withdrawing my finger, so I slide it back in. I crook it slightly, seeking that spot inside, and when I find it, he moans. He's still tight, still tense, but his voice is made of pure pleasure.

"M-more," he whispers again. "Please."

I add a second finger, and damn, the tension is even more obvious now. Though some additional lube helps, I can still barely move my hand. I keep finger-fucking him slowly, gently, letting him relax, but he stays tight as hell. Even as I stroke his prostate, driving soft little moans from him, he doesn't relax.

He shifts, and the sheen of sweat on his shoulders catches the light. The ends of his red hair are darker now too. What the hell?

He turns his head, revealing more perspiration on his

forehead and temple. "I want you..." He pauses, as if he needs to catch his breath. "I want you to fuck me."

But are you ready *for me to fuck you?*

"A lot of this is on Michael, not you," Ian's voice echoes in my head. *"You're not fixing him. You're giving him a safe place to work through the stuff that needs fixing."*

I swallow. Michael knows what he's ready for. If he wants it, and he says he can handle it, then he does and he can. Right?

"Literally all you have to do is be the safe, kind, giving lover that you already are, and let him do the rest."

And maybe that's the key—letting him do the rest. Giving him control so he can call the shots.

I slowly withdraw my hand. "Why don't I get on my back so you can be on top?"

Michael considers it for a second and nods. We change positions—I lie back, and he straddles me. I steady my cock with one hand and cover it in lube with the other. Once I'm good and slick, Michael lowers himself until the head is pressing against his ass.

As he eases down slowly, I grit my teeth. He'll relax. Once he's taken a few strokes, he'll relax. Won't he?

"Breathe," I whisper. "Just breathe and take your time."

He nods. Exhales. Inhales. Lowers himself a little more. The head of my cock breaches him, and my breath hitches. *Fuck,* he's tight.

He doesn't move. Eyes shut tight, lips apart, he's still for several seconds before he lifts off and comes down again. This time, he takes me deeper, but every inch is a challenge. Despite being in control, he's still painfully tight—I can't imagine it's comfortable for him. That taut grimace all but shouts that it's not.

"Michael, are—"

"I can't." The words are strangled, almost a sob. "Fuck, I—"

"It's okay. It's okay. We don't have to."

He lifts himself off me, and I exhale as my cock slides out. A shudder runs through him that sends a chill through me, and he releases a choked, panicked sound.

"Easy." I embrace him gently and guide him down to the bed. Holy fuck, he's shaking. "Michael?"

"I can't. I'm..." He shudders hard. "I'm sorry. I'm—"

"Shh." I press a soft kiss to his forehead. "Just breathe for a minute."

He's breathing, but way too fast, so I hold him close and remind him over and over to breathe, that I'm here, that he's safe and no one will hurt him. All the while, I silently curse Steve. Wherever he is now, I hope to God he's alone and miserable, that he hasn't gotten his hands on anyone else.

Eventually, Michael exhales, and the shaking slows. "Jesus. I'm sorry."

You're not the one who should be sorry.

"You all right?"

He nods, and as I carefully release him, he settles on his back. "I guess I wasn't ready for that after all." He stares up at the ceiling. "Weird. Everything's fine, and then suddenly it's not." He's breathing more steadily now, but his heart's still going a hundred miles an hour.

"We can go slower."

"Question is, how slow?" He turns to me and scowls. "I mean, the thought of you fucking me has had me so turned on all day, I couldn't concentrate at work. Didn't raise any red flags in my head. Didn't make me feel panicky or anything. I just...wanted it. But then when we tried..."

I grimace and kiss his cheek. This really is going to be a minefield, isn't it?

Michael sighs. "I don't know what will be a problem and what won't. For all I know, you could fuck me into oblivion, tie me up, slap my ass, and I'll be fine, but then one kiss in the wrong place, and I'll fall apart." He combs through his hair with shaky fingers. "What the fuck is the matter with me?"

"Nothing's the matter with you. You've been through hell. That's going to leave—"

"It's been *five years*." He rubs his eyes. "Damn it. After the other night, and talking to Dr. Hamilton on the phone today, I felt good about everything, you know? Felt like I could handle anything. But I should've listened to you. When you hesitated."

"You didn't know what was going to happen. We'll get there, Michael."

"Do you know how frustrating that is?" He covers his face with his hands, then lets them drop onto the bed. "I wasn't this wound up when I was a virgin."

"Of course you weren't." I touch his arm, and when he doesn't recoil, I move my hand to the middle of his chest. "Nobody had hurt you then."

He closes his eyes and shudders.

"Nobody's going to hurt you now," I go on, "but it'll take time for your mind to catch up with that. I'll wait as long as it takes."

He sighs. Neither of us says anything for a while. Eventually, Michael breaks the silence. "Can I ask you something kind of weird?"

"Sure."

He opens his eyes and stares unfocused up at the ceiling. It takes him a good thirty seconds to finally ask, "When did you know Steve was..."

"An asshole?"

"Yeah. That."

"Why?"

Michael shrugs. "Just curious." He turns toward me. "I guess I'm trying to figure out how long I was the clueless idiot in the gilded cage."

"You weren't an idiot, Michael. He manipulated you in the beginning, and he scared you in the end. And he fooled us all. Early on, we all liked him."

His eyebrows jump. "You did?"

"Sure. He seemed like a nice guy. Charming as all hell."

"Yeah, he was." Michael sighs, sinking back against the pillow. "And he wasn't always a total asshole. We even had some good days right there toward the end."

"Really? Even after everything he'd done?"

"Stockholm Syndrome will do that to you," he mutters. Then he shakes his head. "Honestly, he was a terrible person, but he could be a good guy at times. You know how some people are perfectly nice most of the time, but sometimes they're just insufferable because they're in a bad mood, or they're drunk, or whatever?"

"I do, and most of those people don't do the things Steve did."

"No, but he was kind of like that. To an extreme. Both extremes, actually. He was really good at making up for it when he was an asshole, and I stupidly ate it up every time." He laughs humorlessly. "If I had a nickel for every time he convinced me he'd changed."

"Like I said, he had us all fooled." I absently run my fingers up and down Michael's arm. "The closer you are to a situation like that, the harder it is to see the truth. Especially when you're being played by someone as manipulative as he was."

"There is that." He inches closer to me. "The fact that

that he wasn't all bad all the time makes it worse. I mean, sometimes..." Michael moistens his lips. "Even now, I have to admit there were times when he was genuinely a good guy. Like when my mom died. He was a fucking *saint*."

"That doesn't negate the other things he did."

"Of course not, but those things don't negate the fact that he got me through that period." Michael turns to me. "I'm not making excuses for him or trying to paint him as a decent guy. To be honest, I *need* to remember those good times because if someone like him comes along again, I'm afraid of not seeing the red flags because, hey, he's such a nice guy."

I shudder at the thought, and take his hand. "Another guy like him comes along, he'll have to get past me. Assuming there's anything left after Ian gets his hands on him."

Michael smiles, though it doesn't reach his eyes. "Well, you'll see it before I did. You saw it with Steve." He pauses. "When *did* you see it?"

Now it's my turn to stare up at the ceiling. It's hard to imagine there was ever a time when I didn't wish a fiery death on that man, but as sickening as it is to look back on it now, there was. Finding the dividing line, that moment when I began to see him for what he was, isn't so difficult now, because there are few things in my life I remember more clearly.

I clear my throat. "Your sister's wedding."

"Really?"

"Yeah. I mean, I'd started getting a weird vibe off him for a while. Ian and I both felt a little 'off' about him, but couldn't put our finger on why. That night..." I shift my gaze toward him. "You'd been acting really strange the last few times I'd seen you." I cringe at my own stupidity. "I thought you were just exhausted from school. It was getting close to finals, and it didn't even occur to me that there was something else going on. And he was kind of short with you whenever I saw you guys together, but... I don't know, I guess I didn't see it, or I didn't want to see it." I lick my dry lips. "But that night..."

Michael fidgets beside me. "What was it that tipped you off?"

Nausea creeps up my throat at the memory. "When you spilled your wine on him at the reception."

He shudders hard. I lace my fingers between his and squeeze gently.

That moment plays through my mind like it's being projected right onto the bedroom ceiling above us. We'd all been having a great time at the reception, even if Michael had been exhausted from—I thought—studying nonstop and his boyfriend had been a little irritable. Michael had just topped off his red wine, and he and Steve had exchanged a few terse words about it. What Steve's problem was, I'll never know. Unlike that jerk, Michael's never been a problem drinker, and if he gets drunk, he gets giggly. He isn't even loud. He just thinks everything is funny—Michael drunk is like me stoned, and I've always thought it was pretty cute.

He wasn't silly or giggly that night. I'm not even sure how much he'd had by that point, but he was still steady on his feet.

His aunt, however, couldn't hold her liquor or walk in high heels. While Michael and Steve stood with Ian and me, she went tottering past, stumbled and crashed into Ian. He and Michael instinctively tried to stop her from falling, and they succeeded, but Michael's wineglass went tumbling out of his hand, bounced off Steve's arm and splashed across his shirt.

And Michael went *white*.

Ian helped the drunk aunt to her feet, but Michael's gaze stayed fixed on Steve, and something in the pit of my stomach had turned to ice as Steve's narrow eyes slid toward Michael.

I'd seen Michael scared before. I'd seen him nervous before plays, terrified before he came out to his parents, shaking as he waited to find out if a knee injury had ended his baseball career. The way he was looking at Steve, shrinking back and pale—I'd never seen him like that before.

Oh God, I remember thinking. *What the hell is going on?*

For the rest of the night, I'd tried to get Michael alone for a minute or two, but Steve was on him like the wine on his shirt. Then I turned around and they were gone, and Michael's mother said they'd taken off because Steve wasn't feeling well. It was two days before I heard from Michael again, and he insisted everything was fine.

"You don't have to answer this," I say cautiously, "But what happened that night? After you guys left?"

Michael rubs his hand over his face, and I can't remember when he started trembling. "After we left, he managed to make me feel two inches tall because of a spilled glass of wine, and..." He squirms uncomfortably. "Remember when I said I encouraged him to drink because drunk and violent was better than the alternative?"

A sick feeling coils in my stomach, and I nod.

"He was designated driver that night. It was the first time he ever got violent with me without the booze." Michael closes his eyes and shudders. "And of course, after he'd calmed down, he was still sober enough for makeup sex."

The sick feeling lurches upward, and I force it back down. "Was that make-up sex consensual?"

Michael swallows, and when he speaks, he's barely whispering: "Not with three cracked ribs, it wasn't."

My jaw falls open. "Holy shit."

He shakes himself and clears his throat. "I mean, technically I consented, but only because in that kind of pain, giving in hurt less—physically—than trying to fight him off."

"My God. No wonder this has all been such a battle for you."

He nods. Then he turns his head toward me. "To tell you the truth, all of this is why I got hooked on hanging out in the hot tub with you and Ian. It was just nice to relax and talk, and be as close as I could get to anyone since Steve."

I cringe inwardly. I can't imagine five years of never getting closer to a man than sharing the same hot tub. "We'll fix this," I whisper. "Even if it takes another five years."

"I know." He lifts his head and kisses me lightly. "And I know it's not like that with every guy. Or even most guys. I know it was a fluke. I won the horrible abusive boyfriend lottery, and that lightning probably won't strike twice." He gulps, meeting my eyes. "But no matter how much I tell myself that, when my brain inexplicably decides it's going to happen again..." He shakes his head.

"I understand." I stroke his cheek. "And I can definitely understand why it's taken you so long to even look this thing in the eye." I pause, then cautiously ask, "When did *you* know?"

"That's a complicated question." He blows out a breath. "Sometimes, looking back on what I thought about things back then, it's like I'm looking into someone else's thoughts.

I would never have accepted the shit he did, and I never would have made excuses for his bullshit. It was like it was me, but someone else was steering."

"Someone else *was* steering, Michael." I kiss him softly.

"Yeah, he was." Michael holds me closer. "He's gone now, but he left a lot behind. It's going to take a while to work through it all."

"I know it will. But we'll take all the time you need. I promise."

"Thank you," he whispers, and finds my lips again. He makes no effort to break the kiss, so I don't either. I clasp his hand between our chests, and we just lie there for a while, kissing lazily and holding onto each other, and it reminds me so much of those afternoons when we were teenagers. When we had nowhere go and nothing to do, and we could tangle up together and kiss like we had all the time in the world. In high school, we were always at least partially dressed, but this time, even completely naked—even with my wedding band sitting on the nightstand behind me—it feels just as innocent as it did back then. We're both in our thirties, and yet it feels like we're two cautious teenagers all over again—exploring, experimenting, gradually working up the courage to go further.

Maybe that's how it should be. Michael's confidence was high when we started tonight, but maybe we should've held back anyway. Crawl before we walk and all of that.

I will if you will.

Then the lightbulb comes on.

I draw back enough to meet his gaze. "Do you still have that massage oil?"

Michael nods.

I push myself up onto my elbow and trail my other hand over his chest. "Maybe I could give you one this time."

He smiles. "I'm not going to say no to that."

I smile back.

He gets up to retrieve the oil, and I sit up too.

My first thought is to have him on his stomach, the same way he massaged me the first time, but as tense as he's been this evening, I want to tread carefully here. The first night, I was pretty sure Michael wanted to give me a massage because the position I was in meant I was completely passive. That may not be such a good idea with him, so as he comes back to the bed, I get up on my knees.

"Instead of lying facedown," I say, "sit on the edge of the bed."

He shoots me a puzzled look but hands me the bottle of oil and does as I suggested.

I kneel behind him. "This way, you still have some control." I pour oil into my hands and start warming it up. "If want me to stop, you can just say so, but you can also get up quickly and easily."

He turns so his face is visible in profile. "I was going to say I can't imagine ever wanting to get away from you like that." He faces forward again, though not before some color rushes into his cheeks. "But I guess after earlier..."

"That's why we're doing this. And I know it's not me you're trying to get away from."

"It never is," he whispers.

I rest my hands on his shoulders. He inhales sharply, and I don't move. The muscles beneath my palms gradually relax. I still don't move. Not until his breathing slows down and evens out.

I only move my thumbs at first. Down slowly. Up just as slowly. Drawing long arcs on either side of his spine. He releases a breath, and more of that tension melts away. Not much, but enough that I can feel it. I'll take it.

He rolls his shoulders beneath my palms, and more tension disappears. I cautiously start moving, making small circles with my hands, gradually making them bigger until I'm touching all over his back.

Little by little, Michael's spine liquefies. When I push against him, he nearly slumps forward, so I tug his shoulders back to steady him. When I do, Michael leans against me. Then a little harder, pressing my cock just right to make my breath catch.

"Fuck!"

"Someone's getting turned on."

"Of course I am." I kiss his feverish, stubbled cheek. "My hands are on you."

"Yeah. They are." He tilts his head back and turns toward me, and our lips meet. Instantly, whatever I'm doing with my fingers becomes priority nothing. He reaches back, sliding his hand around the back of my neck.

His kiss is gentle but not the least bit hesitant. I can't rub his back or shoulders in this position, so I wrap my arms around him, and he twists toward me. Parting his lips, he nudges mine apart, and when I slide the tip of my tongue under his, he shivers.

Michael gently grasps my wrist and guides my hand lower. He closes my hand around his cock, taking in a sharp breath as he does, and encourages me into a slow, steady stroking motion. As if I *need* any encouragement. His kiss, his body, his rejuvenated confidence—there's nothing I won't do for him right now.

His neck has got to be cramping, but he makes no move to change position. Sitting back like this, he can't rock his hips, can't thrust—all he can do is stay like that and let me do everything. Let me have absolute control. And still, he doesn't try to rearrange a thing.

Michael breaks the kiss, and his head falls back against me. "Oh God. Don't..." He whimpers and grabs onto my leg. "Don't stop."

I keep pumping his cock. He screws his eyes shut. His whole body tenses, and he holds his breath. His cock gets even thicker in my hand.

He's so still, so tense.

Please, please, don't panic. Let yourself go, Michael.

He holds his breath. Every muscle is like steel. He's braced against me, digging his fingers into my leg, not moving, not breathing, as if he's gone into suspended animation.

I've got you.

Slowly, he's drawing in a breath.

I promise.

Tense. So tense.

Let go.

So fucking tense.

Michael, I've got—

And then he lets go.

Of his breath. Of my shoulder. Of all that tension.

Hot semen coats my hand and my wrist, and I keep stroking him as he gasps for air and he tries to thrust into my fist. Relief surges through me as if I'm the one who's coming —*yes! Yes, you made it! We can fucking do this.*

Michael sighs and sags against me. "Holy shit."

I hold him, kissing his neck and letting him enjoy the aftershocks for a moment.

"You're awesome," he slurs. "That was..."

I kiss beneath his jaw. "If you think I'm going to get impatient doing things like this, touching and feeling you come, please allow me to liberate you of that notion."

Michael laughs and turns to me. Our eyes meet, and for

a moment, we just gaze at each other. Then he tilts his head back for a kiss.

Eventually, we separate. I grab some tissues off the nightstand, and once we've cleaned off the semen and some of the massage oil, we lie back on the pillows.

I prop myself up on my arm beside him. "How do you feel?"

"A lot better." He reaches up and brushes a few strand of hair off my forehead. "About everything, oddly enough." He pauses, then quickly adds, "But you're probably right about taking things slower. So I don't freak the fuck out."

"You still might." I stroke his cheek. "If you do, we'll just do like we did tonight—step back, catch our breath and start again."

He flinches. "I think..." He closes his eyes. "I *know* you'll never get impatient with me, but part of me is still afraid you will." Before I can get defensive, he meets my gaze. "It's like in high school, when people would lose their virginity too soon because they were afraid they'd get dumped if they didn't put out. We weren't like that. We never were. But some irrational thing in my brain thinks we are now. Even though..." He sighs, shaking his head. "It doesn't make any sense, does it?"

"Probably more than you think. I mean, when we slept together years ago, all we were up against was inexperience." I take his hand and kiss the backs of his fingers. "You've got a lot more to work through now. I'm sure there's plenty of irrational crap that he put into your head, and we'll just have to face it as we come to it."

Michael searches my eyes. "I have no idea how much there is or how long it'll take to work through."

"Neither do I. But I'm not going anywhere."

"But there's also..." He chews his lip. "Look, you're

going out on a limb for me, Josh. Every night you're with me takes away from time you could be with your husband." His eyebrows pinch together. "I guess, in a way, I want to get through this faster to minimize the impact on your marriage."

My lips part. "Michael, my God. I'm not in any—"

"I know. Up here"—he taps his temple—"I know. But it's not rational. So this will probably come up again."

"Then we'll deal with it when it does. As for everything else, you're calling the shots. Please, *please*, don't push yourself too hard for my benefit.

Avoiding my eyes, he nods. "Okay. I'm sorry."

"Don't be." I press my lips to his. "The only one who needs to apologize for anything is—"

He kisses me before I can utter his ex's name, and we both let it linger for a long, long moment. As he draws away, he says, "I hope Ian knows how lucky he is to have you."

I slide my hand into his hair and kiss him again but don't speak.

Because nights like this, as I learn how dangerous and devastating his relationship with Steve really was, I think Ian and I are the lucky ones.

Because as battered as he is, Michael is still with us.

CHAPTER 9

AFTER THAT, WE TAKE IT A LITTLE SLOWER. MASSAGES, making out, hand jobs—it's slow enough to frustrate Michael, but it also seems to keep his demons at bay most of the time. I'm happy to stay in safer territory while he finds his equilibrium, even though part of me is itching to go farther. I'd never dream of pushing him, but I want him to be back to as close to normal as he can get.

And who am I kidding? I want him. This is about him, not me, but the desire definitely exists. I'm only human, and he's one of the most gorgeous human beings I've ever encountered. When he's ready to take things further, he'll hardly need to twist my arm.

Slow and steady, though.

A couple of weeks go by. Another hot tub Sunday rolls around, and I have a few errands to run before Michael comes over to hang out. Ian and I always take turns handling drudgery on the weekends—dry cleaning, grocery shopping and all that other shit that inevitably falls by the wayside during the work week. Especially since lately, my evenings have been a bit...full.

By the time I get home, Ian's car is already in the driveway. I park in the garage, pop the trunk and grab some grocery bags. When I let myself in, Ariel comes thundering and barking to the door as always.

"Careful, baby." I hold up the grocery bags so she doesn't knock them out of my hands. "Down."

She whines a little but stops jumping. As she calms down and follows me toward the kitchen, I can hear Michael and Ian talking.

"...might have a shot, but their bullpen is a fucking disaster."

"Ugh. It is. I've seen stronger Little League pitchers."

"*I* was a stronger pitcher." Michael clicks his tongue, and I can just imagine him rolling his eyes. "I probably still am, and my team was last in the division."

I chuckle as I step into the kitchen, where Michael's leaning against the counter and Ian's pulling some glasses down from the cabinet.

"Are you two still hung up on all this sportsball nonsense?" I ask with a grin and hoist the grocery bags onto the table.

Ian laughs. "It's only nonsense to heathens who don't pay attention."

"Uh-huh." I put my hand on his back and kiss him lightly. "At least it's not football season."

"Not yet," Michael says. "The preseason starts soon."

I groan, and it's my turn to roll my eyes. "Okay, fine. Baseball. Carry on. At least that game makes sense."

"I don't see how football doesn't make sense to you." Michael shrugs. "I mean, even if you don't understand the rules and the plays, it's a bunch of guys in tight, shiny pants throwing each other around. What's not to love?"

"The fact that the refs keep interrupting right when the throwing-each-other-around part starts getting good?"

They both pause, glance at each other and shrug.

"He does have a point," Ian says.

Michael nods. "Can't argue."

I arch an eyebrow. "But this isn't going to put an end to all your conversations about scrimmage and passing games and—"

"Not a chance," they say in unison.

I sigh dramatically. "Damn it."

Ian nods past me. "Need a hand with groceries?"

"Yes, please."

Michael comes too, and between the three of us, the trunk is empty in one trip, even with the giant bag of dog food and two boxes of cat litter. Of course, the minute we start unpacking everything and putting it all away, Michael and Ian are back to analyzing the bullpen and the...the... whatever the hell baseball fanatics analyze. The minute they're on that topic, my eyes glaze over and I tune them out, because *oh my God yawn*.

As much as sports bore me to tears, though, it's good to see the two of them talking like nothing's changed. They're bantering and debating—holy shit, I will never understand how there is so much to discuss about sports— as if we're back to the days before Ian suggested I sleep with Michael.

Maybe nothing *has* changed.

Ian puts a few plates of munchies out on the table beside the tub, along with a couple of bottles of wine. Then he and I run up to the bedroom to put on our swim trunks while Michael changes clothes in the downstairs bathroom.

And finally, it's time to relax for the evening as our weekend winds to a close.

"You boys know the rules." I lower myself into the water. "Sports are banned from the tub."

"*Fine.*" Michael slides in across from me. "No sports."

Ian settles beside me. "Eh, that's okay. It was getting depressing anyway."

Michael grunts in agreement. "Fucking team."

"Right?"

I clear my throat.

"Sorry," they both mutter.

I chuckle. "What can I say? There isn't enough wine in the world to make that topic interesting."

Michael grins. "Well, there's always the new season of The Walk—"

"No." Ian glares at him. "Absolutely not."

Snickering, I pat his arm. "What's wrong, baby?"

"Besides the fact that it's a stupid show that needs to be erased from human history?"

I shrug. "Well, yeah."

Ian rolls his eyes. "Wine?"

"Absolutely," I say.

"Definitely," Michael replies. "I need a drink after listening to such heresy."

Ian mutters something and starts pouring the wine. After he's distributed the glasses, he says, "To Friday getting here as soon as fucking possible."

"Cheers."

We clink glasses and then settle back against our respective sides of the tub.

Ian starts to take a drink but winces and lowers his glass. "Dammit," he mutters, reaching under the water and grimacing.

"What's wrong?" I ask.

"Feet."

"Still?"

"Yeah. It was a *long* week, and they will not let me forget it."

"Huh?" Michael cocks his head. "What's wrong with your feet?"

Ian scowls. "They've apparently decided that standing in front of my classes a few hours a day is bullshit." He brings one foot up and rests it on his other knee so he can rub it gingerly. "The last few months, they're sore as fuck by Friday, and lately, they're still aching by Sunday."

"Why don't you sit while you lecture?" I ask. "I know it's not your favorite way to do things, but it might be easier on your feet."

"Yeah, maybe. I might have to for a little while, just until this stops."

Michael clears his throat. "I could, um..." His eyes dart toward me. "If it's not too weird, I give decent foot massages."

Ian's eyebrows shoot up. I damn near drop my glass in the water.

Michael recoils a little. "Or not. Like I said, if it's too weird, I—"

"No, no. Not at all." Ian sets his glass on the edge. "I was just surprised. You haven't been big on touching people for a while."

I hold my breath.

Michael chews his lip, and some color blooms in his cheeks. "Well, maybe this can help both of us, then."

Ian glances at me. I shrug. To Michael, he says, "If you're sure, yeah, that'd be great."

They both put their glasses aside. Ian leans back, spreading his arms across the edge. Michael scoots to—I assume—the edge of the bench. With the jets running, it's hard to see much below the surface.

He reaches down but hesitates. "Are you ticklish?"

"Not really."

"Okay. Some people are, and I'd just as soon not get kicked by accident."

"No kicking. Promise."

Michael chuckles and then reaches down again.

Ian closes his eyes. He slowly releases his breath. "Wow."

"This okay?"

"Yeah. That's more than okay."

I watch them over my wineglass. The tub's bubbling surface obscures what's going on below, but I can put the pieces together. I've had a foot massage from Michael before, and I've given them to Ian. I know what Michael's hands feel like, sliding over skin and gently working tension out of muscles and tendons. I know how Ian's toes curl, how his other foot won't be able to hold still while the first is getting attention.

Eyes still closed, Ian brings his arm forward and wraps it around my shoulders instead of resting it across the tub's edge. His skin is cool but warms up quickly, and his fingers absently knead my arm, as if mimicking what Michael is doing.

After a while, Michael says, "Other foot?"

They both shift, Michael sitting up for a sip of wine while Ian lowers one foot and brings up the other. When Michael starts again, Ian lets his head fall back.

"Why the hell are you not a massage therapist?" The words are barely more than a groan. But then Ian's eyes snap open, and he tenses, as if he realizes what he's said. "Um, I mean—"

Michael laughs. "You know I don't work with people."

Ian glances at me, and we both relax.

"Fine. Fine," Ian says. "Get your license for animals." He squirms, squeezing his eyes shut. "As long as you'll work on us."

"Yeah, we'll see." Michael glances at me and shrugs, smiling sheepishly. "Maybe I missed my calling."

"You *so* did."

I chuckle, but Michael's words throw me for a loop. We all know he *did* miss his calling, thanks to he-who-doesn't-need-to-be-named, but the fact that he can make an offhand comment about it is...good? And he didn't bat an eye at Ian's comment about being a massage therapist despite the fact that massaging means touching. Which he's doing right now. Without any issue that I can see.

Ian glances at me, and that look sends a jolt straight to my balls. It's just as well the jets are still going, because if I know that smoldering gaze, Ian is hard as a *rock* right now. We always keep the tub a few degrees cooler than normal for that very reason, so we can fool around if we want to, but I'm wondering now if that wasn't a good idea.

Except he'd never let on and make Michael uncomfortable. I know my husband, though—I know what we'll be doing when we're alone later tonight.

He grins and squeezes my shoulder, then closes his eyes and lets his head rest on the side again.

Michael laughs. "If I keep doing this, we can probably talk about The Walking Dead and he'll never notice."

"Talk about whatever you want," Ian says, almost groaning. "Long as you keep rubbing my feet."

"I'll have to remember that when the new season starts." Michael releases Ian's foot. "There. Better?"

"Holy shit, yes." Ian pulls his legs back and sits up. "I'm

serious when I say you would be an amazing massage therapist."

"I think I prefer being an amateur." Michael rolls his shoulders, as if he's stiff from leaning forward, and reaches for his wine. "But any time either of you need it, just say the word."

"And it's okay for you?" Ian's brow furrows. "I mean, with touching?"

Michael swirls his wine. A smile slowly comes to life. He meets my eyes, then Ian's, and he nods. "Yeah. I think it is. So"—he raises his glass—"thank you both."

"You're welcome," Ian says.

I smile. "You're definitely welcome."

Michael meets my gaze as he sips his wine, and my heart flutters.

Maybe he's already come further than either of us thought.

CHAPTER 10

WHEN I WALK INTO MICHAEL'S APARTMENT A FEW nights later, the whole place is dark except for warm light coming from his bedroom's open doorway. The dog greets me as he always does, but then wanders into the living room.

I continue down the hall. "Michael? You here?"

"In the bedroom."

Of course. Heart thumping, I walk into the room. And halt. And stare.

Michael's lying back on the bed, grinning at me. He's completely naked and...

Oh God. Completely hard.

He's grinning at me and stroking himself. Air? Who needs air? Fuck.

"Right on time," he says. "As usual."

"Yeah. And it looks like..." Seriously, air? I clear my throat. "Guess it's a good thing I wasn't late."

He laughs softly, and I'm completely mesmerized as he slowly, *slowly* strokes himself. Why the hell am I still standing all the way over here, anyway? I snap out of it, take off my shoes and socks and join him on the bed.

Michael pulls me over the top of him and kisses me. *Jesus.* Somehow, my clothes haven't evaporated right off me, but I'm okay with that. There is something unspeakably hot about being on top of his naked body while I'm still dressed.

"I want to go further tonight," he says. "Not as far as we tried to that other time. When I..." He shudders.

"How far?"

Michael licks his lips. "Don't know yet. Just further."

This shaky confidence sends my pulse soaring. I can't think straight, and sure as fuck can't speak, so I kiss him again instead. He drags his nails up my back—holy shit, that burn gives me goose bumps. He's out of breath, he's kissing me like his life depends on it, and I'm doing the same to him, especially since every time I move, his erection presses against mine through my jeans and fucks my equilibrium right to hell. I've been here all of two minutes, and I'm already turned on to the point of madness.

I'll take you as far as you want to go, Michael.

As far as you can *go.*

My own thought jolts me—he's been ambitious like this before, and it's backfired. How do I make sure that doesn't happen this time?

I break the kiss and go for his neck. Michael arches, baring as much of his throat as possible, and I explore every inch of it, and even as I'm kissing and nipping his hot skin, my mind is reeling—*how far can he go? How far do I push this?*

It doesn't help that my jeans are unbearably tight. What I wouldn't give to be inside him right now, but he can't possibly be ready for that yet, and this needs to happen at his pace. Small steps. Small, frustrating steps that are driving him insane.

But he wants to go further tonight.

Maybe...

Forcing back my nerves, I lift my head. "Do you trust me?"

"Absolutely."

I sweep my tongue across my lips. "There's a boundary I want to push. If you'll let me."

His eyes widen a little, and he gulps. "Which one?"

I nod toward the door. "When I walked in here tonight, you looked just like you did that first time we were really in bed together. The first time—"

"The first time we went down on each other." His voice is taut and unsteady.

"Exactly. And my first thought was how much I wanted to make you feel like you made me feel that night."

He squirms a bit.

"I know it's a huge step for you," I whisper. "But you said you might be okay receiving, right?"

"I... Maybe?"

"Do you want to try?"

"Yes," he says without hesitation. "I so do."

"I promise, I won't hurt you." I drop a light kiss on his lips. "Say the word, and I'll stop. No questions asked."

"I know." He caresses my face. "I've never doubted that with you."

"So you want me to...?"

He studies me for a moment and then nods slowly. "I don't know if I can handle it." His features tighten for a second, but he starts to relax, and his eyes narrow as a grin comes to life. "I do want to try."

I grin back and lean down to let my lips graze his. Then

I start downward, kissing underneath his jaw before continuing along his throat. His skin is deliciously hot to the touch, and when I reach his collarbone, I can't resist a gentle bite.

"Fuck." Michael arches beneath me. His fingers run through my hair, twitching each time my lips or teeth touch his flesh. "This definitely brings back memories."

I glance up at him. "Good ones?"

"V-very good ones."

I kiss below his collarbone and inch downward. I tease one nipple with my tongue. Then the other. He curses under his breath while I struggle to catch mine—I should be used to the mix of nerves and arousal by now, but tonight, they're both more intense. A lot more intense. This could turn out so incredibly hot, and it could so easily turn into a disaster.

No pressure, Josh.

One kiss at a time, I work my way back to the middle of his chest and start down again. This reminds me so much of that first time, when every light kiss down his beautiful torso gave me the courage to continue. Helped me work up the nerve to suck his cock for the very first time. Now, it's the same, and it couldn't be more different, and I pray with every touch of my lips to his skin that this ends the way it did that very first time. Orgasms. Kisses. Smiles. No ghosts, no demons—only pleasure and innocence.

Michael shifts a bit. I glance up, and he's lifted himself onto one elbow, probably to give himself a better view. He still has a hand in my hair, combing through it in gentle, uneven motions.

"You good?" I ask.

He runs the tip of his tongue across the inside of his lip, and nods.

I keep going. His abs tighten beneath my lips. A flick of my tongue above his navel makes him gasp. His fingers twitch in my hair. Not long ago, I'd have been convinced he was about to grab my hair, jerk my head back and call this whole thing off. This time, though, he's pushing a little, as if trying to encourage me to go farther, faster.

All in good time, Michael. I grin against the thin treasure trail. *All in good time.*

But I want to get there quickly too, so I continue downward. As I follow his hipbone, inching closer to his cock one featherlight kiss at a time, I look up at him again.

His eyes are a little wider now, and his forehead is creased. His chest rises and falls faster than before.

"Sure you're okay?"

He nods vigorously. "Yeah. It's just...intense."

"Good in—"

"Yes. D-definitely good." He bites his lip and lifts his hips, letting his cock brush the edge of my jaw. "Please, Josh..."

Goose bumps. So many goose bumps.

Cautiously, I tease the base of his cock with my lips. Michael moans and fidgets. His hand leaves my hair and drops to the sheets, and his fingers curl as I run the tip of my tongue from the base of his cock to the head. I do it again, even slower this time, to both tease him and give him a chance to get used to this.

The third time, Michael's whole body seizes. His knuckles turn white as he grips the sheets.

My hair stands on end. "Michael? You okay?"

He doesn't answer. And he's suddenly breathing *a lot* faster. "Fuck. Oh fuck." His whole body tenses. His grip on the sheets gets even tighter.

"Michael, are—"

He sucks in a breath that's made of pure panic. "No!"

I immediately stop and join him up by the pillows. His eyes are screwed shut, sweat on his brow catching the light as he hyperventilates and begs me—or maybe not me?—to stop.

"Please, no more. No—"

"Hey, hey." I hold him close—my God, every muscle in his body is completely tense. "Relax. It's me. It's just me." I cradle the back of his head. "Michael. Look at me."

He opens his eyes, but I swear he's looking through me.

"Michael." I run my thumb along his cheekbone. "It's me. It's Josh. You're safe."

He blinks a few times. One by one, his muscles soften. He wipes his eyes. Then his forehead. After a moment, he shifts his focus to me, and cool relief surges through my veins—wherever he went for those few seconds, he's back.

"You okay?"

Sighing, he closes his eyes again and rubs them. "Yeah. Flashbacks are not fun."

I shiver—I've never been through anything traumatic enough to cause my mind to suddenly quantum leap back to it, and I hope I never find out what that's like. Just seeing Michael slip away and snap back is terrifying enough.

He drops his hand beside him. "God, I'm so stupid."

"No, you're not." I stroke his hair. "Just talk to me. What happened?"

He's shaking like mad now, shivering as if all the heat in the room has suddenly vanished, so I pull the covers up over us and hold him close. It's uncomfortably hot while I'm still dressed, but I keep that to myself.

"What happened, Michael?"

"Goddammit." He exhales sharply and stares up—*glares* up—at the ceiling. "It wasn't anything you did. A memory came back to me, and it fucked me all up. It's like, as soon as something like that crosses my mind, there's no stopping it. Pandora's box, in a weird way."

"Maybe we shouldn't push it like this, then." Guilt twists beneath my ribs. I knew oral was a problem for him. Fuck. What did I do? "I am so sorry. I thought—"

"No, no." He turns toward me and cups my cheek. "I wanted to push it."

"But you said oral is specifically a problem."

Lips taut, he nods. "It is. And it's one I want to get past. I can't let this shit in my head own me anymore."

I swallow. "What do you want to do, then?"

"Get back on the horse that threw me." He lifts his eyebrows. "If you're willing to try again, I mean."

"Like *now?*"

He nods.

An uncomfortable prickly feeling starts at the base of my spine and crawls upward. No pressure, indeed.

"I really was enjoying it, by the way," he says. "Right up until I killed the mood."

"You didn't kill the mood. We can still start again." I lean down to kiss his neck, and against his skin, murmur, "If you're really sure you're ready, I'll gladly do it again."

He shivers. "W-will you promise me something?"

I meet his eyes. "Anything."

He touches my face, the apprehension in his quickly vanishing in favor of confidence. And lust. Definitely some burning lust. "This time," he whispers, "don't stop until I come."

My breath halts in my throat. "But if you want to stop, I—"

"I know. I have no doubt." He lifts his head and kisses me again. "But I don't want to stop this time. Just promise..."

I kiss him, letting it linger for a moment. Then, "Promise."

We lock eyes.

One more kiss, and then I start downward just like before. His neck. His collarbone. Down the center of his chest. Down his abs, taking my sweet time because I love the way it feels when a soft kiss makes his muscles tense like that.

"Damn it, Josh," he grinds out. "I want... *Fuck.*"

"Getting there." I glance up, grinning at him. "Patience."

Whatever he says next, I don't understand it, but I'm pretty sure it's profane. Laughing softly, I keep going downward. It's not just to tease him, though. He's not the only one who has to work up the courage to see this through. There's more riding on this than a blowjob, and I've never had such intense performance anxiety before. I know how to suck cock. Do I know how to keep his mind here with me and make this fun and pleasurable when he's got so much trauma tied up with it?

God, I know this probably isn't something you approve of, but please don't let Steve in here tonight.

Then I take a deep breath, glance up at Michael one more time, and go down on him.

The second my lips touch his cock, Michael gasps and tenses. I give him a little more—sliding my lips along the shaft, occasionally teasing him with the tip of my tongue— until he releases his breath. Once he's breathing again, I steady his cock with one hand and start on the head. I run my tongue around it, exploring every ridge and contour just like I did the very, very first time, and I'm rewarded with a whispered, "Holy shit."

His fingers rake through my hair again. I take him

deeper into my mouth, just enough to nudge my gag reflex, and he swears again. The sounds he makes are driving me wild—the little hitches in his breath. The murmured curses. The low, strained groans. Everything he does drives me on, especially the way he keeps his hand in my hair, sometimes running his fingers through it, sometimes grasping it enough to hurt—whatever he does, I'm in heaven.

Michael thrusts up into my mouth. His cock is thicker and harder, his breathing faster, and I give him everything—stroking, twisting, licking, deep-throating now and again.

"Oh God." He sounds like he's on the verge of sobbing. "Oh God, Josh..." He fucks my mouth, gripping my hair tighter and gasping for breath, and then he groans, and semen floods my mouth. I swallow, and he keeps coming, and I swallow again, and he keeps coming until he collapses back onto the bed. "Holy fuck." He exhales, his entire body going limp.

I push myself up on a trembling arm, licking my lips as I move up to join him, and just like I did the first time we ever did this, Michael grabs me, drags me down to him and kisses me. He grips my hair so tight it stings, and he takes the breath right out of me. God, yes—*this* is the Michael I remember.

We finally come up for air. I touch my forehead to his. We both pant, and shake, and I almost cry because there's no demons here now. They'll be back, I'm sure, but for a moment, he's exactly the way I've missed him—trembling with the aftershocks of an orgasm, holding on to me, breathing against me, with no sign of everything that's haunted him all this time.

Welcome back, Michael. We'll make it the rest of the way. I promise.

My arms are about to shake out from under me, so I kiss him once more before I sink onto the bed beside him.

"I haven't told you this in a long time," he slurs, "but your mouth is un-fucking-real."

"Good. Always happy to please."

He laughs breathlessly. I do too, and I'm even more out of breath than he is. I'm still hard, still turned on, relieved beyond words that his fucking demons are MIA for the moment.

But I'm exhausted too. That was the hardest-won blowjob I've ever experienced. Jesus Christ.

Michael feels around, finds my hand between us and grasps it tight. "I honestly never thought I could enjoy a blowjob again."

"That would have been a fucking crime." I turn on my side, nuzzle his neck, kiss his collarbone. "All you have to do is ask, and I'll do it again. Any time you want."

He turns his head, finds my lips and kisses me softly. "You're the best."

Anything for you, Michael. Anything.

He draws back and meets my eyes. "There's still one problem, though."

My stomach lurches into my throat. "What? What's wrong?"

Michael grins, and he nudges me onto my back. As he starts unbuttoning my jeans, he murmurs, "You haven't come yet."

CHAPTER 11

I can barely focus at work, and it's not because of Michael this time.

All I can think about is the sex I had with Ian last night.

It was the first time we'd made love in over a week, which jarred me—I didn't realize until we were in bed just how long it had been. That can't continue. Even while I'm sleeping with Michael, I can't neglect my husband.

But that's not the worst part. It's chewing on my conscience and making me feel like a terrible spouse, but the sex itself was weird.

Ian has never shied away from my touch. He's never recoiled. A shudder from him has always been one of arousal, and a sharp inhalation is a sign he's about to come, not one of impending panic.

Then why...

I blow out a breath, staring at the computer monitor even though I've forgotten what the hell the spreadsheet I'm working on is for. All the words and numbers are gibberish.

I need coffee. Lots and lots of coffee.

I grab my empty cup and leave my desk for the break

room down the hall. As I walk, my body reminds me that Ian *wasn't* shying away or freaking out last night—he was rough just like he always is, and he didn't let up until we'd both gotten off. All the panicking and recoiling was in my mind, not in my bed with my husband.

In the break room, I pour myself some coffee and take a careful sip. I've known from the beginning that things with Michael could potentially cause issues with Ian, and I've tried to be vigilant about that, but this wasn't what I expected.

It's not jealousy. It isn't Michael or Ian. It's...*me*. Specifically, my confidence.

The sexual minefield wasn't supposed to take this much out of me, but it has. As Michael gets bolder and we take things a little further each time, my nerves are fraying. I never know when a touch will ignite some memory in him, or when something we've done a dozen times will make him panic.

And now that's spilling over into my sex life with Ian. Just like Michael knows damn well I'd never do anything Steve did, I know Ian won't pull away like Michael sometimes does, but the kneejerk reaction is there. The irrational certainty is, in the heat of the moment, more convincing than it has any right to be.

Christ. No wonder I couldn't sleep last night.

What the hell am I supposed to do about this, though? I can't tell Michael he's on his own. I can't let this affect Ian either.

Shit.

Well, there isn't much I can do about it here, and getting fired won't do me any good, so I top off my coffee again and head back to my desk.

There, I text Michael and bow out of getting together

tonight. I'll see him tomorrow night, but I need tonight to gather my thoughts.

And do some damage control on my marriage.

THANKS TO MAINLINING COFFEE ALL DAY, I MAKE IT TO six o'clock, and I get the hell out of there. Tomorrow, I will be more productive. I'll even come in an hour early and get some shit done.

Tonight, though, I'm done.

Ian's already home, of course. As soon as I walk into the house, the dog greets me as she always does, and I find Ian in the living room. He's kicked back on the couch, glasses on the table and Rosie curled up on his chest. As I'm coming into the room with the bouncing, woofing dog, they're both waking up—he's blinking and rubbing his eyes, and she's stretching her paws and digging her claws into his chest.

"Hey." He gingerly unsticks her claws. "Guess I fell asleep."

I laugh. "She has that effect on you."

"Yeah, she does." He ruffles her fur and kisses the top of her head. "Up, sweetie. I want to say hi to Daddy."

She glares at him, so he picks her up and puts her on the back of the couch. All of that would've earned me a few bleeding scratches, but she just gives him the look of death, then jumps down and saunters out of the room.

Ian stretches. Then he slides his glasses back on. "How was your day?"

"Not as tiring as yours, apparently."

He laughs. "Yeah, because you didn't have to chaperone a field trip."

Grimacing, I shake my head. "You know, sometimes I

wonder why I let myself be a corporate drone. And then you remind me."

"You're welcome," he mutters. He pushes himself to his feet, comes around the coffee table, and gives me a quick kiss. "You do look tired, though. You okay?"

"Yeah." I wave my hand. "Long day."

He eyes me skeptically but lets it go and gestures toward the kitchen. "Guess we should figure out something to eat. I totally forgot to start anything."

"We could always go out." As soon as I suggest it, I wish I hadn't. I'm too fucking exhausted to think about getting back in the car and going out to where people are. "Or maybe order delivery."

"Hmm. Let's see what's in the kitchen. It might be pizza night."

"I'm fine with that."

I follow him into the kitchen, and as he looks through the cabinets and the fridge, I pour myself a Coke. I sip it, but the taste barely registers. Big surprise, since not much has registered all day. Sleeping should be fun tonight. That's usually the first thing to go when my mind's trying to flail in too many different directions. Hooray. Especially since tomorrow is staff-meeting day, which means—

"Josh?"

I shake myself and turn to him. "Hmm?"

"I asked if you're sure about pizza."

"Yeah. Pizza." I shrug. "Sounds good."

He doesn't reach for his phone, though. "Is everything okay? You seem kind of distracted." His eyes narrow like he's reading me, which he undoubtedly is. "And you seemed kind of preoccupied last night too."

My stomach plummets.

Taking me gently by the hips, Ian looks me right in the

eye. "What's going on?" When I don't answer, he asks, "It's this thing with Michael, isn't it?"

Bull's-eye.

I exhale hard. "I'm sorry. I shouldn't be bringing that home."

"It's kind of inevitable." He tips my chin up. "Like it or not, there's no way something like that isn't going to affect you."

"But it shouldn't affect us. I shouldn't be neglecting you." I struggle to hold his gaze. "Do you realize we hadn't fucked in like a week before last night?"

Ian smiles, and then he kisses me softly. "If it's helping to un-fuck everything Steve did to Michael, then it's worth it. I'll be here when it's over. How is everything going with him, anyway?"

"It's..."

Distracting me from my husband.

Turning me into a goddamned basket case in the bedroom.

Making me second guess every time I want to touch you.

Ian touches my face. "Talk to me, Josh."

I meet his eyes.

And there's nothing to say. Nothing that can be conveyed in words.

So I kiss him.

Ian freezes. For a second, I'm scared to death he's going to push me away and be the adult and tell me we need to talk first, and he'd be right, but...no. Not tonight. Talking can wait. I can't.

I shove him back against the counter, and he doesn't miss a beat—he's got handfuls of my shirt, and he's using them to hold me to him, grinding his hips against mine. His shirt falls away, and it probably hits the floor, but it could've ceased to exist for all I know or care because now my palms are against his hot flesh. I grab on to him, I dig my nails in, I hold him close so there's as much skin touching skin as possible. I can't even concentrate on kissing him, but I damn sure try. Ian's all over the place too, breathing hard and grabbing on wherever his hands happen to land.

"Jesus. Fuck foreplay," I murmur between kisses. "We need to fuck."

Without a word, he grabs my hips, roughly turns me around, and now I'm the one up against the counter. He fumbles with my belt for a second and then shoves my jeans and boxers over my hips. My heart's going crazy now. *Yes, yes. Fuck me.* The sound of his zipper makes me shiver. I grip the counter's edge, digging my teeth into my lip. *Fuck me now!*

Ian reaches past me. Something rattles. Something topples. Then he grabs a bottle and pulls it back to him, and I catch a fleeting glimpse of it.

Was that...olive oil?

Oh hell, I don't care what it is. I bite my lip, trying to stay standing, stay sane, stay breathing. I don't care what he's using as long as—

Ian presses his slick cock against my ass, and my mind goes blank. As soon as the head slides into me, Ian doesn't hold back. He forces himself in, and I'd moan if I could breathe at all. With no prep or stretching, the burn is intense. I shove myself back against him, searching for more, desperately trying to drive him all the way inside me. It burns, it makes my eyes water, and I need more. More. *More.*

Ian presses his lips to the side of my neck, and every hot breath he releases rushes past my skin. I brace a hand against the cabinet and try to push back against him, but he's got me pinned against the counter, and I can barely move.

"Just stay like that," he pants. "Let me...let me..."

Oh, I let him. I hold myself in place as much as I can, and he slams into me again and again, pounding me so hard, it's deliciously painful. I'm begging him not to stop. Or at least I think I am. I want to. Whether my mouth can form the words is another matter. Still, he must know what I want, or maybe he's just so far gone himself that all he wants to do is try to force himself deeper and deeper.

My knees are going to tremble right out from under me. My hand slips off the cabinet. I drop onto my elbows, letting my head fall forward, and I distantly hear myself cry out, and without even touching myself, I come, driven on and on by Ian's powerful thrusts. He grunts, and he thrusts so hard, the edge of the counter bites into my hipbones, and he holds me there, pinning me in place as his cock pulses inside me. "Fuck," he breathes, and one last shudder goes through him.

Thank God for the counter. As we tremble and catch our breath, it's about the only thing keeping us both from melting to the floor.

He pulls out and then kisses the base of my neck. "Go get in the shower. I'll be there in a minute."

Speech isn't possible, so I just nod and make a half-assed attempt at fixing my clothes. My legs are shaky and my head's still spinning, but I manage to get upstairs to the master bedroom. I strip out of my clothes, clean some of the oil off my skin, and then do as I'm told—into the shower.

I don't know how long it's been since we've had sponta-neous sex like that. A blowjob here and there, maybe, but full-on fucking that can't even wait until we find actual lube? Oh God. We need to do that more often.

A few minutes after I get in the shower, Ian joins me,

and it's instantly clear that he's not at all interested in stopping. Though we're making a somewhat concerted effort to get clean, his lips are on me almost constantly—on my neck, my shoulders, my mouth. His hands are everywhere, sliding over wet skin and digging nails in now and then to make me gasp. I love it when he gets like this. When he's demanding and insatiable and utterly fucking relentless. After all the fraught, uneasy sex I've had with Michael lately, I need this. I need to remember what it's like to just let go with someone who *can* let go.

Ian turns off the shower. We dry off—sort of—and then tumble into bed. *God*, he feels good—hot skin against mine, his cock hardening again, his lips skating across my neck and collarbone. Yeah, he's definitely not done. And neither am I. I don't care if I can function tomorrow—I want everything he's willing to give me tonight. We're both hard, and panting, and grinding together, and clawing at each other.

Then Ian reaches for the nightstand. "Knees."

"'kay."

We're down to single syllables. I'm surprised either of us is that articulate.

I've barely gotten myself situated before Ian's against me, and then he's inside me, and he's fucking me again, slamming into me painfully deep and hard, and I can't get enough. My elbows falter, then collapse under me, and I drop onto my forearms as my husband fucks me exactly the way I love it. Exactly the way I've been needing it and didn't even know it. It's just us tonight, no one from the past or the present in between us—it's him, and me, and the violent, bed-shaking sex we've had since day one.

"Harder," I whimper. "F-fuck me harder."

Ian groans, and he pounds me so hard, my vision blurs. My knees burn on the sheets, and every thrust reverberates up my spine, and I dig the heels of my hands into the mattress and push myself back against him, searching for more even though I can't take any more.

I lift myself up as much as I can and reach beneath us. As soon as I start jerking myself off, Ian's dick seems to get even thicker as I tighten around him. He curses under his breath and grips my hips tighter, but his rhythm falters like it sometimes does when he's getting tired.

I find enough breath to murmur, "Let me get on top."

Ian slows, then stops. "Good call."

He pulls out and rolls onto his back. I climb on top, and we both curse as I lower myself onto his cock. I ride him just the way *he* loves it—hard, rocking my hips, trying to force the breath out of him every time I come down. He meets me halfway too. He doesn't hold on to me, but every time I come down, he thrusts up, and even though I've come once tonight, and I'm already sensitive enough that this could get painful in a hurry, I love it.

"Touch yourself," he orders. "Lemme see you get yourself off."

I balance on one arm and, with the other hand, start jerking my cock.

"Oh yeah." He bites his lip, fucking me from below. "Oh God, yeah."

He doesn't stop. I don't stop. We fuck, we touch, and we curse, and I'm in so many levels of heaven, I can't even see straight, and my God, no one but Ian can get me this close this fast after I've already come once. My legs are burning from exertion, my wrist and elbow are starting to ache, but I'm not stopping for anything. Not until I come on him and he comes in me, and the way I feel right now, the way my vision keeps blurring and my body's shaking all over, I'm so damned—

"*Fuck!*"

I fall forward on my free hand, and somehow keep pumping my dick as semen spurts across his abs. Screwing his eyes shut, Ian thrusts up into me. I don't even know who's in control anymore. I don't care. I love the way he feels and looks and sounds, and I want him to feel as amazing as I do, so despite my aching hips and thighs and my spinning head, I give him everything I have—still riding him hard, still rolling my hips just the way he likes it. My rhythm is all over the place. My body's trembling. I'm so dizzy, I'm ready to collapse. But not until Ian's there. Not until he falls to pieces like I just did.

Ian gasps. His eyes fly open. His face is filled with that near-panic of a man on the edge, the telltale *oh fuck there's no stopping it*, and then he pulls me down onto him, forcing himself as deep as I can take him, and shudders.

When he releases me, I lift myself off him and drop onto the bed beside him. He feels around, and eventually finds my hand, and we just lie there, holding hands and panting hard until we can trust our legs to hold us up. As we get up to clean ourselves off, we're shaking and clumsy, but we manage.

Ian groans as he falls back into bed. I collapse beside him.

And we just lie there. Still breathless. Still trembling. My body's aching all over; it's been years since we fucked like that. Two orgasms apiece in rapid succession? I thought we'd left that in our twenties.

"Have I ever told you," I say, barely able to enunciate, "that you're fucking amazing in bed?"

He laughs and lazily takes my hand. "Likewise."

I close my eyes and sigh. "I so needed that tonight."

"So I noticed." He pulls the sheet up over us. "I've been worried about you, you know."

My heart clenches. "I'm sorry. I—"

"Don't be sorry. I'm just worried this whole thing with Michael is taking its toll on you."

I scrub my hand over my face. "I don't see how it *won't* take its toll."

"Yeah, ditto." He pulls me close and kisses my forehead. "Is it helping, though? I mean, is he doing better?"

"Better, yeah. But, God, it's a weird feeling, being with someone who's afraid of being touched."

His fingertips trail down my arm. "I can't even imagine."

"It's like...fucking on eggshells." I rub my eyes with my thumb and forefinger. "And the more he tells me about why..." I drop my hand and look at Ian. "What the hell kind of person *does* this to someone?"

"Someone who needs to be on the evening news," Ian mutters and kisses my temple.

"Seriously." I cuddle against him, tucking my head beneath his chin. "And now I feel like an asshole too, because this whole time, I've been neglecting you."

Ian runs his hand up and down my back. "You've been preoccupied. Under the circumstances—"

"Don't." I lift up and meet his gaze. "If I've been ignoring you, don't make excuses for me."

He purses his lips, then shrugs. "Josh, something like what you're doing with Michael is *going* to take a toll on you. And it's going to pull your focus away from us for a little while." He touches my face. "I knew that when I suggested this."

"Yeah, but I don't ever want to take you for granted or

make you feel like that." I shake my head. "I don't want to do to you what—"

He kisses me, holding the back of my neck firmly. "You are not, and you never will be, anything like Steve."

I swallow. "You know what I mean."

"I do." He loosens his grasp a little and starts stroking my hair. "And right now, the one you're neglecting is yourself."

"And us."

Ian shakes his head. "You need to take care of yourself first."

I search his eyes. "Are you suggesting that I put you after myself and this thing with Michael?"

"No. I'm asking you to make yourself the priority. You keep working with Michael, and you and I will work together to make sure we're not neglecting us. If there's a problem here"—he gestures at each of us—"I'll tell you." He inclines his head. "I always have, haven't I?"

"Yeah. You have." I don't think I've ever been with a man who's less likely to let something fester—Ian is the king of nipping issues in the bud.

"I'll let you know if there's a problem," he says. "All I ask is that you do the same. And be careful, okay?"

"I will. Promise."

"Good. Because Michael needs you, but he needs you to be sane and healthy too. And that's where I come in." He combs his fingers through my hair. "You do everything you can to get him back to a good place, and I'll do everything I can to keep you in a good place. Whenever it gets to you, come to me. I've got your back."

I stare at him, struggling to comprehend what he's saying.

"I care about him too," he goes on. "I *want* you to take

care of him." He brushes his lips across mine. "Just let me take care of you too. Whenever you spend an evening with him, you spend the next one with me. That way you have a chance to decompress, and whatever's happened with him, we can get it out of your system."

I shake my head and trail my fingertips along his five-o'clock shadow. "You are seriously the best husband *ever*, you know that?"

Ian laughs but doesn't say anything. He just holds me closer, and for the longest time, we just lie there, soaking up each other's body heat. Eventually, we'll get downstairs and find something to eat—and feed the animals before they revert to hunters—but for now, we don't move, and I don't object. I've always loved cuddling with Ian, and these days, I need it more than ever. I need *him* more than ever.

Tomorrow, I'll go back to Michael's bed, and I'll keep going back until he's steady on his own two feet. I'm thankful as hell that I can give him what he needs.

But especially right now, I'm grateful beyond words for Ian.

CHAPTER 12

IAN IS A SAINT AT HELPING ME KEEP THINGS BALANCED. A couple nights a week, I'm with Michael. Sunday evenings are wine and the hot tub with both guys. The other nights are reserved for my husband. Thanks to him, I actually have a fighting chance of keeping my sanity. When things are rough with Michael, when his ex has a hold on him and the bedroom turns into that minefield, Ian is there to ground me. That, in turn, makes it possible for me to ground Michael.

Little by little, we push Michael's boundaries. Almost a month into this, we're still barely doing more than making out and jerking each other off, though he's rather enthusiastically letting me go down on him these days. The whole process is painfully slow, and it frustrates him at every turn, but he's come a long way psychologically. The setbacks and flashbacks are fewer and farther between. And thanks to Ian, I'm still on an even keel.

Tonight, like so many other nights, I'm wrapped up in Michael, lying on our sides, kissing, stroking each other beneath the covers. My body still aches in places from everything Ian and I did less than twenty-four hours ago, and when I'm in bed with him tomorrow, I'll still feel Michael too. It's become normal, feeling the phantom touch of one man while I'm with another, and if I'm completely honest with myself, it's become addictive.

Guilt needles at me, but I try to push it aside. There's nothing wrong with enjoying this. It's sex with Michael, for God's sake, and Ian didn't give me his blessing under the condition that I lie back and think of England. And enjoying it tempers all the other emotions I have about it.

And why am I rationalizing this?

"Still awake?" Michael startles me, and when I turn my head, he's watching me.

"Yeah." I rub my eyes. Had I started drifting off? I don't even know. "Is it getting too late?"

"No. You were just quiet."

"Sorry." I lower my hand and turn toward him again. "I was just thinking."

"About?"

I hesitate. Then I shift onto my side and lift myself up on my arm. "Is it wrong that I look forward to coming over for this?"

"I would hope not." He grins. "Even with all the drama going on in my head, I wouldn't want this to be a terrible chore or something for you."

"No, it's nothing like that. I guess... I mean..." My face burns. "I do enjoy this. Being in bed with you."

Michael's expression turns serious, and he strokes my hair. "Does that bother you?"

"I don't know. I'm not sure if it should."

He takes my left hand, runs his thumb along my wedding band, which I don't always remember to take off. He kisses the backs of my fingers. "Ian?"

"Yeah." I sigh and rub my face with my other hand. "I'm probably overthinking things. God knows I've asked him a hundred times if it bothers *him*, and Ian would never keep something like that under his hat."

Michael holds my gaze. His eyes narrow a little, and he smiles as he traces the side of my hand with his thumb. "Well, you are a product of a Puritanical culture just like the rest of us. Maybe you're still adjusting to the idea of bending the rules of monogamy."

"You would think that might've reared its head while I was trolling bathhouses."

"Maybe. Maybe not. But promiscuity is one thing." He lifts my hand and taps my ring. "Sleeping with someone else while your husband is at home? That's bound to strike a few uncomfortable chords." He lowers our joined hands.

I purse my lips. "You know, you're probably right." Shaking my head, I laugh and roll my eyes. "And here I was worried I wouldn't like monogamy."

"I never figured you would." He smiles. "At least, not until you met Ian."

"You definitely caught on to that before I did."

"Well, as you've told me, some things are easier to see from the outside." The hint of sadness in his voice gives me pause.

"Michael, look at what he's done to you," I hear myself pleading in the distant past. *"You've got to get out of there."*

"I can't just leave him."

"Why not?"

"Because I love him!"

I release his hand and draw him into a tight embrace. "After the bullshit cards you've been dealt, karma owes you big-time." I press a kiss to his forehead. "There is one hell of a guy out there waiting for you."

Michael sighs, and when he looks up at me, he smiles. "Let's hope."

Hope, hell. If there isn't a good man out there for Michael, then there's no justice in the universe.

But, gazing into his eyes, I can't quite form the words. So instead, I tip his chin up, lean in and kiss him. And don't stop. And he doesn't stop either.

His arm drifts over my waist. We pull each other closer, kissing deeper and holding on tight. I should know better than to be surprised when we both start getting hard—even after we've already fooled around tonight, and even in the wake of our weird conversations, it's impossible to kiss him like this and not get turned on.

Michael grinds against me, rubbing the undersides of our cocks together. "I want you to fuck me."

"What?" My pulse goes all kinds of crazy and my panicked brain replays what happened last time we tried this. "Are you sure?"

"We can stop any time, right?"

"Any time. Always."

"Then yes. I'm sure." He pushes me onto my back and climbs on top, as if he sees right through me to that weak spot I have for his rarely seen aggressive side. "I like how we tried it before. Me on top."

I nod, sweeping my tongue across my lips. "Hell yeah. I want you in total control." As he picks up the bottle of lube off the nightstand, I add, "I can still get you ready this way. With my fingers."

"I know." He sits over me again. Holding up the bottle of lube, he grins. "Let's do this."

I laugh as I take the bottle from him and put some lube on my fingers. Steadying us both with a hand on his hip, I slip my hand between his legs, and we both exhale as I press a fingertip against him.

My finger slides in. Michael digs his teeth into his lip, his expression wavering between a wince and a look of intense concentration. He lowers himself a bit, taking my finger deeper, and then rises. After a few strokes, I carefully add a second finger. This one doesn't go in quite so easily, though. He flinches but lowers himself and takes them both.

Damn. It's just like the first time we tried this. He's way too tense—there's no way he'll take me without getting hurt.

On the way down again, Michael stops. He closes his eyes, and he takes a few slow breaths.

I touch his thigh. "You okay?"

"Yeah." His lips pull tight for a second. "I'm okay."

He starts to come down again, but I stop him with a hand on his hip. "Michael."

He meets my eyes.

"You don't have to do this," I say as gently as I can. "There's plenty of time."

He nods. "I know. I want to."

"But are you sure you're ready?"

"I won't know until I try."

"That's not very encouraging. We—"

"Please." His Adam's apple bobs. "I *know* I can get past this."

I'm torn between supporting him and helping him over this obstacle, and reminding him that while he can definitely get past it, he doesn't have to do it tonight.

He starts moving again, riding my hand, but there's no way in hell this feels good.

"Wait." I stop him again. As much as I know it's going to frustrate him, I slide my fingers free.

"Josh, we—"

"Let's take a step back. We still have time." I shake my head. "But I can't do this yet. I'm too afraid I'm going to hurt you."

He scowls but doesn't protest, and eases himself down onto the bed beside me.

"I'm sorry," I whisper as I reach for some tissues to clean the lube off my hand.

"I know. It's not your fault." He sighs. "And you're probably right."

Sometimes it sucks being right. I toss the tissues away and lie down beside him. "Why were you suddenly in such a hurry, anyway?"

He releases a long, resigned breath, and rubs the back of his neck, avoiding my eyes. "Honestly?"

"Yes."

Still not looking at me, he whispers, "Because the longer we do this, the worse you're going to feel. About Ian."

My heart stops. "Michael. No." I wrap my arms around him. "You've got a lot of trauma to get past. We're not going to rush this just because—"

"We haven't rushed anything." He lifts his gaze. "We've crawled through this."

"Because I don't want to make things worse."

"But what about you and Ian? Do you really think he agreed to this thinking we'd be at it for months?"

"He knew it would take time."

"Still. You guys have a marriage most people would sell their souls for." He clasps his fingers between mine. "I don't want to damage that. Quite frankly, I'd be happier never sleeping with another man as long as it meant I didn't fuck up what the two of you have."

"No way." I push myself up and kiss him softly. "Ian

and I will take care of things between us. We'll be fine. And I want you to be fine too. That's why I'm here."

He holds my gaze, as if searching my eyes for some kind of unspoken confirmation.

"We'll be okay." I kiss him again. "You and me, and Ian and me. I'm just sorry I made you feel like you needed to rush for my benefit."

Sighing, he shakes his head. "You didn't. I think I'm just used to..." He shakes himself again. "Never mind. Stupid shit my ex put into my head and my therapist has mostly gotten rid of. Except in here. In bed."

I smile. "That's what I'm here for. And we don't have to stop tonight. We can just take it slow."

"What do you have in mind?"

"Roll over." I nod past him. "Facing that way."

He turns onto his side, and I mold myself to his back and drape my arm over him. His body is tense, his spine rigid against my chest.

"We still have plenty of time tonight." I kiss the back of his neck. "Let's just take it slow and see where things end up."

Michael nods.

Holding him close, kissing behind his ear, I take my time. Touching him, tasting his skin, just being naked with him—we stay like this for ages. Slowly, his breathing falls into synch with mine. He covers my arm with his, resting his fingers over the top of mine as I run my hand up and down his chest, his abs, his side, his thigh.

Lying this close to him, it's only a matter of time—as we both relax, I can't help getting turned on. I try to keep my erection away from him, but Michael isn't having any of that. He scoots back against me, pressing his ass against my cock, and at the same time, he guides my hand down to his own erection. I exhale against his neck, letting him close my fingers around his cock as I start gently rubbing against his ass. Then harder. Still harder. The friction is mind-blowing as I fuck against his crack.

All the while, the room is completely silent except for the soft hiss of movement and our no longer synchronized breathing. He's not quite panting, but he's close—deep, uneven breaths, some more ragged than others.

I tug him toward me so he's lying on his back now, and I lean down to kiss his neck. "Remember how you couldn't handle me going down on you in the beginning?"

"Mm-hmm."

"You got past that." I kiss lower. The lube is close by, and I subtly move it so it'll be within reach in a moment, and keep kissing my way down his torso. As his abs contract beneath my lips, I glance up and whisper, "You'll get past this too."

"It shouldn't *be* something to get past." He hisses as I brush my lips over his hipbone.

"But it is. And you will. I promise."

He starts to speak, but as I draw the tip of my tongue along the underside of his cock, he trails off into a moan. Sucking his cock is effortless now—every time I do it, he's more into it than before. That particular demon is a distant memory. There's no tension, no flashbacks, so I just let him enjoy this for a while, listening to him fall to pieces. I swear he's almost purring as he pushes his dick deeper into my throat.

I shift my weight onto one arm. "I'm going to add fingers. That okay?"

"Y-yeah."

I put some lube on my fingers, watching him the whole time for signs of fear, and he shows none. Instead, he's breathing hard and squirming like he does when he's turned on and desperate for an outlet.

I set the lube aside, nudge his legs apart and press a fingertip against his hole.

"Oh my God," he moans.

Stay with me, Michael.

I press harder. This time, he takes my finger easily. As I work a second one in, meeting only minimal resistance, I start on his cock again, and his long, throaty groan brings a shudder out of me.

"Holy fuck," he murmurs. "That feels amazing."

I take his cock deeper in my mouth. At the same time, I crook my fingers inside him. His cock stiffens against my tongue, and his moans reverberate across my nerve endings. More than once, I'm certain he's on the edge—arching, cursing, shuddering. I'm surprised my body isn't trembling just from the exhilaration of hearing and feeling him surrender like this.

"Josh." He moans again. "Fuck me."

My skin prickles and my balls tighten. "Are you—"

"*Yes.*"

I withdraw my fingers, and Michael bites his lip and writhes on the mattress, clawing at the sheets as he does.

"Please," he murmurs. "Fuck me. Oh my God, I want you."

I can barely breathe but manage to whisper, "Likewise." Though my heart is racing with apprehension as well as arousal, I put some lube on me and on him and sit up between his legs.

I press against him. He's tense again, so I start to back off, but he grabs my arm.

"No." He licks his lips. "Just go slow. I want this."

"You'll tell me if it hurts?"

Michael nods vigorously. "Definitely. Just don't *stop*."

"I won't unless you tell me to." I hesitate a few seconds longer and then apply just a little more pressure. He's tight, but not like he was that first time we tried this, when he could barely take me at all.

"Breathe, Michael," I whisper, still leaning against him, though not quite enough to push in. "I won't hurt you. Ever. I only want you to feel good."

Michael swallows.

"There's no hurry. Breathe."

He takes in a long breath through his nose. Lets it out slowly. Draws another. Starts to let that one go.

Then he bears down.

And the head of my cock is inside him.

And we both stop.

My eyes water. My balance wobbles, but I grip his legs to keep myself steady.

"Fuck..." He stares up at the ceiling with unfocused eyes. "Holy..."

I gently press in farther, and his helpless whimper makes my cock even harder. "This good?"

"So good." He bites his lip as I work myself deeper. Before long, I'm moving easily, and he's taking every inch of my cock without that impossible resistance from before.

"Tell me how," I breathe. "Hard? Slow?"

"Slow at first." Michael closes his eyes and arches beneath me. "Just...want to enjoy it."

Oh, I'll let you enjoy it as long as you want.

I ride him as slowly as I can stand it. He's still tight, but with every motion of my hips, he's relaxing. Yielding to me. Taking me deep, biting his lip whenever I pull out and whimpering softly every time I push back in.

"Is this—"

"M-more." Michael's eyes are closed, and he's stroking himself in time with my slow, fluid motions. "You feel...so good."

"So do you." I rock my hips a little faster. Not quite thrusting, but giving him more than before, and he groans as he tightens around me.

"Oh my *God*," he breathes. "So...good..."

"Fuck, yeah. I could—oh *fuck!*" My climax catches me completely off guard. One second I'm taking my sweet time, enjoying the slick, fluid strokes, and the next, I can't breathe. I can't get deep enough inside him. I throw my head back, my hips jerking and toes curling and my vision blurring as release takes over, and then I slump over him with just enough presence of mind to avoid resting my full weight on his chest.

"Holy shit," I murmur, pulling out carefully. "That was, uh, unexpected."

He laughs, letting his fingertips drift up my back, which my suddenly sensitive nerve endings can barely handle. I shiver hard and, without thinking about it, grab his arm and pin it to the bed. Panic prickles the back of my neck. Oh God.

But Michael moans softly and presses his hard cock against me. "If you're gonna be like that, I might have to fuck *you*."

I lift up and blink in surprise.

He grins. "Please?"

"I'm not gonna say no. Are you—" But I don't need to ask if he's sure. Whatever hang-ups he had earlier, they're gone now, and his eyes are filled with more boldness and certainty than I've seen in...hell, years.

"Get on your back." He pulls me down for a quick kiss. "I like this position."

"M-me too." A lot. Holy fuck. Especially when my limbs are still made of rubber. "Go easy, though. Just came."

"Of course." He reaches for the lube, and I roll onto my back. After he's lubed himself up, he positions himself. Twin crevices form between his eyebrows as he steadies his cock with one hand and guides himself to me. He presses against me, glances up to meet my gaze, and a little grin appears on his lips right as he pushes forward. I push back, and for the first time in so many years, Michael's inside me. And I didn't know how much I wanted that, how much I'd missed that, until just now, and as he works himself deeper, my eyes sting.

Aside from the winter when we discovered this in the first place, we never fucked much when we were teens—we enjoyed giving head more than anything. But when we first discovered it, we couldn't get enough, and when we did it, it was always mind-blowing. Gazing up at him now, I hope his mind is going someplace else tonight, and I hope it's going to the same place mine is. Back to that winter when this was as easy as it was new. When anal was still a novelty, and we seized every opportunity to fuck each other senseless. I savor every stroke, my body lethargic and tingling from the orgasm I just had, while he's carefully sliding in and out, well on his way to his own orgasm and still making sure he doesn't overstimulate me now that I'm this hypersensitive. Just like we did back then.

Michael picks up speed. His eyes are heavy-lidded, nearly closed, and he's fucking beautiful—skin gleaming with sweat, red hair damp and disheveled, lips parted as if he'd be moaning if he could just remember how.

"Come here," I whisper, and his eyes open. He meets my gaze as I reach for him, and he comes down to me, and then we're kissing, and moving, and holding each other, and this is beyond perfect. I'm distantly aware of obstacles we still need to work through, but there is nothing about this moment I'd change.

Michael breaks the kiss and buries his head against my neck. His thrusts aren't faster, but they're definitely harder, and though they border on too much for my overstimulated body, they feel good. They feel amazing. And every time his breath hitches or his rhythm falters, I know he's getting closer, and I can't help moaning myself, because *holy fuck, Michael...*

He pulls in a breath. His whole body tenses, but not like all the times he's freaked out. I roll my hips, clench around him, hold him tight, and he exhales hard against my neck just before he thrusts all the way in and groans. Then, like I did earlier, he collapses. He withdraws but otherwise doesn't move.

"That went better than I expected," I whisper.

"Yeah. Same here." He cups my cheek and kisses me tenderly. "Kinda reminds me of the first time we did this."

My heart skips. "Me too." *Quite possibly in more ways than it should.* But I banish that thought. "And it was good for you? Nothing bothering you from the past?"

"Not this time. It was..." He meets my gaze, and his smile does a number on my pulse. "It was perfect."

I just smile back and run my fingers through his hair.

"I know this has been rough on you." He kisses me again and barely breaks that kiss enough to murmur, "But thank you."

"You're welcome, Michael."

CHAPTER 13

After that, we can't stop fucking. Between him and my insatiable husband, it's a wonder I can walk over the next week or so, and I love it. The sex is getting better and better, and so is Michael's confidence.

I've been here more times than I can count now, hard and breathless in Michael's bed, but it feels different tonight.

We've been tangled up together almost since the moment I walked in the front door. That kiss hello didn't stop, and then I had him up against the wall and he was unbuckling my belt. We barely made it down the hallway to his bedroom without tumbling to the carpet and just tearing each other's clothes off right then and there.

And now we're here, struggling to shed clothes as we kiss and grope the way we used to when we were teenagers, back when we'd first discovered sex and couldn't get naked fast enough. When we still had to sneak around and had to make the absolute most out of every stolen opportunity.

We have all the time in the world tonight, but I can't get enough of him. I want him naked, I want his cock in my mouth, I want to fuck him, I want him to fuck me—I just want him.

"Got some more lube," he says between kisses. "We were getting low."

"Already?" I grin against his lips. "Guess we have been going through it pretty fast."

"Uh-huh. And I want to get started on this bottle. Like now."

I push him onto his back and press my cock against his. "I think we should get started on it too. And I want you just like this."

"Yes please." He drags me down to him, gripping my arms painfully tight as he kisses me. Even as we fumble around for that bottle of lube, and as we struggle to remove the cellophane around the top, we're all over each other. Every kiss breaks with whispered cursing, and every new one starts with groans of relief and pleasure. I can't get enough of him, and he's matching me kiss for kiss, grope for grope, and when that bottle comes open, it's a miracle we don't wind up with lube spilled everywhere. Though at this point, I can't convince myself that'd be a bad thing—then we could just keep kissing until one of us slides into the other. Or something. Fuck. I can't even think.

Michael's lips separate from mine. "Finally." He holds up the lube bottle, grinning triumphantly now that it's open and unsealed.

"P-put it on."

He almost drops the bottle, but catches it, and when he closes a slippery hand around my dick, I'm surprised I don't pass out. And we're kissing again. Breathlessly. I thought he was going to fuck me, but now I'm the one with lube on my cock, and he's stroking me like this just turned into a hand job instead, and I'm completely okay with that.

Anything you want, Michael. Just don't stop.

He stops, though, and nudges me, so I lift my hips. He spreads his legs, and we both exhale as I come down between them. With some more fumbling, clumsiness that would've mortified me in my younger days but doesn't bother me in the slightest now, we guide my cock to his ass, and I push in. He's tight since we haven't done a thing to prep him so far, but he slowly relaxes, and I sink into him. After some careful strokes, he's taking me easily, and I start moving faster. Fucking him effortlessly, as if there's never been any physical or mental resistance.

Something's definitely changed tonight. With every stroke and every touch, I've been sure he's going to recoil or tense up, but he hasn't. As I thrust inside him, he holds onto my arms, digging his nails in and rocking his hips to encourage me to fuck him harder, and there's no sign of anything in his expression besides pure lust.

And slowly, it becomes clear why tonight feels different —though Steve is there in the back of my mind, he isn't *here*. For the first time, it's only Michael and me.

He meets my eyes, grabs the back of my neck, and pulls me down into a kiss. Between kissing him and fucking him, I can't find nearly enough oxygen, but I don't care. I'm more than happy to black out if this is the last thing I feel before everything goes dark.

"You feel so good," he whispers.

"So do you. God, Michael, you feel amazing."

He grips my arms tighter. "Harder." He doesn't have to tell me twice. I bury my head against his neck, slide my hands under him, hold on to his shoulders and I fuck him hard, the way he always begged me to when we were younger.

He's damn near sobbing, egging me on with slurred

curses and sharp gasps. Arms around me, he drags his nails down my back, carving lines of delicious burning pain that spur me on.

Then he pulls in a sharp breath. His entire body goes rigid, his muscles tense, his fingers digging hard into my back and his ass so tight around my dick I can barely move, but I keep right on fucking him anyway.

All at once, he lets go. He releases his breath, and he releases me, and hot semen's hitting my chest and stomach, and then I'm coming too, driven by his soft little moans and the way he's trembling beneath me.

With a sigh, I slump over him, holding myself up on shaking arms. Somehow, I manage to pull out, but otherwise, I don't move. Eyes closed, body trembling all over, I rest my forehead against his shoulder and just breathe.

"Oh my God," he murmurs after a while.

"Yeah. My thoughts exactly." Though it's a struggle, I push myself up.

When Michael meets my eyes, there's definitely an extra shine in his, but the smile tells me it's not a bad thing this time. He reaches up with both hands, draws me back down and kisses me so tenderly, he almost moves me to tears too. Then he breaks the kiss and wraps his arms around me, and this time, a couple of hot tears slip free.

Your ex really wasn't here tonight, was he?

It was just us.

Finally.

Our gazes meet again. He smiles. So do I. We both wipe our eyes and, without a word, pry ourselves apart to clean up.

Moments later, we're lying in bed again, facing each other on our sides.

He closes his eyes and smiles serenely. "Jesus. I honestly never thought I'd like it that much again."

I kiss his forehead. "I knew we'd get there."

His eyes open and his expression darkens a little. "So now comes the next hard part."

"Which is...?"

He swallows. "Being okay with all of this when it's someone I've never been with before."

My chest tightens. I hadn't even thought about that part.

"There's always Dr. Klein." He sighs. "Except what if we get to this point and it doesn't work?"

"Michael." I stroke his cheek. "If you get to this point with him, and he can't be patient and accommodating, then he has no business being in bed with you anyway."

"True. I don't know. I'm not sure I'm quite ready for that yet."

"Then don't push it." I kiss him gently. "We can do this as long as you need to."

"You're the best," he murmurs, wrapping his arms around me. "You've made such a difference."

I kiss him again and hold on to him. "Anything I can do to help. I want you to be able to enjoy this again."

"I already do." He smiles up at me, but it fades. "Maybe one of these days, I'll even get to where I can go down on someone again."

My heart sinks. Ah, yes. The one thing he hasn't even tried to face down yet.

I study him. "He really traumatized you with that, didn't he?"

Gaze distant, Michael nods. He gnaws his lip, his brow furrowed as if he wants to speak, but doesn't know what to say.

As much as I don't want to kill the mood and send him back, maybe the answers will shed some light on why this is such a battle for him at every turn. My mouth is starting to go dry as I finally ask the question that's been echoing in my head since day one: "What did he do to you?"

"A lot of things I'd just as soon never talk about again." He gulps. "But oral was his favorite form of punishment."

My stomach turns. "Punishment?"

"Yeah." Michael's lips twist.

I don't push. Something tells me I won't have to.

Michael draws a slow, deep breath. "One night, we were arguing about something—I don't remember what—and he backhanded me."

I hold Michael tighter. Jesus Christ.

He goes on, "It wasn't the first time, and it definitely wasn't the last, but that night, my tooth caught the inside of my cheek. It was one of those cuts that just bled *everywhere*. Not a deep one or one that needed medical attention, but... you know what I mean."

I nod, tamping down the nausea in my throat.

"Anyway, it finally stopped. And we finally calmed down." Michael's eyes grow distant, but he squeezes my hand, as if he's letting himself go back to that place as long as he's got an anchor in this one. I squeeze back. With a subtle shudder, he continues. "He was starting to sober up too, so he decided he wanted to take things into the bedroom to"—he made air quotes with his other hand—"put the fight behind us. One thing led to another, and I was..." He gulps, and shifts as if he's trying not to shudder again. "On my knees. Which is where I always ended up when we were making up."

He runs his tongue alongside his teeth, as if he's

searching the inside of his cheek for a phantom cut. I cringe at the idea of sucking cock like that.

Michael clears his throat. "He got a little rough, and I felt the cut come open again, but he wouldn't stop and wouldn't let *me* stop until after he came."

My stomach lurches. "Fucking bastard."

"Yeah. So of course, my mouth was bleeding, which meant there was blood on him." Michael rolls his eyes. "He freaked the fuck out."

"Even though he was the one who cut your mouth and wouldn't stop."

"Yep. It was actually kind of a blessing in disguise."

"A—*what?*"

"He was kind of a germaphobe, and even though we'd both been tested a million times over, he was absolutely certain we both needed to be tested *right fucking now* for HIV." He laughs bitterly. "Like he thought the virus would spontaneously manifest now that he'd come in contact with my blood."

I arch my eyebrow. "And that was a blessing, how?"

"Because he wouldn't touch me until the tests came back." Michael closes his eyes and scrubs his hand over his face. "The first few days, I felt horrible. Rejected, abandoned. But the longer it went on, the more I realized my body didn't hurt anymore, and I was sleeping better because I didn't have to worry about waking up to..." He pauses, then shudders. "Anyway. I think that was when I realized I needed to get out."

My mouth has gone completely dry. "How long after that did you leave him?"

Michael stares up at the ceiling, and his voice is hollow as he whispers, "Two years."

"Holy shit."

He exhales. "That incident wasn't an isolated one, let's put it that way. He fucked up my jaw a few times. And my gag reflex." Pinching the bridge of his nose, he says, "He took it personally once when I said I needed two or three weeks before I could go down on him again. He decided that wasn't acceptable, and, well, didn't give me much choice." Michael lowers his hand and meets my eyes. "Apparently having your wisdom teeth out isn't a good enough excuse."

I'm surprised my mouth doesn't literally hurt just hearing that. "I think that would put me off blowjobs for the rest of my life too."

Michael's lips tighten, and he nods. "Lucky for me, the blood put him off that time too. But damn." He shakes his head.

"I can't even imagine."

"You don't want to." He inhales deeply through his nose, then lets it out slowly. "It wasn't that horrible all the time. Honestly, we had good sex more often than not. But if he got drunk, or if he got pissed at me for something, all bets were off." He closes his eyes. "And here we are."

I slide my hand up his arm to his shoulder. "And you've come a long way. There's no way in hell someone's going to do that to you again."

"He won't get away with five fucking years of it, anyway."

"He does it once," I growl, "they'll never find the body."

He meets my eyes, and smiles. "If it happens again, I'll definitely take you up on that this time." Then he scowls. "So, you can see why blowjobs are such an issue."

"Yeah. Definitely." I kiss the top of his shoulder. "Question is, how do we get you past that?"

Michael sighs. "Fuck if I know. Because with this one,

there's two things I need to get over. One, I'm afraid I'm going to get hurt. Physically. Two, I can't even think about doing it without feeling like I'm being punished or degraded. Even when I know that's not the case."

"I can see why." I gently draw him into my arms, rolling onto my back so he can rest his head on my shoulder. As we settle, I stroke his hair. "Give it time. It took time to get to where you are tonight, but you made it. You'll get past this, and you'll be able to be with other guys." I kiss his forehead. "And I'm not going anywhere until you do."

"Thank you."

And God help any man who so much as looks at you the wrong way.

CHAPTER 14

Nothing caps off a weekend and gets me ready for another week of drudgery like kicking back with the guys in the hot tub. We toast the fading weekend and the coming week, and relax.

"One of these days," Michael says, sinking in up to his chin and holding up his glass to keep it out of the water, "I am so moving into a place with a hot tub like this."

"You looking to move?" Ian asks.

Michael shrugs. "I've thought about it. I do like where I'm living now, though. It's just tempting to move somewhere with a yard for Cody and, well"—he grins—"a hot tub."

I chuckle. "They're a pain in the ass."

"So are you," Ian says with a smirk. "But you're worth the maintenance."

"Hey!" I playfully kick him under the water, and he laughs and splashes me. Then I turn to Michael again. "If you're thinking of buying, I can hook you up with the realtor who found us this place."

Michael nods. "I'll keep it in mind. Honestly, I do like

my place. And the rent is good, but maybe when I finish off my student loans, I'll start thinking about it." With a quiet laugh, he adds, "I'm not sure if it's a good idea for me to buy a place, though."

"Why's that?" Ian asks.

"Because at the moment, the only thing keeping me from having forty-seven dogs and a bunch of cats is my landlord's pet policy."

"Oh, good point." Ian swirls his glass. "You could always buy in one of those places with a homeowner's association. I mean, they're annoying as hell, but they would put a cap on how many critters you can have."

"True, true. I don't know. Maybe I just need a big chunk of property out in the sticks. The commute would suck, but I'd have room for more than one dog."

"Let me guess." I arch my eyebrow. "So you can have a whole army of horses?"

"And goats."

"And goats. Of course."

Michael laughs. He brings his glass toward his lips, but pauses. "Oh, Ian, I mean to ask. How are your feet doing?"

"Much better," Ian says. "The massage sure helped, and I've been sitting as much as I can during my lectures. Having the summer off should finish the job."

I pat his arm. "Soon."

"Not soon enough," he grumbles and picks up his glass. "Good thing I've got Dionysus to get me through the rest of the year."

"Nerd," I say under my breath.

He snorts. "Oh please. You say that like you don't get turned on listening to me read the classics out loud."

Michael almost spits out his wine. "Say what?"

"It's true." Ian drains his glass. As he reaches for the bottle, he adds, "Isn't it, Josh?"

My face burns. "Only because you read it like you're reading erotica. It could be the damned phone book and it'd have the same effect."

"Hmm. Might have to try—oh shit!" Ian turns the bottle over above his glass, but only a few drops spill out. "Gentlemen, I believe we're out of wine."

"*Again?*" Michael scoffs. "Why does this keep *happening?*"

I set my glass on the edge. "We should just move the wine rack out here. For convenience."

"What?" Ian rolls his eyes. "The temperature would be all wrong. That's why we bought a house with a wine cellar, remember?"

"Right, right." I nod toward the house. "That's also why you get to go get it."

"Of course." He kisses my cheek and stands. "More of the same?"

Michael raises his mostly empty glass. "Definitely. This stuff is great."

"Beats the hell out of the stuff you brought last weekend."

"Hey. *Hey.*" Michael huffs and rolls his eyes. "Excuse me for wanting to try something new."

"Oh, it was a valiant effort, but..." Ian wrinkles his nose as he stands and wades toward the side so he can get out. "A for effort, I guess?"

"Mmhmm. Shall we talk about the pitiful excuse for a shiraz you brought out here before Christmas?"

I can't help gagging at the memory. "Oh my God. He wins, Ian. Nothing will ever out-disgusting that bottle."

"Fair enough. Touché, Michael." Ian laughs and playfully claps Michael's shoulder as he gets out of the tub.

And Michael isn't fazed at all. He chuckles and takes another drink, but he doesn't draw away. Doesn't jump. Barely seems to notice that Ian touched him at all, never mind on uncovered skin. It shouldn't be a surprise after that foot massage a while back, but it *does* get me thinking.

Michael meets my eyes and cocks his head. "What?"

"You don't seem to mind being touched anymore." I nod toward Ian just before he disappears into the kitchen. "Even with him."

"I—well, not with either of you guys."

I smile. "Good. That's good. You used to flinch even from us."

His eyes lose focus for a moment, and then he smiles too. "I guess you're right."

I absently swirl what's left of my wine. "Remember how we talked about you being concerned about getting into bed with a guy you've never been with before?"

"Mmhmm."

"Maybe there's an easier step you could take first. With someone you know and trust but haven't slept with before."

Michael's about to take a sip of wine but freezes, staring at me. Then his eyes dart toward the house, and he nearly drops the glass in the water. "Wait, do you mean—"

"Yes, I do." I shrug, eyeing the kitchen door in case Ian starts heading back this way, and as I speak, tick off the points on my fingers. "You know him. You seem to be okay with touching him and him touching you. And I can vouch for him being completely sane and safe in the bedroom." I lower my hand back into the water. "It's something we can think about. Doesn't have to happen tonight."

Michael watches the kitchen door. "Actually, I like the

idea. And the sooner the better—I want these demons out of my head. Ian's the perfect guy for this if he's on board." He pauses, avoiding my eyes for a second. "I, uh, was kind of thinking of suggesting him myself."

"Really?"

"Really." He moistens his lips. "Do you think he'll want to?"

"Not sure. I thought he was allergic to anything besides monogamy until recently, so anything's possible."

"Worth a shot."

The sliding glass door opens. Ian's on his way back now. Michael and I exchange glances.

"It can wait," I say quietly.

He shakes his head. "No. I'm in." As he watches Ian cross the yard, dressed only in soaked black swim trunks and carrying a bottle of wine, he grins. "I'm definitely in."

I chuckle. "Dirty bastard."

"Not my fault you married a hot guy." He winks.

"Can't argue with that. But—" I glance at Ian, who's nearly at the gazebo, and whisper, "You sure?"

Michael nods.

Ian slips back into the water and tops off all our glasses. As he takes his spot beside me, everyone swirls, sips, swallows, but nobody speaks. The silence drags on, and it's quickly getting conspicuous.

Ian eyes us both suspiciously. "What? You two are quiet all of a sudden." He gives me a good-natured glare. "Did I interrupt a Walking Dead conversation?"

Michael laughs. "No, not quite."

I chuckle, shaking my head.

"Then...?" Ian's forehead creases.

"Uh..." Michael looks at me, eyebrows up. *You got this?*

I guess it makes sense for me to be the one to bring it up. Good thing I'm so great at improv. Wait. Fuck.

I clear my throat. "So, um. About this, uh, arrangement Michael and I have right now."

Ian arches an eyebrow. "Mmhmm?"

I glance at Michael. He nods before taking a deep swallow of wine, and I turn to my husband. "Would you be game to join us?"

"Join—" Ian's eyes have never been wider. "*Join you?*" He turns to Michael. Then me. Michael again. "Spell this out for me."

"Well, we started all this because Michael's been with me before. And now he's comfortable with me again, but that doesn't necessarily mean he'll be okay with someone completely new."

Michael nods. "So maybe a stepping stone would be someone I know but have never been with."

Ian blinks. "Like me?"

"Yeah." Michael cringes a little. "This all sounds insane. If you're not interested, it won't hurt my feelings. I'll find a way to get over all—"

"I didn't say I wasn't interested," Ian says softly. He turns to me. "You're sure about this?"

"I'd be a bit of a hypocrite if I wasn't, don't you think?"

"Still..."

I take Ian's hand beneath the water. "It's ultimately Michael's decision who he's comfortable with, but as far as whether I'm okay with you doing it? I can't imagine anyone I'd trust more. Especially under the circumstances."

Ian turns to Michael. "And you'd really want me?"

Michael nods, and a sheepish little grin forms. "Quite a bit, to be honest."

Ian's blushing now too. "Oh. Wow. Uh, how does..." He

clears his throat. "How do we even start? I'm not exactly a virgin, but I've never had anything start out like this."

I laugh. "I guess it *is* a bit weird."

"Well," Michael says, "we could start out with, you know, kissing or something." His cheeks get a little redder, even though they're already flushed from the wine and the hot tub. "If we like that, we take it from there." He rubs the bridge of his nose and laughs. "My God. We sound like kids playing Spin the Bottle for the first time."

"Eh, I can think of worse ways to break the ice." Ian eyes us both, lips quirked slightly as if he's mulling it over. Then he shrugs and sets his glass on the edge. "All right. I'm not going to say no." He glances at me, eyebrows up like he's waiting for me to shout April Fools! When I don't, he takes a breath, moves across the tub and sits beside Michael.

Michael drains his glass. He puts it aside, shoots me a quick glance and then turns to Ian. Their eyes lock. My heart speeds up. Didn't I just bring this up like two minutes ago? And they're already looking at each other like that?

Ian rests his hand on Michael's shoulder. They inch closer to each other, holding each other's gazes and holding their breath, and I realize I'm not breathing either. Michael's hand slides up Ian's chest and snakes around the back of his neck. Ian tilts his head a little. Closer. Closer. Almost touching.

They stop. Neither pulls away, but they don't move either—as if they're each daring the other to cross the last little gap. My heart could not possibly beat any faster. This is a bad idea, isn't it?

And both suddenly burst out laughing and separate.

Panic and relief both shoot through my veins—what the hell happened? Okay, it didn't turn into a flashback or something for Michael. But...?

Ian lets his face fall into his dripping hand. "I'm sorry. I'm sorry."

"Me too." Michael rolls his eyes. "I don't even know what's funny."

"Neither do I." Ian glares at the two wine bottles. "What did you *do* to us, you bastards?"

All three of us laugh this time, partly out of genuine amusement and partly because, at least in my case, I'm worried as fuck about how this thing might play out. We definitely jumped from discussion to execution way too fast —time to rein it back and talk about it before it blows up in our faces.

I open my mouth to speak, but Ian beats me to it.

"I'm really sorry." He clears his throat, and his tone is completely serious when he continues. "It's just..."

"Nerves?" Michael asks.

"Just a bit."

"Yeah. Me too."

"Look, I really do want to do this. If you think it's going to help you move on, then..." Ian twists around, facing him fully. "I want to follow your lead. What do we do?"

"One thing at a time, I guess." Michael lifts his hand out of the water and reaches for Ian. He pauses, his fingers hovering tentatively as droplets fall in the water right in front of Ian's chest. They lock eyes again, and Michael moves in closer, this time meeting Ian's face with his fingertips.

I chew the inside of my cheek. *We should talk this through.*

But Michael's drawing Ian closer. They're touching, looking at each other—and like Ian, I want to follow Michael's lead. So with my heart in my throat, I watch and hope for the best.

Ian runs the backs of his fingers along the edge of Michael's jaw. "You can trust me. I would never in a million years—"

"I know." Michael smiles, but there's tension written all over his tight lips and in his eyes. "It's PTSD, though. There's nothing rational when that shit kicks in."

Ian gulps. "What do you want me to do, then?"

Michael shivers, eyes flicking toward Ian's lips. "I really want you to kiss me."

Ian's other hand rests on Michael's arm, though I can't decide if he's steadying him, slowing him down, or keeping it there in case he suddenly wants to push him back. "Are you... Is this..." He glances at me, eyebrows pinched together. Facing Michael again, he whispers, "I don't want to make things worse for you."

And right then and there, I thank God for the man I married—he's as concerned about Michael as I have been from the beginning, and if ever there was someone I could trust with Michael, it's definitely him.

"You won't make it worse." Michael's features relax, and he combs his fingers through Ian's dark hair.

Ian isn't convinced, though, and draws back. "I..."

"We can stop any time, right?" Michael asks.

"Of course!"

Michael's smile melts my knees, and he cups Ian's jaw. "Then you won't make it worse. As long as we can stop, it'll be fine." Now he draws back, though, his smile fading. "But I don't want to do this if *you* don't want to."

"It's not a question of wanting to." Ian exhales, running his hand along Michael's forearm. "Trust me. I definitely want to."

"Me too."

They hold each other's gazes. After a moment, Ian's lips

curve into a grin. Then Michael's do the same. He leans in, and Ian mirrors him, and I hold my breath, not sure if this is going to be the hottest thing imaginable or a hot mess.

Good God, they're really doing this. Drawing each other in, gazes darting from eyes to parted lips and back— *please, please, don't let this backfire.*

They're both all smiles and confidence right up until they're close enough to kiss, and then they slow down. Michael bites his lip. Ian's forehead creases.

Damn it. Another attempt to move too far, too fast, and it'll only be a setback that'll—

Michael kisses Ian.

And my glass nearly tumbles into the water.

Michael grips the sides of Ian's neck in both hands, as if he's afraid Ian will pull away. At first, I'm certain Ian will. His spine's rigid, and his shoulders tense as if he's about to bolt. Then he wraps one arm around Michael. And the other. His hand slides up to cradle the back of Michael's head, and...

Wow.

One second, he's hesitating.

The next, Ian tilts his head and moves in for more. His cheek hollows. Michael's jaw relaxes. Across the tub, my balls tighten because I know how *both* men feel and taste when they kiss that deeply.

They pull apart and stare at each other. Both are out of breath.

No need to ask for a verdict. Their eyes say it all even before Michael licks his lips and Ian shivers.

"I have to say," Michael murmurs, "that wine tastes even better like this."

"No arguments here," Ian growls, and kisses Michael again, harder this time. Together, they shift around, and

Michael's suddenly in Ian's lap, straddling him. Without breaking the kiss, he grasps Ian's wrist and guides it beneath the water. My blood pressure soars. Ian groans as Michael inhales sharply through his nose. Ian's shoulder dips. Rises. Dips again. Michael shudders, digging his fingers into Ian's arm. I can't see Ian's hand below the surface, but whatever he's doing is driving Michael insane.

For all I know, they've forgotten I'm here, but I'm totally okay with that. There is officially nothing in the world hotter than watching my husband and my best friend making out in a hot tub. Jesus. Why didn't we think of this years ago?

Because Michael wasn't ready for it.

A chill cuts through the warmth of arousal and the hot tub, and memories flood my mind. How this all started with him. How he shied away from me. How he still flashes back sometimes when things get intense.

But...there he is. After the briefest possible conversation about it, he's in. Arms around my husband, rubbing against him and kissing him as if that earlier flinch and all the ones before it never even happened.

Michael tilts his head back, and my skin tingles as Ian takes the cue and kisses his way down that beautiful bared neck.

"So, um." Michael turns to me as Ian damn near bites him. "Yeah. That, uh, this'll work."

"You don't say." Shit, even I'm out of breath.

"I think we should go upstairs," Ian murmurs against Michael's throat. "Because I really, *really* want to suck his dick."

Panic shoots through me—Michael's okay with me going down on him, but Ian?

Michael drags his nails across Ian's shoulder. "In that

case, we should definitely go upstairs. Or else your neighbors are going to get a show."

Relief replaces panic.

And then arousal takes over. Nothing but pure, electric arousal.

Holy fuck, this is going to be hot.

CHAPTER 15

WE WAIT UNTIL WE'RE INSIDE TO SLIP OFF OUR SWIM trunks. Our privacy fence keeps out most prying eyes, but it'd be just our luck that the night someone decided to look would be the night we'd traipse naked into the house with hard-ons and a third guy. So, in the interest of keeping neighborhood barbecues from getting awkward, we step into the laundry room and peel off what little clothing we have on.

On the way upstairs, Ian steals a glance at Michael. Michael steals one at him as we step into the bedroom. And in the split second I turn away to close the door, they're kissing. I don't know who grabbed who, or who's in control, or what, but the two most gorgeous men in the universe are naked, dripping wet and kissing next to my bed.

At first, all I can do is stare. I've fantasized about this plenty of times over the years but never imagined it would actually happen, and now, there they are. Soaked. Naked. Erect.

And why the hell am I just staring?

As I come closer, they break the kiss and turn to me,

both grinning. They start to let each other go, but I put up my hands.

"No, no. Don't stop on my behalf." I lower myself to my knees beside them. "I can keep my mouth busy." Closing my fingers around each of their cocks, I add, "Hands too."

"He's good at that," Ian murmurs.

"Mmhmm," Michael says. "Really good."

Ian might've had a smart remark or something to add, but then I've got his cock in my mouth, and the only sound he makes is a soft whimper, which Michael promptly muffles.

I switch back and forth from Ian's cock to Michael's while they kiss above me. Someone's hand is in my hair. Someone groans. I can't tell one from the other, and there's something ridiculously hot about that. It's been years since I've had a threesome, and I've never imagined I'd actually have one with these two. This is going to be *amazing*. It already is.

Please don't let this night end. Ever.

Michael's hips rock. Fingers twitch against my scalp— they must be his, since they're encouraging me to take him deeper in my throat.

"We should..." He pauses, and when I glance up, he's kissing Ian again. Then he breaks away. "Bed. Before I fucking collapse."

"Good idea," Ian says.

I release them both, and they each extend an arm to me. My legs are a little tingly from kneeling for so long, but they still work, and with help from the guys, I manage to get upright and onto the bed.

Michael winds up in the middle, and he's barely horizontal before Ian and I both start on him. I kiss his mouth while Ian starts down his neck, and I lose track of Ian after that. All I'm aware of is Michael's kiss, his hot body next to mine, his hand finding—and now stroking, oh God—my cock. Hands and mouths are everywhere. Skin on skin. Fingers in hair. Teasing nipples, stroking cocks, nipping skin here and there—I've never been in bed with two men as passionate as these two at the same time, and every second promises to drive me out of my mind.

Ian starts kissing his way down Michael's chest. He did say he wanted to suck Michael's dick, and my whole body is on fire just imagining the sight of it.

Michael bites his lip and squirms. "Fuck..."

Then Ian kisses above Michael's navel.

And Michael sucks in a sharp breath.

His body goes stiff. My blood goes cold.

Ian and I both lift our heads.

And there they are—Michael's nerves.

"You all right?" Ian asks.

"Michael?" I touch his face.

He closes his eyes, and the breath he draws this time is deep but controlled. Steady. He inhales, puts his hand over the top of mine on his face and exhales slowly.

"Easy," I whisper. "It's just us. Just you, me and Ian."

Ian comes back up and eases himself down beside Michael. "You okay?"

"Yeah. Yeah." Michael shakes himself and opens his eyes. "Oral is a weird thing for me. I should've said something."

Ian glances at me, eyebrows up. *What do I do?*

"Do you want him to try again?" I ask Michael. "Or hold off for tonight?"

Michael scowls. "I want you to," he says to Ian. "God, I do. But..." He shivers, lips pulling tight as he does, and I caress his face again.

"It's just us," I remind him. "Nothing has to happen. You're not obligated to do anything."

"I know." Michael inhales. Exhales. Opens his eyes. Then he licks his lips and grins sheepishly. "I know. I'm sorry. It's this—"

"Don't apologize." Ian kisses Michael's forehead. "This is a new thing. I'm new to you."

"You are. But I like this. Just have to get past—" Michael taps his temple.

"Take all the time you need. There's absolutely no hurry. Tonight or any other night."

"Thank you." Michael curves his hand around the back of Ian's neck, and he kisses him. Gently at first, but then they both come back for more. Michael opens to him, and Ian takes the invitation, deepening the kiss as Michael's hand drifts lower. When Michael starts stroking Ian's cock, Ian groans and kisses him even harder, and Michael gives as good as he gets—oh yeah, he's definitely back.

I can't believe what I'm seeing. Not just the fact that my husband and best friend are kissing and turning each other on, but that Michael's actually okay. His nerves have raised their heads, but he's tamped them down, and *fast*. I can't help smiling as I watch the two of them kiss— Michael's definitely come further than he thought. Of course I'm not surprised he trusts Ian, but his demons showed up when it was just him and me too, so they were bound to make an appearance or two tonight. The fact that he's banished them so quickly, and recovered enough to get back in the game after just a moment of calming himself down—he can't possibly know that's nearly moving me to tears.

You really are back, aren't you?

Oblivious to me, Ian breaks the kiss and meets

Michael's eyes. "All of this is at your speed. Whatever you want to do."

"Good," Michael pants against Ian's lips. "Because right now, I want to fuck you."

Ian and I both stare at him. My heart goes haywire—Ian's not much of a bottom, though he's not opposed to it, but it's this aggressiveness from Michael that turns me on like *whoa*. And blows my mind in the wake of that brief setback.

"You're sure you're ready for that?" I ask.

Michael's gaze stays fixed on Ian. "Yeah." He strokes Ian's cock, biting his lip when Ian shudders and curses. To me, Michael says, "I'm definitely ready for it."

"Thank fuck," Ian says. "So am I." He kisses him again, briefly this time. "There's lube next to the bed." He grins. "How do you want me?"

"Depends." Michael's eyes gleam with lust. "You want it hard or slow?"

Ian shivers. "Is that even a question?" The grin broadens. "*Hard.*"

I'm surprised Michael doesn't come right then and there. Hell, I'm surprised *I* don't.

"If you really want it hard"—Michael nods toward the foot of the bed—"get on your hands and knees." To me, he says, "Could you hand me the lube, please?"

Despite my hands forgetting how they're supposed to work, I somehow manage to get him the lube from the nightstand without dropping it.

Ian gets on his hands and knees and holds on to the footboard. I lie down beside him, holding myself up on my elbow, and watch, my pulse soaring as Michael kneels behind Ian with the bottle of lube in his hand.

Michael puts some lube on himself. He inhales sharply

—just stroking lube onto his cock is enough to make his breath hitch. As he positions himself behind Ian, Michael's eyes are heavy-lidded, and he's breathing hard already, but evidently he's still focused enough to push into Ian.

"Oh...*God*." Ian moans, closing his eyes and gripping the footboard. He rocks back, driving Michael deeper. They're breathing almost in unison now, and their bodies are falling into synch like they've done this a million times before.

My mouth waters. Apparently there is something hotter than watching them make out in a hot tub. Jesus Christ.

"Josh." Ian beckons to me, and then taps the footboard in front of him. I quickly get up off the bed and come around in front of him. As soon as I'm within reach, he grabs my arm, pulls me closer. Before I know what's happening, my cock is between his lips. I grab the footboard and Ian's hair for balance. I've experienced his mouth countless times before, but all my senses are heightened tonight, and every touch sends lightning bolts through my veins.

Over Ian, I meet Michael's eyes. I can't tell if his skin is still damp from the hot tub, or if he's sweating now, but either way, the sheen just adds to that primal gleam in his eyes. When he licks his lips, I can't help shuddering, and inadvertently push my cock deeper into Ian's mouth. He groans, though, and he starts teasing my balls with his fingers as he deep throats me.

"Shit," I breathe. "That is so..." Words. Fuck words. Fuck thoughts. Ian's sucking my cock and Michael's fucking Ian right in front of me, and I don't know or care how to articulate anything beyond a long, helpless moan.

The harder Michael fucks Ian, the more enthusiastically Ian sucks my cock. The more I curse and gasp, the harder Michael fucks Ian. I have just enough presence of mind to hope they're both as overwhelmed with pleasure as I am, that they're both as close to the edge. My eyes don't want to focus, but I force them to, and it's worth it— Michael's definitely getting close to the edge, and the sight is unbelievable. His eyes screwed shut. His lips apart. Sharp, uneven breaths. Hard, frantic thrusts. Every muscle is tense, his knuckles blanched as he holds on to my husband's hips, his skin shining with sweat. And God, I can feel his thrusts—every time he slams into Ian, Ian jerks forward, his lips and hand tightening around my cock like an echo of Michael fucking him.

And then Michael forces himself in as deep as Ian will take him. Ian moans, the sound reverberating through me as Michael throws his head back and releases a choked half cry, half whimper, and shudders. Ian doesn't let up, and between his mouth and the sight of Michael coming undone, I lose it. I grab onto the footboard for balance as the world shifts beneath my feet and everything goes white for a moment. Ian keeps stroking me and teasing me with his tongue, drawing my orgasm out until my legs nearly drop out from under me.

Ian stops. I blink a few times. Michael's dropped back onto his heels, breathing hard and also blinking like he can't quite focus. Ian's grinning up at me as he licks his lips.

"Oh my God," I moan.

"Yeah." Michael exhales. "That. But we still..." He puts a hand on Ian's hip. "Still gotta make you come."

"I don't think that'll be difficult." Ian gets up on his knees, and he reaches for me, but Michael puts an arm around him and pulls him back. Ian turns his head, and as soon as they kiss, I swear an aftershock of my orgasm almost puts me on my knees. Michael's out of breath, but that doesn't stop him from kissing Ian deeply, just the way he does after I've sucked him off.

Ian grips the back of Michael's head with one hand, and strokes himself with the other. Oh yeah. We definitely need to get that man off.

"Put him on his back," I say. "I think he deserves one hell of an orgasm."

Michael breaks the kiss. "I think you're right." While they shift position, I come around the bed and join them, and Ian's shoulders have barely hit the bed before my mouth is around his cock.

"Oh yeah," he groans. "*Fuck*."

I nudge his thigh, and he parts his legs for me. When I slip two fingers inside his ass, he grips my hair. He moans, but it's a muffled sound, and I glance up to see Michael kissing him deeply, and the two of them make out as I suck Ian's cock and fuck him with my hand. Ian's already close to the brink when I start; I'm tempted to stop, let him calm down completely, and then give him the kind of long blowjob he loves, but that would be cruel at this point, so I don't hold back.

In almost no time, he's nearly there. His cock gets thicker, harder, and he curses and gasps as he tries to thrust into my mouth. I crook my fingers, and—

"*Fuck!*" He nearly comes up off the bed as semen jets across my tongue. "Oh my—" He's muted again, his cries reduced to barely audible moans by Michael's mouth, and between us, we keep him coming until he breaks the kiss to whisper, "S-stop...please..."

I swallow as I carefully withdraw my fingers.

Ian sinks back down to the mattress. He covers his eyes for a moment, just catching his breath. "Wow."

"I agree." Michael nuzzles his neck. "You two are fucking *hot* in bed."

I chuckle as I come up to join them. "You say this like it's a surprise."

"Oh, it's not." He grins at me over my panting, trembling husband. "But you've gotta admit—experiencing is believing."

"Good point."

Ian lowers his hand. "Don't know. Might have to do it again. Just to be sure."

"You want to catch your breath first?"

He nods vigorously. "Yes. Please."

Once Ian can stand, we all get up to clean ourselves off, and then collapse on the bed again, Ian and me on either side of Michael. We're all still lethargic and relaxed, but I feel more coherent now. Michael's eyes are clearer. Ian has returned to planet Earth. None of us are quick to fall asleep after sex, so as the dust settles, we're all wide awake. Just relaxed. Really relaxed.

Michael glances back and forth between us. "So I guess this means I'm good with other guys. Not that Ian's a stranger, but..."

"I know what you mean," Ian says. "I'm new to you. In this sense, anyway."

Michael nods. To me, he says, "You were right. This was a good idea."

Ian arches an eyebrow. "Oh, so this was *your* idea?"

"Are you surprised?" I ask.

"Hmm. Well. Now that you mention it..."

"That's what I thought." I smooth Michael's hair. "You did still get nervous. Maybe this is something we should keep doing. Just until those nerves settle."

"So, all three of us?" Ian asks.

I nod. "Or the two of you. Whichever works."

Michael runs his fingers along Ian's arm. "Well, I'm definitely not opposed to one-on-one with either of you. But both together?" He grins. "I'm not going to say no to that either."

Ian laughs. "Yeah. What he said."

They both turn to me. I show my palms. "Hey, don't look at me for the voice of reason. I've been fantasizing about the two of you at once for ten years."

"Oh, *have* you now?" Ian asks.

"Are you really surprised?"

His lips quirk. "Actually, no. And I may have thought about it once or twice myself."

"Uh-huh." Michael raises an eyebrow. "Is this why you guys kept inviting me over to hang out in the hot tub?"

Ian and I both laugh and shake our heads.

"No, of course not." I shrug. "But, I mean, it didn't *hurt...*"

Michael snorts, rolling his eyes. "Guess I should've brought over some stronger wine."

Ian wrinkles his nose. "Assuming it didn't taste like the horse piss you brought last time."

Shaking a finger at him, Michael says, "Shiraz. Christmas. Your argument is invalid."

We all laugh again, and they nudge each other playfully.

As the moment passes, Ian turns to Michael again. "In all seriousness, this arrangement"—he gestures at all three of us—"obviously works. And if this helps exorcise some of that jerkoff's demons, then I'm definitely in."

"Thank you," Michael whispers, caressing Ian's face.

Ian kisses his wrist. "You're welcome to stay here

tonight if you want." He meets my eyes and his eyebrows flick up. *Right?*

I nod. "Definitely."

Michael smiles but shakes his head. "I can't leave Cody for the night, or I definitely would."

"Completely understandable." Ian turns Michael's head toward him and gives him a tender kiss. "Why don't you bring him next time? Ariel wouldn't mind some company."

Michael laughs. "Well, Cody hasn't had a playdate in a while."

I chuckle. "Guess that means he gets one, and so do you."

"Perfect."

"Yes, it is." Ian kisses Michael again. "The dogs will be entertained, and we can have you all night."

Michael just shivers.

So do I.

CHAPTER 16

MICHAEL ISN'T JUST COMFORTABLE WITH IAN AS WELL as with me—the three of us can't get enough of each other. I can't even say for sure if it's in the name of helping Michael anymore, or if we've just turned something loose that doesn't want to be contained again. Our hot tub nights take on a whole new dimension. And Michael's at our house—and in our bed—more evenings than not. I don't think Ian's ever been so insatiable, not even back when we were both bathhouse sluts, and Michael's in heaven.

We aren't even having sex all the time. Dinner. Movies. Trips to the dog park with Ariel and Cody. But even when we're clothed and out in public, that undercurrent remains. Subtle touches. Less than subtle looks. We've spent time with Michael for years, and we're doing a lot of the things we've done all that time, but it's never been quite like this. As if there's always an unspoken *Just wait until we get home.*

The evenings when we don't go out are almost comically routine. Ian gets home first. Michael usually shows up around seven. I get there shortly after that. There's small talk in the kitchen, maybe a bottle of wine if anyone wants it, and someone finally makes a move. A flirtatious comment here. A playful ass grab there. Then we're off and running until Michael has to drag himself out to his car and head home. Unless, of course, he stays over—I love those nights. Falling asleep naked between Michael and Ian is becoming such a comfortable, sexy part of our routine, it's starting to feel strange when he's not here. Rosie's even getting used to the idea of an extra dog hanging around.

So when I get home from work this evening, my whole body gets warmer at the sight of Michael's car in the driveway and Cody playing in the backyard with Ariel. As I pull into the garage beside Ian's car, my pulse shoots skyward as if this is the first time. The novelty definitely hasn't worn off.

I can't help grinning as I get out of the car.

I step into the foyer, and—

Stop dead.

Oh my God.

I've seen a lot of incredibly hot things in my life, especially recently, but all that pales in comparison to what's playing out right now—my husband kneeling in front of the couch, head bobbing over my best friend's lap.

Michael's been resistant to oral since the first night. They've tried a few times, but he's shied away, and Ian never, ever pushes.

And now…

This?

Neither of them responds to my presence. Maybe they don't hear me. Maybe they're too caught up in the moment. Knowing how talented Ian's mouth is, I wouldn't be surprised if Michael's forgotten his own name by now. His fingers rake through Ian's dark hair, and his eyes are closed and his teeth are digging into his lower lip, and my cock is getting hard before I've even toed the door shut.

I set my jacket down and loosen my tie. My legs don't quite remember how to work, but somehow, I convince them to carry me across the foyer and into the living room. And from the doorway, I just stare.

Michael exhales slowly, running his fingers through Ian's hair. It's impossible to tell what Ian's doing—deep-throating, licking his way up and down the shaft, focusing on the sensitive head—only that Michael loves it. If the two of them had to banish any demons before they got this far, it doesn't show.

"Oh, shit, that's good." Michael's head lolls to the side. His back arches as his fingers twitch in Ian's hair.

I ease myself onto the couch beside Michael, and his eyes slide open. He reaches for me, draws me in—I swear to God, if I wasn't hard already, his mouth would have changed that in an instant. His kiss sends shivers all the way through me, curling my toes inside my shoes.

Between kisses, I murmur, "I hope you're not gonna come quite yet." I'm surprised I get the words out at all, never mind audibly.

"If he keeps..." Michael looks down and sweeps his tongue across his lips. "If he keeps doing this..."

Ian's eyes flick up. My body temperature soars.

"Maybe he should." I hook a finger under Michael's chin and turn him back toward me. "Then we'll just have to make you come again later."

Michael whimpers, and I silence him with a kiss. He wriggles against me and slides his hand over my lap, and now it's my turn to squirm.

In front of us, Ian moans softly. I look down, and he's picked up speed, taking Michael deeper in his mouth and adding a little twist with his hand, and Michael's palm presses harder against my cock.

I nibble Michael's earlobe. "Don't hold back. This isn't going to be the last time you come tonight."

He presses the heel of his hand against my dick and kneads my balls with his fingers—not enough to hurt but damn sure enough to make my breath catch. His head falls back against the couch, and I kiss his exposed throat, my cock getting even harder beneath his hand as my lips explore that hot, smooth flesh.

"B-both of you. Don't stop. Please..."

We're not stopping for anything. Michael's breathing so fast now, and when I slide my hand over his chest, his heart is pounding. His sharp huffs of breath turn to whispered curses. He squeezes my cock, the touch bordering on painful and turning me on like crazy, and I murmur *"fuck"* against his neck.

He inhales. Holds it. His fingers twitch. His heart pounds.

And then he releases a ragged breath and shudders hard, fucking into Ian's mouth as much as he can in this position, and if I know Ian, he's on the verge of coming himself as Michael lets go.

"Jesus Christ." With one last shudder, Michael sinks back against the couch. He covers his face with a shaking hand, and Ian and I exchange grins as Michael trembles between us.

"We should really go upstairs." I gently remove Michael's other hand from my groin so I can think. "Much more room up there."

"Good idea," Michael murmurs.

"Agreed." Ian gingerly stands, cursing under his breath as his knees and ankles pop. As he does, Michael gazes longingly at the thick bulge beneath Ian's jeans, and I know that look—he wants to blow Ian. He made it past one barrier tonight, and now he can handle Ian going down on him, and I can see in his eyes how badly he wants to return the favor.

But he doesn't. That's one line he just hasn't been able to cross yet. Not even with me.

My stomach tightens. Night after night, the three of us fuck like rabbits, Michael getting more and more confident with every touch, and *still* Steve manages to keep a choke-hold on him.

We'll get there. I refuse to believe we won't.

And for now, there are plenty of other ways to keep Michael's mouth entertained.

I gently turn his head toward me, grin and pull him into a kiss.

Afterward, the three of us lie beneath the sheets, Michael in the middle again. Ian gets up to let the dogs in—though they stay downstairs—and joins us again, draping an arm over Michael and propping himself up on his elbow, facing us both.

"Are they tired out?" Michael asks.

"Pretty sure they'll sleep well tonight." Ian kisses him. "Pretty sure *you'll* sleep well tonight."

"Kind of hard not to after you guys are done with me."

I chuckle and kiss the top of his shoulder. "I don't think there'll be any insomnia in this house any time soon."

"Definitely not," Ian says.

I watch them both for a moment. "So, I see you two have gotten comfortable with each other."

"We already were," Michael says.

"But enough for oral?"

Michael nods as he runs his fingers along Ian's arm. "I think it was a foregone conclusion that it would happen eventually."

I smile. "That's probably the most optimistic thing you've said since we started out."

He smiles too. "I guess you guys are fucking the cynic right out of me." He and Ian exchange grins, and Michael shrugs. "Tonight, I decided I was tired of getting so hung up on oral. Because I *know* I love it—I just had to get past that mental barrier. We started kissing before you got home, and—"

"That was fucking hot," Ian whispers. "One minute, we're kissing on the couch. The next, he's asking if the offer is still open to suck his dick." He shivers, running a hand over Michael's hip. "Damn right it was."

"Yeah, it was." Michael lifts his head and kisses Ian lightly. "Thank you, by the way. It seems like such a stupid thing to get hung up—"

"You don't have to justify any of this, Michael." Ian rests his hand in the middle of Michael's chest. "You've been through hell. Getting past that is a process."

"Still." Michael swallows. "Thank you."

"You're welcome." Ian kisses him, then turns to me. "You're, um, not upset, are you? About us starting without you tonight?"

"No, definitely not." I shake my head. "I was just thinking." I study them both. "Out of curiosity, when you guys started fooling around tonight, would it..." I hesitate. "Would it have been different if I hadn't been on my way?"

They exchange puzzled glances.

"How so?" Michael asks.

"I mean, do you think you'd be completely comfortable one-on-one with Ian?"

Ian's eyebrows jump.

Michael's eyes lose focus. "I hadn't thought of that."

"Josh does have a point," Ian says. "Whenever you and I have been together, Josh has been here, or he's been well on his way. We didn't even get started tonight until, what, ten minutes before he got home?" He trails the backs of his fingers up Michael's arm. "If you want to see what it's like without him as a safety net, then—"

"I don't see how I'd freak out with you, though." Michael smiles. "I know you. I trust you."

"Exactly," I say. "So it makes perfect sense. If some nerves or past trauma come out at an inopportune moment, you'll be in good hands. I know it's kind of baby steps, but that's probably the best thing, you know?" I search Michael's eyes. "Only if you want to, though. Of course."

"I do." Michael chews his lip. "But you guys have already gone above and beyond for me. I don't this to turn into something that'll cause problems between you two."

"It won't." Ian squeezes his arm. "If there was a problem, none of us would be here in the first place."

Michael's eyebrows pull together. "So..."

"If you're game to try," Ian puts a hand over Michael's. "There's one way to find out if you're comfortable with just me." To me, he says, "If you're really okay with it."

"Yeah, of course."

We both turn to Michael, and he shrinks back slightly, as if the double scrutiny is more than he can handle.

I slide my hand under his and Ian's. "It's up to you. If you'd rather keep to all three of us..."

"No, I trust Ian." Michael glances at me, then turns to

Ian. "Meet me at my apartment tomorrow night? After work?"

"Let's do this." Ian grins, and I hope to God Michael feels the same tingle of anticipation I do.

After a moment, he returns Ian's grin. "I can't wait."

CHAPTER 17

Tonight's the night.

Ian isn't home when I get there. His car is gone. The dog is whining and bouncing, eager for attention. The laptop on the table is closed, all the papers tucked away in an attaché case. Rosie is peering at me as if it's my fault that Ian isn't here, and how *dare* I come home without him?

"Sorry, sweetie." I scratch her ears but stop before she swats me. "He'll be home later."

How much later? I stop in my tracks. My visits with Michael haven't been overnight, but no one explicitly decided whether this one would be. Do I wait up?

I shake my head and head into the kitchen to make myself something to eat. This is hardly the first time I've come home to an empty house, and I can handle it. I always have.

But his absence is painfully conspicuous tonight.

This is a good thing, I remind myself. Michael's comfortable enough with Ian to be alone with him. I trust Ian—Michael's in good hands, and Ian will come home to me. If not tonight, then tomorrow.

Now if I could convince my brain to stop panicking over it and turning it into something it's not, I'd be in good shape. Ian isn't having an affair any more than I was. Michael isn't going to wind up traumatized all over again because Ian won't let that happen. Ian will come home at the end of the night, and everything will continue as normal. Well, some shade of normal, anyway.

Thinking about it isn't going to accomplish anything, so I do the best I can to distract myself.

After a quick dinner, I take Ariel out into the yard. Immediately, she grabs a stick and runs up to me, tail wagging so hard she's whipping herself in the sides. I'm glad she doesn't have her tail docked like most boxers, but damn, that's gotta hurt. When I toss the stick, she turns, and her tail cracks me in the knee.

"Shit, dog," I mutter, eyes watering as she takes off to get the stick.

She brings the stick back and drops it, and since I'm still leaning over to rub my knee, she slurps me in the face for good measure. Laughing, I gently nudge her away and toss the stick again. The pain fades, of course. I can't even be mad at her—hell, I'm impressed. That tail's a damned weapon.

I throw the stick a couple dozen times, but my arm's getting tired well before my dog is.

"You need someone who can throw it farther," I tell her as I put the stick in the box where all her outdoor toys end up. "Michael's a pitcher—ask him when he comes over."

Michael.

Fuck.

So much for distracting myself.

I take Ariel back inside and do a double take.

"Rosie." I snap my fingers. "Get off the counter."

She glares at me, as if to say *Make me, asshole.*

I roll my eyes and reach for her. She lifts her paw, daring me to actually pick her up.

"Really?" I return the glare. "You never get up there when Dad's home. What the hell."

The paw stays up, her blue eyes narrow and her ears start to go down. All Ian would have to do right now is give her a look, and she'd jump down without a fuss. Then again, she wouldn't have gotten up there if he were here, so it would've been a moot point.

"Down." I put my arm over her and scoop her off the counter. Naturally, she bites me—not hard enough to draw blood, but hard enough to let me know she is displeased. When I set her on the floor, she hisses.

"Sorry, kiddo. Dad's not here. You're stuck with me and Ariel tonight."

Her ears go all the way down, and I wonder if she actually understood me or if it's just her usual disdain. Either way, she didn't authorize Ian's absence this evening, and if I know what's good for me, I'll conjure him from thin air to do her bidding.

Then she turns away and saunters out of the room. She'll probably go terrorize Ariel now, but at least she doesn't use her claws on the poor dog.

Alone in the kitchen, I drum my fingers on the counter where the cat was defiantly sitting a moment ago. Between the two guys, I haven't had much time to myself in ages. Really, not since Michael and I started sleeping together. And now, I probably have a few hours. Knowing Ian and Michael, they'll fill any downtime with talk about baseball or football, so I don't expect him home any time soon.

So now I just...need to figure out...what to do...

I blow out a breath in the silent kitchen. Is this how Ian

feels every time I'm alone with Michael? If it bothered him, he'd have said something, but it's weird to be in his shoes this evening.

A few chores around the house keep me busy for a while. Dishes. Some routine cleaning and tidying upstairs. Sorting a month's worth of junk mail. Litter boxes. Topping off water dispensers for both animals. Ian and I keep the place pretty neat, though, and our animals are relatively low maintenance, so there's only so much to do unless I want to start pressure-washing the driveway or something.

It does kill some time, though. Once I'm done, I park on the couch to catch up on some Walking Dead. Can't exactly watch that with Ian around. Ariel jumps up beside me, flops down and rests her head on my leg. Rosie sits on the back of the armchair, peering down at us.

For the next couple of hours, I lose myself in watching a bunch of allegedly intelligent people routinely paint themselves into corners and fall victim to zombies. Ian's probably right that it's a stupid show, and I can't get through an episode without at least one facepalm and a muttered "Are you kidding me?", but it's entertaining as hell. And Daryl's hot, which makes up for pretty much everything.

Halfway through the sixth episode of the evening, my phone vibrates. A million imaginary texts flood my mind, and for the two seconds it takes me to get the phone from the coffee table and look at the screen, I'm suddenly and irrationally convinced that every possible worst case scenario is taking place.

But Ian's name comes up, followed by: *On my way home*.

All the worry vanishes in favor of the fluttery, giddy feeling I used to get when we were dating. When he'd text me to let me know he was heading over to my apartment, and I'd start counting down the minutes until he was there. Because I knew exactly how long it took for him to get from his place to mine, just like I know down to the nanosecond how long it takes to get here from Michael's.

Maybe I left a chore or two undone. There's got to be something I can do for the next forty-seven minutes.

I look at the TV screen. This episode is halfway over, but that'll kill at least some of the time. Hmm.

I click off the DVR to see what's on TV. After flipping through a few channels, I land on a baseball game. It's in the fourth inning, so he'll be home long before it's over. And at least it isn't football. I kind of know what's going on.

But holy shit, boring. Forget it.

I turn off the TV completely and start playing games on my phone instead. Just as I hoped, they hold my attention, and before I know it, Ariel's head snaps up, making her tags jingle. A second later, the garage door rumbles to life, and Ariel is off the couch, bounding toward the door.

It's just as well she has no dignity and does the running, jumping and barking. At this point, it's either her or me.

Christ, what the fuck is wrong with me? He's been gone a few hours.

Having sex with another man.

Having sex with Michael.

Just like I've been doing for weeks.

Then Ian steps into the foyer. Ariel goes crazy—*I know the feeling, sweetheart*—so he crouches down to pet her and at least try not to get whipped in the face by that tail. Meanwhile, I sit up but don't stand yet. Can't look too eager, right?

Get a grip, idiot.

On the armchair, Rosie stretches and yawns, looking as indifferent as possible, then sits up and stares at Ian expectantly. When he's done greeting the dog, he stands, and on his way to the couch, stops to pet her, and she bumps her head against his arm, purring loudly.

I shoot him my most pitiful expression. "So I'm third in line?"

"Hardly." He rolls his eyes, sits beside me and puts an arm around my waist. "But I have to appease them so that when I say hello to you..." He draws me in for a kiss, and it's one of those deep, languid kisses that turns my brain to mush. When our lips separate, he finishes: "...we don't get interrupted."

"G-good point."

"So." He winks. "Hello."

We both laugh, and he kisses me again, briefly this time.

"So, um." I clear my throat. "How was he? I mean, how was it? The night. With Michael."

Ian chuckles and touches my cheek. "You're adorable when you're flustered, you know that?"

"Flustered. I'm—"

"Yes, you are." He kisses the tip of my nose. "And to answer your question, everything went fine."

"It went fine?" I fold my hands in my lap because I can't remember how to look casual. "It wasn't a surgical procedure, Ian."

He laughs nervously. "What do you want me to say? I had a great time, and I'm pretty sure Michael did too. There isn't much more to tell."

"You enjoyed yourselves, though, right?"

Color blooms in his cheeks, and he can't quite look me in the eye. "We had a good time."

"Ian?" I tip up his chin. "You okay?"

"Yeah. Yeah." He kisses my hand, and this time he does

meet my gaze. "I guess it's just a little weird coming home from another guy's bed. Even his."

"Tell me about it."

He's about to say something, but Rosie picks that moment to stomp across me and flop down in Ian's lap.

I chuckle. "Somebody missed you tonight."

He scratches her tummy. "How badly did she terrorize you?"

"She only bit me once."

"She bit you?" He eyes me. "What did you do?"

"Told her she couldn't sit on the kitchen counter."

"What?" He wags his finger at her. "What have I told you, kitty?"

She swats at his finger but keeps her claws in. Of course.

He laughs, then picks her up and deposits her on the other cushion. When he faces me again, the humor is gone. "So, tonight." He swallows. "There *was* one point where Michael started to freak out."

My blood turns cold and my spine straightens. "What happened?"

He loses focus for a second. Slowly, he shakes his head and meets my gaze again. "I'm not even really sure, to be honest. Everything seemed fine, and then..."

"And then it wasn't?"

"Basically."

Sighing, I nod. "Yeah, I've had that happen many times. But, he was okay afterward?"

Ian nods. "We stopped for a little while. He calmed down, and then we got started again."

"What set him off? I mean, what were you guys doing when it happened?"

Ian swallows. "Missionary. Or, trying to, anyway."

"You on top? Or him?"

"Me." He chews his lip. "When we tried again, he wanted to do the same position again, so we just took it slower."

"He does like that position," I say quietly. "We've done it quite a few times."

"Why would it set him off this time?"

"It's hard to say. That fucking PTSD can just come out of nowhere."

Ian's lips twist. "Now I get why you called it a minefield."

"Uh-huh. He's come a long way, though. It's amazing to see the difference in him. How he was so nervous and self-conscious early on, but now..."

Ian shivers.

So do I.

"It's a damned shame he was ever like that," Ian says. "I swear, if I ever see Steve again..."

"You and me both. And I'm going to be chewing my nails to stumps the first time Michael's out with another guy."

Ian nods. "Me too."

"Well. We'll all cross that bridge when we get there."

"Yeah. For now..." Ian takes my hand. "Bed?"

"Bed."

We go through our evening routine, cat and dog underfoot as always. I can't quite settle down for the night, though. I'm relieved to have him home, even though I don't know why—I knew he'd be home, and I knew where he was the whole time anyway. But I'm also restless. Maybe because I know there's not a chance in hell that we're having sex tonight. We always want what we can't have, after all.

Once we're in bed, Ian doesn't kill the light. He tugs on my shoulder, so I roll onto my back. He's on his side, arm draped across my chest. "You all right tonight?"

"Yeah. Of course. Why wouldn't I be?"

"I don't know. You just seem a bit tense."

I chew the inside of my cheek. "I guess it was just a bit weird, switching roles with you." Meeting his eyes, I ask, "Has it been weird for you? When I'm over at Michael's place?"

"It was a little in the beginning. Just an adjustment, I guess."

"Maybe that's it."

"We've been strictly monogamous for a long time. Shifting gears and accepting the idea of your husband sleeping with another guy... It's gonna make you stop and think, you know?"

"Yeah. It does." I touch his face. "I'm sorry if this has been stressful for you."

"Don't be." He turns his head and kisses my palm. "The only one who needs to apologize for anything is Steve, and he's beyond redemption anyway. The adjustments and stress for us have been worth it to help Michael."

"I agree. As long as we're okay."

Ian smiles, sending a warm jolt of electricity through me. "We're definitely okay." His fingertips drift over my abs and continue downward.

I bite my lip. "I thought you were tired."

"I am." He kisses the side of my neck, and then starts downward again, his lips following the same path his fingers took. "But you're not."

"No, but—"

But I love those soft little kisses down my chest. Over my stomach. Across my hipbone. And Ian may be completely spent after everything he did with Michael tonight, but when he closes his lips around my cock, the fatigue doesn't show at all.

And I just lie back, close my eyes and enjoy my husband's skilled, enthusiastic mouth.

CHAPTER 18

AFTER THAT, MICHAEL AND IAN SPEND THE occasional night together, and Michael and I sometimes have a bed to ourselves. More often than not, it's all three of us, but it seems they're as addictive as they are addicted—we all want each other all the time. Some nights, I all but forget this is meant to help Michael repair damage from his past—he's on an even keel most of the time, with only the slightest pauses now and then, and his avoidance of giving blowjobs. The line blurred a long time ago between doing this for fun and doing it for therapy.

Which I suppose is good. The less it's at the forefront of my mind—and hopefully Michael's—the less it's a problem. The farther his demons are behind him. The more that jackass's memory fades.

So I should feel good about all of this. And I do.

But something isn't sitting right. It festers beneath my ribs for a few days, getting steadily more noticeable. I can't quite put my finger on what's causing it, though, only that I always feel worse after a night with Michael. What the hell is wrong? Because everything seems to be going just fine. Right?

It makes sense one morning when I roll over and find Ian's side of the bed empty. That in itself isn't unusual, and I know he's here because the shower is running. The cat is still on Ian's pillow, the dog slowly taking over his side—everything is normal.

But his absence in our bed resonates with me in a weird way. I've gotten used to him occasionally being at Michael's, so why should this—

Ah. That's it.

He's here, but...not. And it's been like that a lot recently. Almost constantly, if I'm honest. My stomach clenches—I can't even remember the last time we slept together. We've had a few quickies before going to bed, especially if one of us has been out with Michael, but beyond that...

Nothing.

As I lie there, my thoughts unnerve me. I fully expected to be engrossed in helping Michael, and I knew there'd be some physical exhaustion involved. But it hadn't occurred to me that Ian and I might neglect our marriage in the process. That we might get so caught up in Michael, we'd forget how much we enjoyed being together. Even after more than a decade, our sex life has always been amazing, but lately...

Lately it's been nearly nonexistent outside of the things we've done with Michael. When we have had sex on our own, it's been a reprieve—a chance to enjoy some effortless physical intimacy after seeing firsthand how hard it is for Michael. That's not how it's supposed to be. That's not how I imagined it could ever be.

What the hell is happening to us?

We're getting too tangled up with Michael, that's what.

Fuck. Didn't I swear up and down this wouldn't happen again? That everything with Michael would not distract me from Ian? I don't want to leave Michael to his own devices until he's sure he's back on track, but I need to fix this. And it can't wait.

I carefully slip my leg out from under the dog. She grumbles a bit, wriggles farther onto Ian's side, but that's it.

I step into the bathroom. The sight of Ian on the other side of the frosted glass makes my chest tighten. How long *has* it been?

He turns his head, though the semi-opaque door obscures his features. "You're up early."

"Yeah. I know." I pause. "Mind if I join you?"

"Sure."

I step into the shower with him.

"Couldn't sleep?" He leans back to rinse some shampoo from his hair.

"Not really." I wait until he's done rinsing off, and then put my hands on his waist. "I wanted to see you before you go to work."

He glances down at my hands and blinks a few times. "What are—"

"We haven't been spending enough time together." I draw him in and run my fingers through his wet hair. It's too early in the morning to kiss, but I need to touch him. "We were having so much sex before, and now that we're with Michael all the time, we've barely had anything left for each other."

Ian frowns. "I know. And I want to keep spending time with him, but..." He swallows. "To be honest, I miss you."

"I miss you too," I whisper.

"Call Michael when he's up." He kisses my fingers. "Tonight, we're shutting off our phones and staying home."

"Good idea. I'm sure he'll understand."

"I have no doubt."

We exchange smiles.

"You know, as long as I'm in here." I snake a hand between us.

Ian sucks in a breath. "Josh, I need to... I have to get to..."

I trail my fingers along his cock. "You have time, don't you?"

He shudders, pressing against my hand. "I need—"

"Turn around."

He hesitates, and I'm expecting him to insist he really doesn't have time, but then he does turn around. I pull him against me so I can reach around and stroke his cock while I kiss up and down his neck.

Ian braces his arm against the wall, and he pushes back, and a groan escapes my lips as he rubs against my dick. I had only intended to jerk him off and give him a little preview of tonight, but like this, with my cock pressed between his wet skin and mine, I'm losing it too.

His other hand closes around mine. He's not taking over, not controlling how I stroke his cock, just making contact, and I stroke him faster. Ian moans and thrusts into my hand—our hands—which only increases the delicious friction against my cock. I bury my face in his neck and rub harder against his wet skin.

"*God.*" He shudders, and I hold him tighter as my own orgasm rocks my whole damn body. So much for just getting him off, but I'm not complaining.

We rinse off and then pull each other close, and for the longest time, we just stand there, holding each other beneath the warm shower, lazily kissing each other's necks. Fatigue—from both my orgasm and being up at the break of dawn—sets in, and I'm getting sleepy in his arms, but I don't care.

"Why did we *ever* stop fucking in the morning?" he says.

I kiss his forehead. "Because you went and got a job that makes you get up too fucking early."

"Oh right." We both laugh breathlessly.

"Tonight's a good idea," Ian murmurs. "I can't wait."

"Neither can I."

"Gotta go to work, though." He lifts his head and meets my gaze, his eyelids heavy and his lips curving into the most delicious grin. "I'll be counting down the hours."

"Me too." I smile sleepily. "Love you."

"Love you too." Ian kisses my cheek, then steps out of the shower.

With the stall to myself, I close my eyes and let the hot water rush over my skin for a minute or so. Then I reach for the shampoo and start getting myself cleaned up. It's early, but now that I'm awake, I might as well get ready for work.

Not that I'll get much done today. I suspect I'll be a distracted idiot for the next several hours.

Because tonight, I have a date with my husband.

As I PULL IN THE DRIVEWAY AFTER WORK, anticipation crackles along my spine—Ian's always home first, so I have no doubt he's ready and waiting for me. In bed? On the couch? Hell, he could be in the garage, ready to fuck me across the hood or in the backseat.

I shiver. I don't care where or how, I just want him.

In the house, Ariel greets me as she always does, but Ian

doesn't answer when I call for him. I take off my jacket in the foyer, and on my way into the kitchen, slip off my tie.

And there, beside his laptop and briefcase on the kitchen table, is a bottle of wine, a pair of glasses and a piece of paper with two handwritten words:

Hot tub.

Oh, hell yes.

Glasses in one hand, bottle in the other, I step out onto the deck, and there he is. He's lounging in the tub, arms stretched out across the edge, watching me.

I hold up the bottle. "Should we even bother with the wine?"

"Maybe afterward." He beckons to me. "Get in here."

Neighbors be damned, I strip out of my clothes and slip into the water. My feet have barely touched the bottom before Ian wraps his arms around me and pulls me onto his lap. His wet hands run all over my back and shoulders, up and down my sides and my thighs.

Under the water, his erection brushes mine, but it's his mouth that has my attention right now. I've always loved the way he kisses.

After a while, Ian breaks the kiss and gazes up at me. Sliding wet fingers through my hair, he says, "I don't want to hurry. We have all night, and I want to use it."

"Agreed. Question is, what do you want to do with it?"

He flashes a wicked grin. "I think what we're doing now is perfect."

"Me too."

We haven't made out like this in *years*. This is exactly the way he kissed me the night we met, when we'd caught each other's eye in a bathhouse and found ourselves pressed up against a wall, kissing and panting before we'd exchanged so much as a hello. Memories rush through my mind of where that first kiss went—a frantic hand job in a corner, a blowjob in front of guys whose names I'll never know—and I shiver against him.

At some point, we pull apart, and our eyes meet.

My spine tingles.

He licks his lips. "Bedroom?"

"Bedroom."

We dry off just enough to keep from slipping and falling on the linoleum, and somehow Ian's coherent enough to bring the untouched wine bottle back in the house.

Then it's up to the bedroom.

I lie back against the pillows, and Ian goes right for my cock. True to his word, though, he's in no hurry—he licks and teases me, as if he wants to savor every taste. No one on the planet can make a blowjob last as long as Ian can without it getting boring and tedious—and a blowjob from him is *never* boring or tedious.

After just a few minutes, though, he stops. "I've got a better idea."

"Oh yeah?"

"Mmhmm." He gestures for me to sit up. I do, and then let him guide me back down so we're lying in opposite directions, facing each other on our sides. Oh yes. This will do quite nicely—now I can suck his cock while he sucks mine.

The only downside is that it's difficult to concentrate while he's driving me crazy with his mouth, but I try anyway. Ian moans softly, and his hips start moving, not quite thrusting into my mouth, but definitely trying to get deeper. I do the same, and we fall into a slow, steady rhythm, sliding in and out of each other's mouths. Our hands roam over each other's asses, hips, legs. No one's in any hurry—I could lie like this and please him like this all night long. Lips, tongue, hands, doing to him the same things he's doing to me and vice versa. Time doesn't exist anymore. Nothing does except this beautiful man beside me and all the little moans we're drawing out of each other.

After God knows how long, Ian stops. "Come up here." He turns onto his back, and I join him, climbing on top. His hands on my hips nudge me into motion, and silently, breathlessly, we're moving together, my cock rubbing against his. The friction is insane, but quickly becomes too intense, so I get the lube off the nightstand.

I pour some into Ian's hand. He strokes some of it onto his cock and some onto mine. As we start moving together again, the undersides of our dicks rubbing together, that slipperiness is mind-blowing.

His other hand curves around the back of my neck, and as he draws me down, he lifts his head to meet me halfway. As soon as our lips meet, I'm nearly there—his body, his mouth, everything about him turns me on, and I can barely stand it as we kiss and rub together.

Ian breaks the kiss, but he doesn't let me go. Forehead to forehead, panting and trembling, we're both getting close—I swear I can feel his orgasm building just like I can feel my own.

Then he gasps. A shudder runs up his back, lifting him off the bed, and I kiss his neck as semen spurts between us, and in seconds, I'm coming too, groaning and shaking until I can't even fucking move anymore.

He collapses. I collapse. We hold onto each other, we breathe, and I'm surprised I don't black out.

When my arms and legs finally agree to hold me up, we separate, we wipe ourselves off and then pull the sheets up over us.

Neither of us says anything for a while. Lying beside him, head tucked beneath his chin, I don't want to get up.

Even now that we've reconnected again, I'm almost afraid to let him go. This is the second time I've let our arrangement with Michael pull my focus away from my marriage, and it's left me rattled that we both let it happen this time.

Ian's hand slides up my arm. "Still awake?"

"Yeah." I rub my eyes. "Just"—*distracted*—"drowsy."

"Me too." He holds me closer. "We really need to do this more often."

"Yeah, we do." I kiss beneath his jaw.

"I don't want to stop what we're doing with Michael," he says. "But we can't forget about us."

I close my eyes and exhale, relieved we're on the same page even though I shouldn't be at all surprised. "No, we definitely can't. Maybe we need a night or two a week that's just for us."

"Probably. Or even keep playing it by ear, but make sure we're still spending time one on one. I have no doubt Michael will understand."

"More than most guys would, I think." He nudges me gently. "We should eat something."

"Yeah." I drape my arm over him and cuddle closer. "But I don't want to move yet."

"Neither do I." He nuzzles my hair. "This is comfortable."

"Mmhmm."

"Come on. Let's go make some dinner before we fall asleep."

I want nothing more than to lie here with him, but I nod and start to get up. "Yeah, good idea."

Ian stops me with a hand on the back of my neck, and he grins. "Maybe a light dinner. I don't know about you, but I could go for some more tonight."

Goose bumps spring up along my spine. "You can have as much as you want."

The grin broadens, and he draws me in for a kiss. "Maybe dinner can wait, then."

"Hmm. Maybe it can…"

CHAPTER 19

IT'S NO SURPRISE THAT MICHAEL'S COMPLETELY supportive when Ian and I tell him we need a couple of nights a week to ourselves.

"Like I've said from the beginning," he tells us over dinner, "I don't want to cause any problems between you two. I'm happy to make whatever adjustments help you guys."

Funny how I was so worried about this being a bad idea. I'm married to and sleeping with two of the most level-headed, laidback men on the planet. While I get worried and convince myself we're on the cusp of disaster, they adapt as if they can't imagine why not.

So on an evening when Ian's swamped with papers to grade—which he neglected for a few nights in a row because of both Michael and me—he gives me a kiss, tells me to have a good time and reminds me to kiss Michael for him. And it's completely normal. This has become normal in our house. Which is weird when I think about it, but living it feels exactly that: normal.

As does walking into Michael's house, saying hi to Cody

and continuing into Michael's kitchen, where he's waiting with a glass of wine in his hand.

"Right on time." He sets the glass down and wraps his arms around me. "As always."

"Couldn't possibly be late." I kiss him lightly. "By the way, Ian says hello. And he sends"—I cup Michael's neck and kiss him again, longer and deeper, just the way Ian likes it—"that."

Michael grins. "I'll definitely make sure to send one home for him too." He holds my gaze, and the grin falters a bit. "I, um...I'm actually glad it's just you and me tonight, though."

"Oh yeah? Why's that?"

He rests his forearms on my shoulders. "Because I want tonight to be different. It's been all about me from the beginning. Tonight, it needs to be about you."

"But we—"

He kisses me, and my resistance doesn't stand a chance. Some nights, we talk for a while, and maybe go through a little bit of wine, but sometimes we cut right to the chase. This is going to be one of those nights, according to this languid bedroom kiss.

After some long, undefined expanse of time, he draws back and meets my gaze. "I know this has been stressful for you. Fun, yeah, but let's be real. I know you've worried about me, and about your marriage." He takes my hand and leads me toward the bedroom. "I just want you to know that I appreciate it."

"I know you do, Michael. I've never doubted that for a second."

"Still." He pauses. "I think we should finish this conversation in the bedroom."

It seems like a topic that can easily kill the mood, but I

do what I've done since the start—follow Michael's lead. Into his bedroom. Out of our clothes. Into his bed. Into another long, tangled kiss.

Without breaking the kiss, Michael rolls me onto my back. Then, he moves from my lips to my jaw, and continues down my neck. "I've told you time and again how much you've done for me, and how much it means to me." Kiss by kiss, he inches down my torso. "Tonight, I want to show you."

"Show me? How are..."

As he starts down my abs, his eyes flick up to meet mine, and the pieces snap together.

He's really...

He passes my navel, pausing now and then to flick his tongue across my skin.

Oh my God.

His lips mark a slow, gentle path along the edge of my hipbone.

He is.

He starts at the base of my cock, drawing little circles with the tip of his tongue, and my breath is gone. Just gone. My eyes water, and it's more than arousal. I can't even believe what I'm seeing, what I'm feeling—Michael's going down on me?

He works his way from the base to the head, kissing and teasing. Just like that very first time a lifetime ago, he's taking his time, working up the confidence while he's turning me inside out.

He rests a hand on my hip, quite possibly to keep me still, and runs the tip of his tongue along the underside of my cock. And when he reaches the head, I expect him to go back down, but instead—

Holy. Fucking. *Hell.*

His lips slide down over the head. Before I can catch my breath from that, he runs his tongue around it. Again, back the other way. He doesn't take me very deep, but that's just fine by me—what he's doing is...so...*good*.

I want so badly to grip his hair, to run my fingers through it, but I don't know if that's welcome. Not when it's taken him so much just to work up the nerve to do this. So I grab the pillow and hold on, forcing myself to stay still even when my hips desperately want to rock in time with his strokes. On the plus side, staying still keeps me from coming too fast—thank God, because this really is our first time all over again, and I want to savor it even more than I did then.

There's no putting off an orgasm indefinitely, though. I grip the pillow tighter and try to stay still. Try to hold back. Not a chance.

"K-keep doing that," I slur. "And you'll make me come." I'm half-expecting him to continue anyway, like he did the first time, but he stops. He lifts his head and pushes himself onto his arms.

"I do want to make you come," he breathes as he moves up over me, "but I want to fuck you." He shudders, pressing his rock hard cock against me. "I want to be inside you when you come."

Oh fuck yes.

I moisten my dry lips. "How?"

"My favorite position, of course."

"Perfect." I love it when he fucks me this way. The angle, the view—it's all perfect. And it means I don't have to move, which is even better, since he's turned my spine and limbs to jelly.

Michael sits up and puts on some lube. My pulse is going crazy as he pushes my legs apart and positions himself.

The head of his cock breaches me, and as thick as he is, it makes my eyes water. Then he pulls out and does it again. And again. And again. I want him all the way inside me, every last goddamned inch of him, but that shallow fucking is enough to drive me insane.

Michael rests his weight on his hands, pushes with his hips and slides all the way inside me. And just in case I have any sanity left, he withdraws almost completely and does it all over again. He fucks me painfully slowly, drawing out each stroke until I'm ready to come unglued.

"Like that?" he asks as he pulls out again.

"So much. You fucking tease."

"Me?" He flashes a toothy grin and then *slams* into me. "I have no idea what you mean."

I can't think of a comeback. My brain's gone blank, and he's pulling out again, and...*yes, please, please, do it again. Do it—oh fuck!*

He doesn't let up now. He's pounding me deep and hard, relentlessly, reducing my vocabulary to helpless near-sobs. I manage to grip the back of his neck with one hand, pump my dick with the other, and I'm in heaven. He's kissing me, he's fucking me, and everything's...everything's perfect.

A tremor ripples through my whole body. I break the kiss with a gasp, and arch off the bed. Whatever rhythm my hand had, it's gone now, but I don't care.

And suddenly Michael pulls out.

And he pushes my hand away.

What the—

His mouth closes around my cock. He slides his fingers inside me and crooks them, and he's fucking me with them, and...and...

"Oh my God," I whimper. "Michael, I'm—"

Gone.

Just...gone.

The whole world explodes. He keeps going, keeps sucking my cock and finger-fucking me, and I just keep coming, and coming, and coming.

"S-stop." I gasp for breath. "Fuck. Stop..."

Michael stops. Gives me a moment to breathe. Then he slips his fingers free. He comes back up, and even more than the very first time, I have to kiss him. I have to taste this and convince myself it's real. That Michael really did knock down that last obstacle.

God, yes. It is real. The salt in his mouth is as real as the fading shockwaves of my orgasm. He really did it.

"I thought..." I gulp, trying not to kill the mood. "I thought you wanted to be fucking me when I came."

"I did." He kisses me again, lightly this time. "I changed my mind."

"Jesus." I blink a few times. "You haven't come yet, though." I reach for the bottle of lube. "Let me do something about that."

"Don't have to tell me twice." He rolls onto his back. I lie beside him, pour a little lube on my hand and then close my fingers around his cock.

Michael kisses me, but before long, he's too out of breath to keep kissing me. Instead, he gazes down, watching me pump his dick, and then he closes his eyes and lets his head fall back. "Oh yeah... Oh..." He groans and bites his lip.

I stroke him faster, adding a slight twist to my strokes.

Michael grabs on to my shoulder and thrusts into my fist. "Fuck, Josh. Keep..." He trails off into a choked whimper, and a split second later, he comes, fucking my hand erratically until he shivers and sinks back onto the bed.

I kiss him lightly. "Have I ever mentioned how hot it is to watch you come?"

He grins even as he's catching his breath. "Any time you wanna watch, I'm more than happy to oblige."

"Of course you are. Dork."

He just chuckles, and I turn away to grab the tissues off the nightstand.

After the dust settles and we're tangled up under the sheets, I meet his gaze. "You went down on me."

He laughs. "You noticed."

I roll my eyes and tousle his hair. "You know what I mean."

"Yeah, I do." He kisses me softly. "I've been trying to work up the nerve for a while, and part of me just realized how stupid it was to be afraid to do anything with you." He caresses my cheek. "Because you've proven time after time after time what I've known without a doubt since we were kids—that there's no one I trust more than you."

"Of course you can trust me," I whisper. "Always."

"I know." He smiles tightly. "The thing is, I kind of feel stupid for not coming to you about this years ago. Or even telling you what happened."

"You didn't have to."

"No, but it would've done me some good. I didn't know how badly I needed my sexuality back until I started *getting* it back. For the first time in years, I actually feel like *me* again. Completely. I didn't even realize how important it was to me, and how much I missed it until...until you..." He exhales, and then he kisses me, letting the soft contact linger for a moment. "Josh, you and Ian gave me back the last thing Steve took away from me."

I'm...speechless.

Michael sweeps his tongue across his lips. "What he

did, it'll always be there. What's done is done. But now it's like when I fucked up my knee in high school. There's still some damage, and it still gives me trouble once in a while, but it's *healed*. And that's how this feels too. Like it's less of an open wound now and more of a scar." He clasps both his hands around one of mine, and the intensity in his eyes damn near drives me to tears even before he whispers, "Which means I can finally move on."

I still can't speak, so I just free my hand and wrap my arms around him, and that doesn't really help me get my emotions under control.

After a moment, I clear my throat. "He didn't deserve a single piece of you. I'm so glad Ian and I helped you get this one back."

"Me too." He holds me tighter. "Thank you, Josh. This means the world to me."

I kiss the top of his head. "You're welcome."

Because you *mean the world to me, Michael.*

CHAPTER 20

A few days after Ian and I reconnect, I'm meeting Michael for lunch. That's not unusual; we've been having lunch together a couple of times a week ever since I started working on the same side of town as the vet clinic.

But when he walks through the door of our usual restaurant, I do a double take. There's a grin on Michael's face that he can't quite suppress, and he's definitely trying. When he takes his seat across from me, he's practically bouncing.

I cock my head. "What?"

"Hmm?" He presses his lips together, but that only makes it worse. "What?"

"You know what."

He stops even trying, and that smile takes my breath away. "Dr. Klein was in the clinic this morning."

"Oh yeah? And did you talk to him?"

"I did." He's beaming now. God, he's beautiful when he's this happy. "And uh, I told him I got cold feet before, and asked if the offer was still open."

My jaw drops. "*You* actually asked *him* out?"

Michael laughs. "Come on, don't sound quite so surprised."

"Well, I..."

"It's okay." He reaches across the table and puts his hand on my arm. "It kinda surprised me too."

"So, was the offer still open?" As if I need to ask.

Michael squeezes my arm, then withdraws his hand. "We're having dinner tomorrow night. Then I guess, um..." He laughs, sounding nervous and relieved at the same time. "I guess we'll see what happens."

I chuckle, arching my eyebrow. "You don't have to call him Dr. Klein over dinner, do you?"

"No. It's just a habit at the clinic." He smiles, and I'm surprised little hearts don't appear in his eyes. "I guess I'll have to get used to calling him Ben."

The sound of the doctor's first name hits me in the chest for some reason. "I'm sure you'll get used to it."

"Just have to remember not to call him that at the clinic. Ah, hell. If I do, who cares, right?"

"Though hey, what better way to remind yourself you're dating a doctor?"

"We're not dating. It's one—"

"Not yet." I grin. "But after tomorrow..."

"We'll see." Michael picks up the menu, even though he and I have both memorized it a hundred times over. He gives it a cursory glance before he lays it down again and meets my gaze, that grin still crinkling the corners of his eyes. "This is so weird. I haven't been on an actual date in ages."

"Well, don't expect me to come over and help you pick out what to wear."

Michael snorts. "Right. That'll be the day."

"So where are you guys going?"

His lips quirk. "I don't know. We didn't get that far. We're meeting at the clinic since we both know where it is." He half shrugs. "I guess we'll see what happens after that."

I smile, though I'm not sure why it takes so much work. "I guess we will."

AFTER LUNCH, WE BOTH NEED TO GET BACK TO WORK, but neither of us is in a huge rush on the way out to the parking lot. The walkway seems shorter today, though, and too soon, we're at the curb.

Our eyes meet. This is usually the moment for "have a good one" and "see you next time" and "try not to choke anyone at work" before we both walk away—him to his car, me to my office. But we're not moving, and we're not speaking, and we're not leaving.

My heart speeds up. "So, um..."

This silence is fucking stubborn. I need to get back to work before my boss gives me the evil eye, but I can't make myself say good-bye.

Suddenly, Michael steps forward, puts his arms around me and hugs me tight. "Tomorrow night wouldn't be happening if it hadn't been for you." His voice wavers a bit, and he whispers, "Thank you so much, Josh."

"You're welcome." I hold him close and squeeze my eyes shut. "I'm so glad you're back on an even keel."

"Me too."

He doesn't let go. Neither do I.

"Good luck tomorrow," I whisper. "I really hope this works out for you."

"So do I." He finally releases me, and when our eyes meet, his are clearer and brighter than they've been in a while. "Even if it doesn't, I think..." He shrugs. "I think I'm okay with that. If it doesn't work out with him, it will with someone else."

"Of course it will. Any guy would be lucky to have you."

Michael smiles. "Well, I'll let you know how it goes."

I smile back. "I can't wait to hear."

Be good to him, Dr. Klein...

CHAPTER 21

THE NEXT NIGHT, AS WE HAVE SO MANY TIMES OVER THE years, Ian and I cuddle up on the couch with the animals to watch TV. Ariel is taking up more space than she has any right to. Rosie is on the armrest, letting Ian pet her while she stays firmly out of my reach. In front of us is a rerun of The Big Bang Theory—I can almost lip synch the dialogue because we've seen this one five hundred times, but the jokes are still funny. This is as normal as it gets in this house, but it feels all wrong.

I glance at my phone. It's eight thirty.

By now, Dr. Klein and Michael are probably sitting in a restaurant somewhere, making conversation over drinks and appetizers, shyly fumbling their way through first-date nerves even though they've known each other for ages.

And that's the problem, isn't it? We're here, and Michael's out there, and I wonder if I'm even more nervous than he is tonight.

But it's not just nerves. I can't get comfortable. Can't settle. Even when I remind myself a hundred times over that Dr. Klein is arguably the safest, gentlest man any of us know, there's something else still tugging at my consciousness.

It's almost like the letdown that comes after an exhilarating experience, but it doesn't make any sense. This process with Michael has been about getting him back on his feet. What he's doing tonight is exactly what we've been trying to help him achieve—the confidence and courage to take a chance with another man.

So why do I feel so empty?

Empty. That's what it is.

And here comes the guilt. I resist the urge to fidget beside Ian and draw his attention to my discomfort, because this is something I really don't want to explain. I'm not entirely sure I *can* explain it, but I damn sure don't want to. How the fuck would I tell my husband I feel down and sad because Michael's not here tonight? Because Michael's out with another man, and all three of us have our fingers crossed that it works out?

I cuddle closer to Ian, ostensibly to give our ever-expanding dog some more room, and rest my head on his chest. Ian kisses the top of my head and adjusts his arm around my shoulders.

This is perfect. What the fuck is wrong with me? I've never once felt like there was anything missing in my marriage. Ian isn't perfect, but he's the perfect man for me—I'd sworn off marriage and monogamy alike right up until I realized I was in love with him.

There's nothing missing from my marriage to Ian, but where is this hollow feeling coming from? I've always been thrilled when Michael finds somebody—even that asshole, before I knew what he was really like—but tonight, I'm floundering.

Out of nowhere, Ian says, "You think he's having a good time?"

My head snaps toward Ian. "Huh?"

"Michael." He looks at me like I've lost my mind. "What?"

"I'm just, uh..." *Surprised you're thinking of him too.* I clear my throat and shrug. "I hope he's having a good time. God knows he deserves it."

"Yeah, he does." Ian's expression hardens a bit. "And God help that vet if he doesn't treat him right."

That protectiveness sends a tingle right through me, and I fidget to mask a shiver. "No shit."

"It sounds like he will, though. My fingers are definitely crossed for him."

"Mine too."

Ian eyes me. "You don't sound all that enthusiastic?"

"I am." My face burns. "Is it wrong that I'm going to be kind of disappointed when Michael moves on?" I cringe at my own words. "I mean, the sooner he's in a good place, the better, but..."

"I know what you mean." Ian takes my hand, and a little smile works its way onto his lips. "I think we'd both be lying if we said we haven't enjoyed being with him, particularly now that it's not so rough on him anymore."

"True." Why doesn't that explanation feel like enough? "I guess it has been pretty fun for all three of us, especially the more he's recovered."

"It has." Ian grins. "Let's face it—our sex life is better than it's been in a long time."

I can't really argue with that. We've been having more sex lately than we have for the past few years, and it's been absolutely smoking hot. Not that it was ever lacking, but lately it's been better. Just like our marriage—nothing has been missing all these years, but tonight it suddenly feels like there is.

Shame turns my stomach. It's just an adjustment, that's all. There is absolutely nothing missing in my marriage.

"Damn," Ian says. "How is it already quarter to ten?"

Where is Michael now? Are he and Dr. Klein—

No, no, no. Don't need to think about that.

"Time flies, I guess."

"It always does." Ian kisses my temple. "We should head to bed. Some of us have to be up at the crack of dawn."

"Sucks to be you," I say with a halfhearted laugh. "And what the hell? It's not even that late yet."

"Uh-huh. But if we go to bed now..."

Oh.

Oh.

Ian's alarm startles me awake. I usually sleep through it, or if I wake up at all, it's not for long, but this time, he may as well have kicked me.

As he always does, he slips out of bed almost silently and goes into the bathroom to take a shower and get ready for work. That's my cue to start drifting off again. He'll wake me briefly with a kiss good-bye, murmur "I love you" in my ear, and then he'll leave me to sleep until my own alarm screeches.

Except that drifting-off part isn't happening. At all.

I listen to the shower come on. A few minutes later, it turns off again. The faucet runs. His razor clinks against the edge of the sink.

Fuck. I'm not going back to sleep, am I? With as much time as I spent wide awake last night, I could've used that extra hour or two of sleep, but it's not happening. Might as well get up.

Rosie is still curled up on Ian's pillow, and Ariel is sprawled across the foot of the bed. I carefully pull my legs out from under her so I don't wake her up. She's not much of a morning dog, though, and just grumbles and fidgets a little.

Sitting on the edge of the mattress, I rub my eyes as if that'll actually banish the fatigue. At this hour? Not likely.

Coffee, we're going to be really good buddies today.

I grumble some profanity as I push myself to my feet.

Like he always does, Ian's got the bathroom door open to let the cool air in now that the shower has steamed everything up. He's halfway through shaving when I lean against the doorframe. He glances at me as he rinses his razor.

"You're awake."

"Well, that's being generous." I yawn and rub my eyes again.

"Can't sleep?"

I shake my head. "Might as well get up and get moving."

"Thinking about Michael?"

"Am I that obvious?"

"No." He tilts his head back and draws the razor up his neck. "But I was thinking about him a lot last night too."

I shift uncomfortably. "Were you?"

"Kind of hard not to." He glances at me, but then continues focusing on shaving. As he works his way along the side of his throat, he says, "Even if I hadn't gotten physically involved, I'm still worried about the guy. And after I got involved..."

I raise my eyebrows.

He rinses his razor and glances at me again. "I don't know. I guess I just felt more...invested. I've always cared about him, first because he was your friend, and then because he was also mine. And I guess getting physical with someone..."

It's a struggle not to shift and fidget, especially as we both silently watch his reflection while he finishes his neck and jaw. If Ian's gotten in deeper now that they've gotten physical, what does that mean for me?

That's probably not something I want to think about. Especially not before I've had coffee.

Ian finishes shaving and dries his face. "Sink's all yours."

"Thanks."

In silence, we go about our routines, and despite the tight quarters, we don't get underfoot. After all this time, we've mastered the art of staying out of each other's way. Especially since we've had to do this with a rambunctious boxer and, at times, a tripping hazard cat in the way.

As I finish brushing my teeth, Ian comes back in, buttoning his crisp white shirt, his shirttails untucked and his tie draped over his shoulders.

"You going to be okay today?"

"I'll manage." I shrug as I rinse my toothbrush. "We've got that high octane coffee at work now. I should be able to stay awake."

"That's not the part I'm worried about."

I meet his eyes in the mirror. "Yeah. That. I'm, um, having lunch with him today. I'll find out how last night went."

He rests his chin on my shoulder and wraps his arms around my waist. "Let me know?"

"I will. Definitely."

Neither of us speaks, and he doesn't let me go. It's way too early in the morning for awkward silence, but there it is.

After a while, Ian finally says, "Listen, um..." He breaks

eye contact but nuzzles the side of my neck, as if he wants to avoid my gaze but still maintain this affectionate embrace. "Maybe it's just as well that Michael's back on his own two feet now."

Of course it is. It's great that he's confident enough to pursue something with another man. But I don't think that's what Ian's getting at.

I reach back and rest my hand in his short hair. "Why's that?"

"Because I'm starting to think this isn't healthy anymore." He kisses the back of my shoulder. "For you. It's eating you alive."

I lower my hand and sigh.

Ian keeps his eyes down. "If he does need more of this, we need to think about how long we let it continue. Before you start doing more damage to yourself than—"

"I'll be fine." I gently free myself and turn around. "Really. I will."

He scowls and rests his hand on the back of my neck. "I want to believe that, but I know you." He draws me in for a soft kiss. "You're the kind of person who'd get yourself killed pulling someone out of a burning building."

"I'm not saving him from a burning building."

"Not literally, but you are going to be collateral damage if you're not careful."

"Then what do you think I should do?" I wrap my arms around his waist. "What should *we* do?"

"Well, last night will be a test of how far he's really come. Maybe he's ready to move on, and that's great. But if he's not..." Ian chews his lip. "That's where things could get tricky. Because I want us both to see this through for his sake, but I also want to put a stop to it for yours. Except if he still needs us after last night, then that's the worst possible time for us to call time on it, and..." Ian shakes his head. "How am I supposed to tell a wounded man he can't have more of what helps him?"

My heart falls into the pit of my stomach. Pulling my husband close, I whisper, "I don't know. I have no idea what we're supposed to do now."

"Talk to him. See how last night went." Ian kisses my forehead. "Then we'll all figure out where to go from there."

I nod, not sure what else to say. I can't explain my feelings to Ian. Not until I sort them out in my own head, anyway.

Ian glances at his watch. "Damn. I have to go." He cups my neck in both hands and presses his lips to mine. "We'll talk over dinner tonight. Okay?"

I nod. "Okay."

"I love you."

"I love you too."

He leaves the bathroom, and I listen as his footsteps continue down the stairs and across the hardwood foyer. When the door shuts, I release my breath. As the garage door rumbles open beneath my feet, I lean over the counter, holding on to its cool faux marble edge for balance.

I need to get my head together. I have no business feeling like this. Michael went on a date last night, and there is nothing in the world I want more than to hear that it was perfect. I hope like hell that I get a text from him before lunch. Something like, *Can't make it. Long night.* ;)

I hope and pray he spent the night with Dr. Klein, and the two of them are still lying there and enjoying each other's company. He wasted enough of his life with a man who caused him to call in sick too many times because of ER visits. He deserves nothing less than someone who makes him call in sick because they can't get enough of each other.

And somehow, for the sake of my friendship, my marriage, and my own sanity, I have got to get rid of this sudden jealous bone.

CHAPTER 22

"So how did it go?"

Across the booth at our usual restaurant, Michael
doesn't answer. He's not looking me in the eye, and he's not
touching the food that showed up a couple of minutes ago.

My pulse ratchets up—it's a struggle not to prod him,
and at the same time, I'm afraid to hear the truth. With
everything Michael's been through, I hope to God it was
only a disappointing first date. Maybe Dr. Klein was less
attractive without the stethoscope around his neck, or he
had some heinous political views, or he turned out to be
estranged from his toothbrush. Maybe he ordered veal at
dinner—that would be a one-way ticket to Nopeville in
Michael's book.

I nibble on a fry, mostly because I need to do something
besides sit here and stare him down. He seems uncomfortable enough without my scrutiny.

Then, releasing a breath, Michael pushes his untouched
plate away. "Well, the date went fine. I had a pretty good
time, and I think he did too." A smile tries to work its way
onto his lips. "Ben's an awesome guy."

"You don't sound happy, though." My chest tightens—*please, please, don't let him say it went* that *kind of wrong*.

Michael's eyes lose focus. "It seemed like it was going okay. We had dinner, and then we went to a comedy club. After that, he took me back to my car." He releases a long breath. "And he kissed me."

I can't breathe. *Klein, if you did anything to fuck with him...* "What happened?"

Michael rests his elbow on the table and rubs his forehead. "God, it actually started even before that. The thing is, the whole night, I felt like something was missing. I wasn't bored, but I wasn't as into it as I thought I'd be. Like I couldn't get into it even though I wanted to." He drops his hand on the table and exhales. "I was on a date with Ben Klein, for God's sake!"

I stare at him, completely at a loss for words.

Michael leans back against the cushion. "And then as soon as he kissed me, I got it. I figured out what was missing."

"And that was..."

His eyes meet mine. "You and Ian."

My heart stops. My mouth has gone dry, but I manage to choke out, "What?"

He flinches, looking out at something across the restaurant instead of at me. His voice is so soft, it's almost timid as he murmurs, "As soon as he kissed me, all I could think of was the two of you."

"But you've been wanting him for—"

"I know. And when I finally had a shot with him..." He laughs humorlessly. "All I could think of was how much I wanted to be with you and Ian. Because I—" His voice cracks.

I can't even fit all this in my brain, never mind put my

finger on what it means. All I know is the way I felt last night, and how I feel now looking at him. There are some pieces in my head threatening to come together, and I keep trying to push them apart because I have a feeling the big picture isn't one that'll help this situation. Even while I'm hurting for him because I know how much he wanted his date to work out, why is there...relief? Guilt? Shame? What the fuck?

"So, yeah." Michael groans. "I fucking blew it. Because I..." He buries his face in both hands. "This must sound incredibly stupid."

"You'd be surprised."

Michael lowers his hands and searches my eyes. "Meaning?"

"Meaning..." *I love you.*

The thought hits me like a fist to the gut.

Oh shit. Oh. Shit.

I can't. But I do.

Oh God. I do.

Staring at Michael, holding his gaze from across the table while he waits for me to tell him why his feelings aren't as stupid as he thinks they are, everything I felt last night suddenly makes way too much sense.

Fuck.

I rub the back of my neck. "Maybe things got more complicated than we thought they would. For all of us."

His eyebrow slowly rises.

So does my pulse.

I scramble to collect my thoughts and explain myself, but there's no easy way to say it. Knowing he's got feelings like this too, that doesn't help the situation, because I don't know how to tell him I love him in the same breath I need to tell him I'm terrified for my marriage. There are two men in this world who I'd step in front of a bullet for, and I'm scared out of my mind that there's no way we're all getting through this without one of them—all of us—getting hurt.

Before I can find the words, Michael puts up his hands. "Look, I think we can both agree this got really complicated, but I need to cut to the chase. Whatever's going on, I need to put on the brakes. On all of this."

A weird mix of disappointment and relief and hurt twist in my stomach. Like I've been issued a pardon and a kick in the balls at the same time. "Oh."

He puts his elbows on the table again and steeples his fingers in front of his lips. "I'm sorry." He closes his eyes and releases a long breath. "The thing is, over the course of five years, Steve convinced me I was trash. And since we started this whole thing, you and Ian haven't just made me feel like I can have an actual sex life again." He opens his eyes. "You've made me feel like I'm worth loving again."

I swallow the lump in my throat. *Why do you think I've been in love with you for twenty years?* But I can't say that. It'll only complicate this conversation, and I'm not so sure I can get the words out anyway. It's hard enough to convince my mouth to form, "Michael, you *are* worth loving."

"Maybe I am. But it's been a long, long time since I've been able to feel anything for anyone. And I'm not sure I trust those feelings."

I tilt my head. "Trust them? What do you mean?"

He chews his lip for a moment, staring at the table between us. Without lifting his gaze, he says, "Dr. Hamilton told me early on that she's had problems with patients who've fallen in love with her. One of her colleagues has had the same thing happen. They're not really in love with *her*, they're..."

My heart sinks as I realize where he's going with this. "They're in love with the person who helped them."

Michael nods. "She said it's kind of like the Florence Nightingale effect, but in reverse. The patient falling for the caregiver."

"Transference?"

"Yeah. That."

And the sinking feeling gets even worse. Is that what's happened to me? And Ian, for that matter? Is that all this is?

No. That's not possible. Not when I've had feelings for Michael since we were kids.

Except they've never been as intense as they are now. As they've been since that first night I joined Michael in his bed.

I'm still collecting my thoughts, but Michael continues. "Listen, I can't thank you and Ian enough for everything you've done for me." He holds my gaze, though he struggles. "I'm in a much, much better place now because of you guys."

"I'm glad we could help," I say numbly.

"Me too. But I think I need to spend some time on my own. So I can, you know, sort out what I feel and..." He sighs. "I don't even know. But I don't want to fuck up your marriage, and I don't want to fuck up our friendship." His eyes flick up again, meeting mine through his lashes. "So this isn't forever. I just need to figure a few things out."

Now it's definitely feeling more like a kick in the balls than a pardon, and I fight the urge to reach for his arm. How weird—he's so much more comfortable with physical contact than before, and everything that made him more comfortable with it adds up to why I can't make myself touch him now. We got too close. We let this get too deep. And I will not be the one who makes him second guess his decision—not after I've seen just how hard it is for him to walk away from someone he shouldn't have been with in the first place.

"When you're ready," I say, willing my voice to remain even, "you know where to find us. The door's always open."

He nods but doesn't look at me. "I know. And that means a lot. But I need..."

"Some time?"

"Yeah."

What can I say to that? "Anything you need."

Michael searches my eyes for a moment. Then he looks down at his plate, and his nose wrinkles a bit as if he's wondering why the hell he ordered anything in the first place. "Listen ..."

My stomach twists as he reaches for his wallet.

"I'm gonna go." He fishes out a twenty and sets it beside his untouched meal. "I'll be in touch, though. I promise."

When?

I just nod. "Okay. Take care of yourself, all right?"

"I will." He slides out of the booth and glances at me, but doesn't let the eye contact linger. "Give Ian my best?"

"Absolutely."

Our eyes meet again. I don't know what to say, and he doesn't offer anything. After several long, uncomfortable seconds, he turns to go, and it takes every bit of restraint I have not to jump up and run after him. As he walks down the narrow row between tables, hands in his pockets and head down, my chest physically aches.

This doesn't hurt as bad as all the times I watched him go back to Steve.

But damn, it's a close second.

CHAPTER 23

Lying by omission and a quick subject change get me out of an uncomfortable conversation with Ian.

"How did Michael's date go?"

"Sounds like it went fine, but there probably won't be a second date."

"Damn. That's too bad."

"Yeah, it is. Have you eaten yet?"

Then it's dinner I can't taste, TV shows I can't focus on and wine that doesn't do me a damned bit of good.

And now we're in bed. Ian's sound asleep even though Rosie has almost pushed him off his pillow. Between us, the dog is snoring.

I haven't even started drifting off yet. I've been listening to my husband and pets breathe while the conversation with Michael replays over and over and over inside my head. The guilt and shame keep burrowing deeper. I want to wake Ian, tell him everything and beg forgiveness. I want to call Michael and do the same.

I check my phone for the thousandth time. 2:28 a.m. Two minutes since the last time I checked. This night is either going to last forever, or it's going to eat me alive before dawn.

Finally, I can't take it anymore. My conscience can't handle being this close to my husband while I'm pining after someone else. Because whether I want to admit it or not, that's exactly what I'm doing. I miss Michael.

I move as carefully and quietly as I can, put on a pair of sweats and slip out of the bedroom. By the grace of God, I don't wake the dog, because she would've woken Ian.

While everyone else sleeps, I make my way down to the kitchen, fully intending to pour myself a drink. But by the time I get there, I can't do it—I have to work in a few hours. I'm going to be a waste of space, but I don't want a DUI during my morning commute. And if I start drinking now, it'll be enough to get me a DUI in six hours.

I rest my hands on the counter's cool edge and stare out into the darkness of the backyard. What little moonlight there is hints at the outline of the gazebo and hot tub, and my mind's eye fills in the rest. Relaxing with Ian and Michael. Fooling around with Ian. Watching them kiss for the first time. Fooling around with both of them.

I shiver.

There's got to be a solution to this situation. Feelings are what they are. I'm not obligated to act on them, and neither is Michael. Once he collects his thoughts and reestablishes contact, we can talk it out and agree that we don't have to cross more lines than we already have.

But can I look Ian in the eye and tell him that things didn't go too far? And can I look Michael in the eye and not hurt because I can't touch him?

How the fuck do I make this work?

A chill works its way through me. My heart's racing and my stomach's definitely glad I didn't have that drink after all. It's like I'm watching a train wreck in slow motion—it's happening, the wheels are in motion, and there's nothing I can do except hold my breath and wait for the inevitable.

I'm not panicking yet, but it's coming. I've felt Ian slipping away before. I've felt Michael slipping away before. Never both at the same time. The thought of losing either of them is devastating—both? Oh fuck.

My heart pounds even harder. I'm overreacting. Right? This is bigger in my head than it is in reality. It doesn't have to play out badly. It doesn't have to play out at all. Michael will respect that I want to be faithful to my husband. I'll respect that he wants to maintain our friendship. It's that simple. Isn't it?

Soft footsteps raise the hairs on the back of my neck.

No, no, no. Go back to bed, Ian. Please, go back to bed.

"Josh?"

I cringe. I can't even look at him, and my throat's so tight, I can barely breathe, never mind speak.

He stops behind me. "It's almost three in the morning."

"I know." I still don't turn around. "Sorry. I didn't mean to wake you up."

"Never mind that. What are *you* doing up?"

"Couldn't sleep."

"You okay?"

I can't even produce an automatic *Yeah, I'm fine*, and every second of silence gives the answer I didn't want to— no, I'm not okay.

"Josh?" He steps closer. "Is this about Michael?"

The sound of Ian saying Michael's name snaps whatever tenuous thread has been holding me together.

"Fuck." I whisper, and I lose it.

"Whoa, hey." Ian wraps his arms around me. "Easy." He gently turns me around and holds me close, tenderly stroking my hair and completely oblivious to what he's doing to my conscience. "Take it easy."

There's no reining this back in and pretending nothing's wrong. Ian's only seen me cry a handful of times, so he knows damn well my tears aren't on a hair trigger. Which means we're talking about this. We're talking about it tonight. And he won't take *it's nothing* or *I'm really okay* and let it go.

"This really has been hard on you, hasn't it?" he whispers, and goddammit, I can't do it.

I pull in a deep breath, clear my throat and try to collect my composure. "Yeah, it's about Michael. Ever since he went out with Dr. Klein, I..."

"I understand."

No, you don't. Trust me.

But he goes on. "You've seen firsthand the damage someone did to him. It's okay to have a hard time with him going to someone else who could hurt him again."

There's that, yes. But there's... But I...

How am I supposed to tell Ian there's so much more to it than that? That I'm not just scared of Michael getting hurt again? That it hurts like hell to watch him go, especially now that he's admitted to feeling things that I feel too, things that Ian would divorce me over if he knew?

Except I can't lie to him. If I do, he'll see right through me and drag out the truth anyway. But what will he do when the truth comes out? How the fuck do I tell my husband I love someone else and convince him I still love him too?

Because that's the crux of it, isn't it? I love Michael. No two ways about it. But my feelings for Ian haven't changed. If anything, I've fallen even more in love with him recently. His compassion for Michael, the way he's so patiently and gently helped me guide Michael back to a place where he can be intimate with men again—how could I not?

"I need..." I step back, safely out of his embrace, and wipe my eyes. "I need to be honest about something."

Ian's eyebrows jump above the frames of his glasses. "Okay?"

Where do I even start? "Everything we've done with him, I..."

Ian tenses, as if he's on the verge of folding his arms across his chest, but he doesn't. And he doesn't speak.

I clear my throat again. "I am so sorry, Ian. I thought I could do this without feelings getting involved, but—"

"Feelings?" His voice is quiet and completely neutral.

"Yeah." I slump back against the counter and let my head rest against the cupboard. "I don't know if it's..." My conversation with Michael flashes through my mind again. I close my eyes. "Maybe it's the whole Florence Nightingale thing. I don't know."

"You're in love with him." It's not a hard-edged accusation—more like a resigned statement of fact.

A fact I can't deny.

Swallowing hard, I meet his gaze. "Yeah."

"I see."

"This doesn't change how I feel about you." Why does it sound so fucking pathetic when I say it?

He studies me. I can't tell if he's angry, hurt, skeptical, or if nothing's quite settled in his brain yet. Then, without speaking, he pulls out a chair and sits at the kitchen table, gesturing for me to do the same. I hesitate but finally join him.

If I'd manned up and broached this subject last night, we both could've had a drink, but at this hour, Ian has to be up soon for work. He'll probably be showing up at school with red eyes as it is; no sense adding a hangover to the mix. It's both too early and too late for coffee, so there's nothing to do except face each other across the table.

Ian takes off his glasses and rubs his eyes. "So what happens now?"

"I don't know. I've been trying to make sense of everything. Guess I hadn't gotten that far yet." My stomach is threatening to climb up my throat, and I try my damnedest not to get sick. "The last thing I want to do is leave, though."

He lowers his hand, puts his glasses back on and meets my gaze.

The sick feeling gets even worse. *I don't want you to leave either.*

"I'm sorry," I say again, as if that might somehow magically fix anything.

Ian's face still betrays nothing, and neither does his voice. "There's something I'm curious about." He thumbs the edge of the table, watching that instead of looking at me. "Even though I'm not really sure I want to know the answer."

I gulp. "Okay."

He's quiet for a long time. Every passing second makes me itch—it's never good when Ian isn't sure what to say. Finally, he lowers his hand into his lap, and he looks me in the eye. "If you and I had never met, do you think—"

"Ian." I shake my head. "Don't go there. Please."

"No, I think we need to go there." He holds my gaze. "How do you think things would have turned out with him?"

He never would have met Steve.

I banish that thought as quickly as it materializes, and I stare at the table between us. In ten years, I've never struggled this hard to look my husband in the eye, but it's a challenge tonight. "I don't know, to be honest. I really don't." I run a hand through my hair, and with some more effort, meet his gaze. "It wasn't in the cards. And it's impossible to say what would've happened if I'd never met you, because I *did* meet you, and my whole life's been different since then."

His lips are taut, but he doesn't speak.

"I love you, Ian," I say softly. "Yeah, Michael and I have a long past, and yeah, there was a time when I thought we'd have a long future. But that was before I met you."

"So this isn't new. How you feel about him."

I blink. "I—what? Look, you know he and I dated in the past, and yeah, I've always felt something for him."

"But not like this."

That stops me in my tracks. No, not like this. Not even close.

Abruptly, though, Ian scoots his chair back from the table. "It's three in the morning. We both need to get some sleep."

"But what about—"

"We'll talk about it tomorrow." There's still no anger or hostility in his voice. It's still that same quiet resignation that cuts right to the bone.

He stands. So do I.

Sleep is a lost cause, but I follow him upstairs anyway. Maybe we'll have one of those miraculous "I'm too upset to talk, but let's fuck anyway" moments, and then we can talk a little more before we try to go to sleep. Somehow it's always easier to see eye to eye when we're both covered in the same sweat.

But Ian doesn't even look at me. Neither of us speaks as we rearrange the animals and climb back into bed. I'm used to sleeping with fifty pounds of boxer in the middle. Now, we might as well have an entire team of sled dogs between us.

"Ian."

"Hmm?"

I try to make out his features in the darkness. "I meant what I said. This doesn't change how I feel about you."

He's quiet for a moment. "We'll talk tomorrow."

"I know." I pause, my heart speeding up again. "I love you."

For the first time, I'm not sure if he believes me.

And deep down, I'm not sure if I blame him.

CHAPTER 24

UNSURPRISINGLY, DESPITE THE LATE HOUR, SLEEP doesn't come easy. When it does, it comes in fits and starts, and it's fucking awful. In my dreams, Michael's walking away again, and Ian's right on his heels this time. I don't know how many times I wake up in a panic and reach for Ian, and then fall asleep and do it all over again.

It's the longest, most restless night I've had in years.

Asleep or awake, I can't get rid of this feeling that my husband and my best friend are both slipping through my fingers, and I don't know how to make it stop. Especially now that I've fessed up and told Ian the truth. The proverbial cat is out of the bag, and it likes me about as much as Rosie does.

My own sleep-deprived, overstressed, semi-delirious thought almost makes me laugh. Almost. I waver between sort of awake and not quite asleep, and exhaustion finally takes over, apparently, because at some point, the dreams stop waking me up and I don't open my eyes again until my alarm goes off.

Ian's already gone. That's expected, of course, but something doesn't sit right. I don't remember him giving me a kiss before he left for work. There's no way I would've slept through that. Not after last night.

That's not a good sign.

There's not much I can do about it at this point, though, except get out of bed, get dressed and pour enough coffee down my throat to make it through the day. Worrying and obsessing didn't help me sleep, and it's not going to help me work.

By the time I get to the office, it's pretty clear that nothing short of a miracle is going to help me work. I'm absolutely useless. All day, I'm either struggling to stay awake or trying not to obsess over Ian and Michael and the conversation Ian and I need to have when I get home. Assuming he's there. He wouldn't overreact and just walk out, would he? Of course not. Ian's the rational one. He's the one who'll want to talk this all the way through, no matter what. Even if he's already made up his mind and has one foot out the door and a U-Haul on the way.

No, he won't make up his mind just yet. Talk first. Decide later. That's his MO. Now if I can convince my stomach to settle, maybe I can make it through the rest of the day in one piece. Or at least without puking up what little I've eaten throughout the day.

And of course, my go-to tic when I'm uncomfortable—playing with my wedding ring—is only making everything worse.

Good God. I'm a wreck.

When the two-thirty slump shows up, I'm done. Just done. I don't usually play hooky from work, so hopefully my boss will forgive me just this once, and after a quick phone call and some lame excuses, I'm out of there before three o'clock.

All the way home, I'm on the verge of shivering even though I'm not cold. I stay in the right lane on the freeway, not because I want to drive slower than everyone else, but because I want easy access to the shoulder in case this nausea suddenly gets worse.

I make it, though. Up the driveway. Into the garage. Out of the car. Deep breath. Into the house.

Ariel greets me at the door, bouncing and wiggling as she always does, and she gets me to crack the first smile I've managed all day. "Hey, sweetie." I tousle her ears. "You miss me?"

She whips herself in the sides with her tail, and when she spins around in her excitement, she cracks me in the back of the knee with it.

"Hey! Watch it with that thing!" I laugh and pat her side, trying to stay out of the line of fire as her tail continues wagging. "Come on, let's go see—"

Daddy.

My stomach flips. It's go-time. Ian's home, and it's time to have this out. I scratch Ariel's back and then continue into the house. Ian's not in the living room, so with Ariel hot on my heels, I go into the kitchen.

He's at the table with his laptop, the screen reflecting on his lenses, and he's surrounded by neat stacks of white pages. As I step into the room, our eyes meet. He doesn't seem surprised to see me home early, and he doesn't look thrilled either. Just like last night, his poker face offers nothing.

Without a word, he closes his laptop. He takes off his glasses, sets them on top of the computer, and stands up.

Now that his glasses are off, the heavy shadows under his eyes are unmistakable. My guilt burrows deeper—guess I wasn't the only one who couldn't sleep last night.

Beside me, Ariel's tail slows, no longer making whip-whip-whip sounds through the air. Ian's got one of her toys on the table, one of the ones that can be filled with kibbles, ready and waiting as if he's been prepared since he got home to gently distract her while we fight it out, so she doesn't get as stressed. He picks it up and hands it to her. She grabs it out of his hand, drops onto the floor by the sink and starts pawing at it to get the treats out.

For a moment, we stand there, facing each other from miles apart. The only sound is Ariel rolling the toy around and crunching on the treats that fall out, and even that's barely audible over my thumping heart.

"We should..." Ian swallows. "We should talk. About last night."

"I know." My throat tightens, and I take a deep breath. I run a shaky hand through my hair and can't make myself look him in the eye. "I'm sorry. You trusted me to do this with Michael and not get involved like that, and I..." There's no explanation. No rationalizing it and making it nice and pretty so he can brush it off and pretend it never happened. The cold hard truth is that my husband trusted me to have sex with another man, and to keep it as sex and nothing more, and I fell for that man anyway.

I make myself meet his gaze. "I'm sorry, Ian. I wish there was something else I could say. But I'm sorry, and I love you, and I don't want to lose you."

Please tell me I haven't already lost you.

Ian comes closer, and my knees are shaking as badly as they did the day Michael forced us to hash it out after that stupid breakup years ago.

He doesn't say a word. His eyes tell me nothing.

"I'm sorry," I whisper again, sounding so goddamned useless and pathetic.

"I know." He wraps his arms around me, and my knees almost collapse out from under both of us. I want to believe this is silent forgiveness, but I'm waiting for the other shoe to drop. I'm scared to death he's just waiting for the right moment to calmly, quietly tell me that he's going to move in with his brother, and we can talk to attorneys next week, and that he hopes we can do this amicably.

Though I'm not sure I want to know, I ask, "What do we do now?"

He doesn't answer right away, but finally says, "Come on. Let's go sit." He leads me into the living room. Rosie is on the couch, so Ian moves her to the back of one of the armchairs. We sit down, a full cushion dividing us. There's still a lot of space between us, much more than I'm comfortable with, but Ian takes my hand. At least that's something —at this point, I'll take it.

Ian takes a deep breath. "I've been doing a lot of thinking since last night." He watches his thumb running back and forth along the backs of my knuckles. "And maybe this whole thing with Michael... Maybe we went about it the wrong way."

The wrong...huh?

I cock my head. "What do you mean?"

He wets his lips and lifts his gaze. "Maybe what we've been doing with him shouldn't be just sex. And maybe it shouldn't be...temporary."

I blink, not sure I heard him right. "What?"

"Maybe you need him." He swallows. "Maybe we both do."

Okay, I definitely heard him right that time, but... *What?* "I don't understand."

Ian takes a deep breath. "The thing is, Michael's been a part of your life forever, and he's been a part of ours ever since we met. He's never tried to intrude. Hell, he kept us together when we fucked up."

"Yeah, true."

"He's never been a third wheel. More like...more like the third corner. And when we started getting physically involved with him, it was..." He's quiet for a moment, eyes unfocused. "The thing is, look how fast he was willing to let me join the picture, even with all that trauma still hanging over him. And I cared from the start about him getting past all his flashbacks and panics, but when I was really involved in it..." He grimaces.

"It hurts. To watch someone you care that much about going through that."

"Yeah, it does." His voice wavers, and he clears his throat. "Maybe that should've told me something. And I guess I can't help wondering if this—the feelings and wanting more—was inevitable."

My heart speeds up and my stomach flips. "Inevitable? What do you mean?"

"For the three of us to get to this point. Where it's not just two husbands and a friend. Where we're...three guys together."

"Like, three guys in one relationship?"

Ian nods.

I stare at him but then put up a hand and shake my head. "Look, I know marriage is all about compromise, but I can't ask you to—"

"You're not. And this isn't compromise." His lips twist a little, as if he's searching for the right words. "Quite frankly,

I was pissed last night when you told me how you felt about him."

I flinch, but he's not done yet.

"And I spent a lot of time thinking about it. All night, and throughout today, right up until you got home. And the thing is, the more I thought about it, the more I realized that I have feelings for him too."

"You do?"

Ian nods. "I guess what drove it home was when I caught myself freaking out that you might leave me for him, and it hurt to think about losing him too." He slides a little closer. "Josh, I don't want to lose either of you. I thought last night was the come-to-Jesus moment for you, where you needed to think about whether you want to be with me or with Michael. But I think it was that moment for all of us to realize there's an option we hadn't considered before."

Speechless. Completely fucking speechless.

Ian laces our fingers together on the cushion between us. "I don't think I could ever feel for him or anybody else what I feel for you. And I know there's something between the two of you that can't exist anywhere except there." He shifts his weight. "But maybe it doesn't have to be a hundred percent equal on all sides. Maybe the way it is...works."

"But..." I shake myself, certain this is all some sort of sleep-deprived hallucination. "How the fuck would something like that even work?"

Ian shrugs. "I don't know. I guess if any of us knew that, maybe we'd have done this a long time ago. Up until we started..." He pauses, cheeks coloring a little. "Until this, uh, arrangement with Michael, I thought it was either monogamy or the casual fucking around we did when we were younger." He waves his hand. "Maybe there's a sweet spot somewhere in between that we didn't think about before."

I can't believe what I'm hearing. Part of me is still bracing for the worst case scenario, which makes it almost impossible to believe the solution Ian's suggesting. "Are you..."

He squeezes my hand. "Yes, I'm serious."

I slide closer and wrap my arms around him. "God, I love you."

"I love you too." He kisses my cheek and holds me tighter. "And I want all three of us to be happy, even if it means doing things that are a bit unusual."

"I don't know if Michael will go for that."

Ian strokes my hair. "It's worth a shot."

I sit up and meet his gaze. "But...your job. The school district barely puts up with the fact that you're gay."

Ian chuckles, and he shrugs. "Well, what they don't know won't hurt me." Turning serious, he cups my face and kisses me again. "We can be discreet. It's really none of anyone else's business."

"And if they find out anyway?"

"We'll cross that bridge when we get there." He meets my gaze. "We were both freaked out about the school district figuring out I was gay, and yeah, they don't like it, but there isn't a damned thing they can do about it."

"An arrangement like this, though..."

"Then, like I said, we'll be discreet. If it comes out..." He shrugs again. "We'll deal with it. But I think this has the potential to be something really amazing for all three of us. I'm not going to pass that up just because someone who's stuck in the Dark Ages might find out about it. The only ones whose opinions matter are you, me and Michael."

"Question is, what will he think of the idea?"

"All we can do is talk to him."

"Except I'm not sure if he'll even take my calls right now." Just saying it makes me sick to my stomach.

Ian's eyebrows jump. "What do you mean? Did something happen?"

"When we talked, he said he needed some time. He didn't come out and say it, but it was kind of a 'don't call me, I'll call you' type of thing."

Ian scowls. "Well, all you can do is try. If he isn't receptive right now, then we'll wait until he comes out of the woodwork." He runs his fingers through my hair. "He isn't gone forever. We both know he'll come back."

That damned lump is rising in my throat again. "I know. I just..." I shake my head. "Fuck."

"He'll come back." Ian gathers me in his arms. "And if by some chance he doesn't, I'm still here. I'm not going anywhere."

I close my eyes and hold him tight. This isn't over yet, not until we've talked to Michael, but all I can feel right now is the most profound relief. After being so terrified that Ian was ready to walk out the door, I should be dragging him upstairs and fucking him into the ground just to make sure this is real and we're both really here, but I can't move.

Truth be told, I don't want to move. We've joked in the past that the best part of fighting is making up, and we've had some explosive makeup sex over the years, but I don't see that part happening this time. I'm physically exhausted. I'm emotionally exhausted. More than that, though, I just want to hold him like this for a moment. Right here on our couch, fully dressed and not even a little bit turned on, this is all I want.

Ian lifts his head and tips my chin up so we're looking in each other's eyes.

And then he kisses me, and it's chaste and gentle, and I don't have to ask if he feels the same way.

The sex will come later. Just...don't move.

I want to believe Michael will come back, but right now, I'm just grateful Ian's still here.

CHAPTER 25

IT TAKES ME UNTIL ALMOST BEDTIME TO FINALLY WORK up the nerve to text Michael.

We'd like to talk—dinner?

Of course, that's a mistake. Now I'll be up all night wondering what he's thinking, if he'll respond, if he'll be upset that I broke the silence. His departure wasn't hostile by any means, but especially in the years since he left Steve, Michael has been fiercely protective of his space. If he wants to be left alone, he wants to be *left alone*.

As I'm getting ready for bed, I have visions of him looking at the message and then shoving his phone in his pocket without responding.

"Give him time." Ian snaps me out of my thoughts with a gentle hand on my shoulder. "He's got a lot to think about."

"I know." I toss my shirt in the hamper and sigh. "But you know I'm going to freak out about it until—"

Ian kisses me softly. "I know. And there's nothing I can say that'll stop you, but *you* know I'm still going to try."

I meet his eyes and can't help laughing. "Yeah, true. I don't know why I bother trying."

He smiles, and then hugs me gently. "It'll be—"

My phone buzzes on top of my dresser, and both our heads snap toward it.

"Is that...?"

"Maybe." I grab the phone, and sure enough, there's a text from Michael.

Are you sure that's a good idea?

I gulp.

"What'd he say?" Ian asks.

I show him the message, and he frowns.

"How upset was he when you guys talked?"

"He was pretty shaken up." I look at the screen again. "He might be afraid to face you."

"Me? Why would—" He pauses. "Because of how he feels about you."

I nod.

"Maybe I should message him," Ian says. "So he knows I'm not upset."

Gnawing my lip, I try to think of a better idea but come up empty, so I sigh and lower my phone. "It's worth a shot."

He takes out his own and starts typing out a message. Before he sends it, he turns it so I can see it.

There's no hard feelings. Just want to talk.

I nod, and Ian sends the message. We both stare at our screens, waiting for the icon that indicates he's responding, but nothing happens.

Until my phone suddenly comes to life with his ringtone, and a smiling picture of him that seems so out of place right now.

I quickly answer. "Hey."

"Hey." He pauses. "So, Ian knows? What we talked about?"

My heart speeds up. "Yeah."

"And he's..."

"He's not angry. No one is." I glance at Ian for reassurance, and when he nods, I continue. "This just seems like something we should all talk about. Face to face."

He goes quiet for so long, I'm sure I dropped the call. Or worse, that he hung up.

But finally, he says, "If you guys really want to talk about this in person, let's do it sooner than later. I know it's late, but..."

"Now?"

Ian's eyebrows jump, but he shrugs. *Why not?*

Michael sighs. "I can be there in twenty."

"We'll be here."

After I hang up, I meet my husband's gaze. "Well, I guess if we're gonna lose sleep..."

"Might as well be doing something other than staring at the ceiling."

"Yeah." I put my hands on his waist. "Before he gets here... We're really okay, right? You and me?"

"I wouldn't even consider adding someone else if we weren't." He gathers me into a tight embrace. "Whatever happens tonight, nothing changes."

I just pray to God he's right.

ALMOST EXACTLY TWENTY MINUTES LATER, MICHAEL'S at the door. As I let him in, Ariel goes crazy, barking and whapping herself in the ribs with her tail. Michael leans down to pet her, and though he's tense, he laughs—it's hard not to when she's being crazy like that.

He glances up at me, and his laughter vanishes. He clears his throat. "I hope this isn't too late at night."

"No, definitely not."

Ian steps into the foyer. "Better to clear the air now than lose sleep over it."

Michael recoils slightly, as if he's expecting Ian to lash out at him even though he's never seen Ian lose his temper, not even when I've pushed him to the point where anyone in his right mind would have.

"Let's go sit," I say softly. "In the living room."

Michael nods. "Okay."

He follows us into the living room and takes the armchair. Ian and I take the couch, Ian on the end closest to Michael with me on the middle cushion.

Almost immediately, Rosie crawls into Michael's lap and curls up. Even from here, I can hear her purring. Though Michael's obviously tense—aren't we all?—he still pets her, and he doesn't even flinch as she kneads his leg.

No one's speaking, and everyone's focused on Rosie. She soaks it all up, of course. Nothing better for a smug cat than three people sitting in silence and admiring her.

Michael is still focused on her when he takes a breath and sets his shoulders back. "So, you guys wanted to talk."

Ian and I exchange glances. He takes my hand.

I shift my gaze to Michael. "It's about the conversation we had at lunch yesterday. About..."

Michael winces, drawing back a little as his eyes dart toward Ian.

"He told me what you guys talked about," Ian says softly.

I glance down at our joined hands, then meet Michael's

gaze. "The thing is, everybody's feelings got more intense than we thought they would. But we're..."

Ian squeezes my hand gently.

I pull in a breath. "We're not so sure that's a bad thing."

Michael's eyebrows jump, and his gaze flicks back and forth between us, but he doesn't speak.

"We..." My pulse is out of control. "The thing is..."

Ian breaks in: "We want you to be part of our family."

Michael's eyes widen.

"Actually, that's not even accurate." Ian clears his throat, and he's holding my hand even tighter as he says, "Michael, having you here is what *makes* this"—he gestures at each of us in turn—"a family."

My heart flutters. God, now that he says it like that, it's so true. "He's right."

Michael chews his lip. Then he exhales and absently unsticks one of Rosie's claws from his jeans. "Look, guys. I appreciate everything you've done for me recently. It's made such a big difference, I can't even put it into words. But this was just a temporary thing. So I could move on from my ex."

"Do you want it to be temporary?" Ian asks.

I hold my breath, not sure I want to know the answer.

"You two are married." Michael's barely whispering. "I can't... I don't want to be the third wheel."

Before I can speak, Ian says, "You're not the third wheel. If anything, I am."

My head snaps toward Ian, and Michael and I both say in unison, "What?"

Ian glances at me, then Michael. "You guys have had something special for a lot longer than I've been in the picture." Slowly, his smile comes to life. "And Josh and I, we've had something special for a long time too. It almost seems like—"

"You're not the third wheel, Ian," Michael cuts in. "The two of you... That was fate if I ever saw it. I knew the minute I met you that you and Josh were in it for the long haul."

"Then maybe there isn't a third wheel here," I say. "Does there have to be? Just because there's three people involved, does there have to be an odd man out?"

Michael shifts, petting the cat and not looking at either of us.

"He's right," Ian says. "The three of us just make sense. I mean, the nights we all spend with a bottle of wine in the hot tub? I look forward to that. And I thought it was just because it's a chance to relax and get away from everything, but honestly, I could do that alone. I could take a bottle of wine into the hot tub by myself. Or with Josh." He traces my thumb with his. "But it's not the same." He hesitates, chewing his lip, before he adds, "Looking back, I'm just surprised it took this long to figure out that there's a lot more here than a married couple and a good friend. I guess the sex just..." He glances at each of us. "It just sealed it."

Michael rests his hand on top of Rosie. "I don't even know what to say. I mean, *if* we went through with this, how would it even work?"

"We'll make it up as we go," I say.

Ian nods. "I don't think it'll be much different from what we've already been doing."

"Exactly," I say. "I think it'll pretty much work how it's *been* working all along. Quite honestly, how it's been working since even before we all started sleeping together."

They both look at me, eyebrows up.

I clear my throat. "Think about it. We can all function

on our own. We can all function as pairs—Ian and me, Michael and me, you two together. But if we miss a Sunday night, we're all bummed out until we can finally do it again. Because it just feels like that's how everything should be."

Ian chews his lip for a moment. To Michael, he says, "He's got a point."

"I know he does. But it's... I..." Michael exhales hard. He picks up Rosie and carefully sets her on the armrest. Then he leans forward, resting his elbows on his knees and covering his face with his hands. "This is a lot to take in."

"Nothing has to happen overnight." Ian runs his thumb along the side of my hand. "If you need to think, then by all means, take whatever time you need. If we're all on board, then the only thing that really changes now is we just accept what we're doing. Let it evolve. You don't have to move in or anything like that."

"But we can discuss that option in the future," I say quietly. "If you want to."

Michael rubs the bridge of his nose. "Couldn't this get really complicated?"

"I think it already has."

Ian nods. "I can't think of anything more complicated than trying to ignore feelings that obviously don't want to be ignored."

Michael lowers his hand. "You know what I mean."

"Yeah," I say. "And neither of us is pretending it'll be bliss and perfection all the time. No relationship is."

"It'll definitely be an adjustment." Ian grips my hand tighter. "Hell, Josh and I still butt heads sometimes. It just means three people squabbling over who takes out the trash and getting annoyed over leaving empty milk cartons in the fridge."

Michael laughs. "Honestly, a relationship where the

worst bone of contention involves household chores... That kind of sounds like heaven to me." He pauses, gazing at both of us, and releases a breath. "Especially if it's with the two of you."

I slide over and gesture for Michael to come to the couch. "Then join us."

He tenses, eyeing both of us and the vacancy between us. "You guys really are serious about this."

"Absolutely." Ian pats the cushion. "We both love you, Michael. We want you to join us."

Michael eyes that vacant spot again. Slowly, tentatively, he rises. Ian moves his legs aside to give him room as he makes his way around the coffee table, and my heart goes crazy as Michael sinks down onto the couch between us.

He glances at me. Then at Ian. He swallows, pressing his lips together as if he's struggling to keep his emotions in check.

I curve my hand over his leg. "Ian's right. We want you to stay with us."

Michael puts his hand over mine, and for a long, silent moment, he stares at that point of contact. "I can't..."

My heart sinks. *Michael...*

Then he laughs, shakes his head and looks me in the eyes. "I can't think of anywhere else I'd rather be."

Ian and I both laugh too. It doesn't seem like the right thing to do in that moment, but I'm not sure there is a right thing to do except be happy. And relieved. And pull Michael into my arms and hug him the way I did the day he left Steve for good.

I was so afraid you'd never come back.

"I love you," he whispers.

"I love you too." I kiss the top of his head, and when he meets my gaze, we both smile. Then I kiss him for real.

As I deepen that kiss, Ian slides his hand over the top of mine on Michael's back, and I open my eyes. Over Michael's shoulder, I meet Ian's gaze. His eyes have tears in them, and I realize mine are stinging a bit too.

Michael draws back, wiping his eyes.

He turns to Ian and takes his hand. The air between them is taut. They hold each other's gazes, I hold my breath, wondering what they're thinking and what one might eventually say.

Ian reaches for Michael's face, but hesitates. His hand hovers there, just inches away, before finally settling against Michael's cheek. Michael closes his eyes and presses against Ian's hand, clasping his own over the top of it.

Then Ian lifts Michael's chin, draws him in and kisses him.

And now I get why so many fairy tales use a kiss to break enchantments. The second those two make contact, it's like a spell is broken. The standoff is over. The uncertainty is gone. Michael is here, and Ian is here, and nobody's going anywhere.

Well, sort of.

I slide my hand higher up Michael's leg. "You know, we do have some furniture that's more comfortable than this couch."

Michael laughs and turns to me. "Is that your not so subtle hint that we should all go upstairs and fuck?"

"Is that a not so subtle yes?"

"You're damn right it is."

CHAPTER 26

NONE OF US WASTE ANY TIME CAREFULLY UNDRESSING each other. As soon as we're in the bedroom, the clothes are off, and it's on.

And what a fucking relief, just being naked in our bed with both Ian and Michael. I can't stop touching either of them. Even when I'm kissing one, my hands are all over the other, and there's hands all over me too. How did any of us think for a second that this wasn't the perfect arrangement? The way things belong?

Better late than never, I suppose.

"It hasn't been that long," Ian breathes in between kissing Michael's neck. "But God, I've missed you."

"I've missed you both." Michael slides his hand into Ian's hair and pulls his head back. "Come here, you." He kisses Ian, and holy shit. Any worries I have left about this being a compromise, about either of them taking one for the team just for the sake of peace, evaporate in the heat of that kiss.

And then Michael drops to his knees, steadies Ian's cock

in both hands and closes his lips around the head. Effort-lessly, without reservation, he sucks Ian's cock.

My jaw drops. My God. He really can handle this. The demons are still there, I have no doubt, but he's made it over this wall, and not just with me.

Ian glances at me, and he grins. He reaches for me, and when I step closer, he draws me in for a kiss. Before our lips meet, though, he pauses, and he smiles.

We are *okay, aren't we? All three of us.*

Then he starts to lean back in but stops again, closing his eyes and exhaling hard. "Whoa."

I glance down and have to do a double take. Michael, who had to fight hard to even think about oral sex at all, is eagerly deep-throating Ian. His eyes flick up to meet mine, and he stops what he's doing just long enough to flash me a grin. Then he slowly swallows my husband's cock as if he never had a reason not to. And before I can even process that mouthwatering sight, he turns and does the same to me—lips tight around my cock, slowly taking it until I'm sure I'm pushing his gag reflex.

"Oh my God, Michael. You're—"

Ian grabs the back of my neck and drags me into a kiss that's as breathless and passionate as the one he shared with Michael a moment ago. I hold on to him because I'm lucky I'm still standing now.

At our feet, stroking us each with one hand, Michael alternates between sucking my cock and Ian's. He teases Ian right to the edge, getting his breath to catch and making his knees shake, and then he switches to me and works nothing short of magic with his lips and tongue, swirling and flut-tering and licking until I'm cursing into Ian's kiss. Jesus Christ—sex just does *not* get any better than this.

Michael releases me, and I break the kiss and look down

as he sits back on his heels. "We should really take this to your bed. Before your carpet chews up my knees."

Ian laughs and offers Michael his arm. "That the only reason you want to get in bed?"

"Of course it is." Michael clasps his hand around Ian's forearm and gets up, wincing slightly as he straightens the knee he injured years ago. "But it's as good an excuse as any, right?"

"You're damn right it is." Ian drags Michael into a kiss. Michael gasps, but he's gripping Ian's shoulders and kissing him back. They stumble toward the bed while I watch, getting more and more turned on with every breath they steal from each other.

When they reach the bed, Ian shoves Michael back and pins him to the mattress, and panic shoots through me for a split second before I realize Michael's still returning Ian's kiss with as much—if not more—fervor. He's unafraid, and he's unrelenting, and when he wrestles one arm free, he throws it around Ian's neck and drags him down to him. He hooks his leg around Ian's, and Ian groans and shivers as Michael pulls their bodies closer together.

My mouth waters as I watch them. Ian's this rough with me all the time, and he must've gotten caught up in the moment and thought Michael wanted the same, and apparently he's right.

As I lie down beside them, they finally come up for air.

"You guys are..." Michael gasps for breath. "Jesus fuck."

"Tell us what you want," I whisper.

He shakes his head. "No. It's..." He pauses, taking a few more breaths. "It's been about me since day one. And none of us would..." More breaths. "None of us would be here if it hadn't been for you." He licks his lips. "Tell me what *you* want."

Ian meets my gaze, eyebrows up. *Well?*

"I want to fuck you, Michael." Enunciate. I can do this. "While you suck Ian off."

Beside me, Ian shivers. "Yes, please."

Michael's grin almost melts my bones. "Hell yeah."

Without hesitation, we change positions. Ian reclines against the pillows, and Michael gets on his hands and knees while I turn away to get some lube. I've barely started putting it on when a throaty groan from Ian turns my head. Good God. There's the Michael I knew before—sucking cock, moaning with pleasure.

I can barely think about anything except watching the two of them. Even lubing up my own dick is too complicated when Michael's going to town on Ian and Ian's trying to watch him but has to keep blinking as if his eyes are already watering.

"Fuck 'im," Ian moans. "I want...I want to see that before..." His eyelids slide closed. "Fuck."

I can sure as hell move now. Lubed and ready, I kneel behind Michael and put some lube on him. Then I press against him. In the back of my mind, I'm irrationally sure this will be the moment when Michael panics, that he's going to suddenly tense up and return to that bad place.

But he doesn't. Moaning around Ian's cock, Michael pushes back, and I can barely breathe as my dick sinks into him.

The view is spectacular—my cock sliding in and out of Michael. His gorgeous, lean torso. His head bobbing up and down above Ian. Ian lying back and going out of his fucking mind. Everything about this is perfect. And hot. So ridiculously hot.

"Oh my God..." Ian arches, squeezing his eyes shut. "That's so good. Holy shit."

Michael groans. He rocks back and forth, riding my dick faster, and Ian curses under his breath. He's gripping Michael's hair, staring down at him, his lips apart and his forehead creased, and I fuck Michael a little harder so he'll give Ian even more.

"I'm gonna come," Ian slurs. "I'm gonna...I'm gonna..."

Much more of this, and I will too. I grit my teeth and hold Michael's hips tighter, fucking him for all I'm worth while he drives Ian insane.

"Oh...shit..." Ian's head falls back. "So fucking good." He gasps. His eyes fly open, and Michael tenses around me as he bobs his head even faster.

I struggle to keep my eyes focused, but my own orgasm is closing in fast, so I grit my teeth as I pound Michael's ass for all I'm worth. He groans, and he shudders, and apparently that's more than Ian can take—he squeezes his eyes shut again, curses and trembles as his back arches. I don't know how he doesn't take me over the edge with him—God, I love the sight of Ian falling to pieces—but somehow, I keep going, and I keep fucking Michael.

Ian takes a few seconds to catch his breath. Not long, though—he's barely wiped the sweat from his brow before he shifts around, grabs the back of Michael's neck and kisses him. He reaches beneath Michael, and I don't have to see to know he's stroking Michael's cock. The way Michael clenches around me tells me everything I need to know. And besides, *fuck, fuck*—watching those two make out is hot enough. Knowing Michael has Ian's semen on his tongue? Knowing how Ian kisses right after he's had an orgasm?

That's it. I can't take another second.

With a roar, I slam into Michael, and I come so hard, I very nearly black for real out this time. And just as I'm coming down, Michael cries out, and he gets almost painfully tight as I take a few last thrusts before my body can't handle anymore.

I stop. Michael stops. Ian's arm stops moving. They're not kissing anymore—Michael presses his forehead to Ian's shoulder, and Ian holds him, stroking his hair. Our eyes meet. We both grin, and when Ian presses a soft kiss to Michael's damp red hair, my skin prickles with goose bumps.

I pull out carefully. None of us are all that steady on our feet, which is to be expected, but we manage as always. When we finally settle into bed, Ian and I are both on our sides, facing Michael, who's between us.

Michael exhales. "You guys are seriously unreal."

Ian grins. "You're not so bad yourself, you know."

Michael sweeps his tongue across his lips and looks at us. "I don't just mean in bed. I mean..." He reaches across me and takes Ian's hand. "Letting me in like this."

I put my hand on top of theirs on my stomach. "This isn't something we'd do with just anyone. It took someone pretty amazing to make life better with three people instead of two."

Ian nods. "That's not to say the end justifies the means. What happened to you never should have happened. But—"

"But this is one hell of a silver lining," Michael says. "If that's how things were going to work out, then I'm just glad they eventually brought me here."

Right then, Rosie leaps onto the bed, stomps over Ian and me and flops down on top of Michael.

"Seriously, cat?" Ian rolls his eyes. "We feed you, we house you, but *no*, you want *him*."

Michael laughs, tousling Rosie's fur, which would have gotten me or even Ian a claws-out swat. "I see how it is. You guys just want me here because I'm the only one your cat doesn't hate."

Ian bursts out laughing. "Oh come on. She doesn't *hate* us." He reaches across me, and she bats at him but misses. "Okay, okay. Maybe she does."

I start to speak, but Ariel jumps up behind Ian. "Shit! Watch that tail!"

He ducks and just misses a smack in the face. "Ariel, down." He points at the floor, but Ariel just flops down next to him and rests her head on his arm. Ian groans. "Seriously?"

I snicker. "I think we might need a bigger bed."

Michael laughs, but it doesn't last. He gently lifts Rosie and sets her on the edge of the bed. Then he turns on his side and looks at Ian. "For the record, you are not, and never have been, a third wheel. You and I aren't as close as we both are to Josh, but it doesn't have to stay that way." He clasps Ian's hand in his, and kisses the backs of his fingers. "It'll take time, but I think we'll get there."

Ian's smile is slow to form, but his eyes definitely echo it. "You're probably right. I guess, like everything, it'll be a process."

Michael nods. "Yeah, and I'm a bit more optimistic about the process than I was about the sexual exorcism one." He pauses, the smile turning to a playful smirk. "Well, okay, that process was fun *most* of the time too. But you know what I mean."

"Yeah, I do." Ian leans over me to kiss Michael's lips. "And I agree."

Michael turns to me and touches my face. "You were right, you know."

"About what?"

"You said karma owed me big-time. That there was a

good guy out there waiting for me." His smile gets bigger, and I swear his eyes tear up as he says, "Turns out there were two right in front of my face."

And suddenly my vision is getting blurry for some reason. I wipe my eyes. "Well, let's hope we can live up to the karma you definitely deserve."

Michael sniffs and wipes his eyes too. "I'm not worried about that at all."

"Neither am I." Ian kisses Michael's cheek, then mine. "We've got all the time in the world to get it right."

"You don't need it," Michael says. "You've already got it. But I'll definitely take all the time I can get with the two of you."

"Likewise," I say.

Ian nods. "Ditto."

It's a little crowded in our bed with the three of us, the cat and Ariel, and I imagine it won't be any better when Cody is added to the mix, but that's okay. There's nothing about this moment I would change, because I have the two men I love more than anyone else in the world. Ian's still here. Michael's part of our family.

And everything is perfect.

Even if the cat still hates me.

For more books by L.A. Witt, please visit

http://www.gallagherwitt.com

Romance * Suspense

Contemporary * Historical * Sports * Military

Titles Include

Rookie Mistake (written with Anna Zabo)

Scoreless Game (written with Anna Zabo)

The Hitman vs. Hitman Series (written with Cari Z)

The Bad Behavior Series (written with Cari Z)

The Gentlemen of the Emerald City Series

The Anchor Point Series

The Husband Gambit

Name From a Hat Trick

After December

Brick Walls

The Venetian and the Rum Runner

If The Seas Catch Fire

...and many, many more!

ABOUT THE AUTHOR

L.A. Witt is a romance and suspense author who has at last given up the exciting nomadic lifestyle of the military spouse (read: her husband finally retired). She now resides in Pittsburgh, where the potholes are determined to eat her car and her cats are endlessly taunted by a disrespectful squirrel named Moose. In her spare time, she can be found painting in her art room or destroying her voice at a Pittsburgh Penguins game.

Website: www.gallagherwitt.com
Email: gallagherwitt@gmail.com
Twitter: @GallagherWitt

Printed in the USA
CPSIA information can be obtained
at www.ICGtesting.com
LVHW042148231023
761949LV00006B/55

9 781543 073300